# RUTHLESS MONARCH

AVA HARRISON

*Ruthless Monarch*
Cover Design: Hang Le
Editor: Editing4Indies, Karen Hrdlicka
Proofreader: Marla Selkow Esposito, Jaime Ryter
Formatting: Champagne Book DEsign

If you know the enemy and know yourself, you need not fear the result of a hundred battles. If you know yourself but not the enemy, for every victory gained you will also suffer a defeat. If you know neither the enemy nor yourself, you will succumb in every battle.

—Sun Tzu, *The Art of War*

# PROLOGUE

## Matteo

I CAN SMELL DEATH IN THE AIR. ITS PUNGENT AROMA THICK and heavy in my nostrils as I amble across the warehouse.

Each step through the crimson terrain reminds me of all I lost and why I am here now.

My father died.

My mother died.

Fuck, even my brother died.

The war to maintain my family's control over the East Coast has been long, bloody, and jam-packed with casualties.

But in the end, I won.

I always do.

I know this reprieve from violence won't last long. Another enemy is always lurking in the shadows.

The underworld is like the Hydra. You cut off one head, and two more grow in its place.

I know this time is no different. I need to prepare for war.

There has been a lull for the past few months.

I pay a great deal of money to be apprised of my cousin's dealings.

There is no question he is coming for me. He's been coming for me for years.

Ever since my father died, and I was put in charge.

He believed he should have been the one to take over.

Deeming me not the rightful heir.

Technically, he's not wrong. Had his father lived, this kingdom would have been his.

But regardless of what could have been, I'm in charge and the best option.

At thirty-five, I have already lived more than most. I had been raised half my life to take over my family's business.

On the books, we own a legitimate enterprise.

Behind that, we own everything.

The door swings open, and in walks my right-hand man and cousin, Lorenzo.

"What do you have for me?" I spit out.

His dark eyes are narrowed. As soon as they look at me, I know something is wrong. The thing about him is that he doesn't just work for me. He's like a brother, which is why I'm already on edge with the rigid, cold stare he gives.

"Nothing good," he states, and the customary humor he only allows himself to show me is gone.

I lean forward in my chair. "Go on."

"He's moving on Chicago."

"What the fuck does that mean?" I draw in a deep breath, trying to calm myself down, but no amount of oxygen will fix this. I should have killed that fuck when I had a chance. Maybe it's not too late.

"He's got his mitts on every dirty politician. He's got the ear of the governor. We might have won Boston, but he's got the ear of the Irish."

"Fuck."

"What do you think that means for us?"

"It means he's not done."

"What do you want to do?"

I lean back in my chair, a bitter smile on my lips.

"We need to take him out before he succeeds."

# CHAPTER ONE

*One year later . . .*

DESPITE EVERYTHING I THOUGHT, I LOST CHICAGO.
That was enough to send my ego and bloodthirst spinning. But that wasn't all. Salvatore is rumored to be making another play for the East Coast.

This is where it stops.

The East Coast is *mine*.

I don't give a fuck who he thinks he is. I won't let him take it from me.

The door to my office swings open. The sound of Italian loafers hitting the marble ricochets through the room.

I don't have to look up to know it's Lorenzo, and by the way he stomps in, it's not good.

"What now?" I lift my head from the papers I'm looking over and see his scowl. In the year that has passed, he's grown up a lot, and is no longer the happy-go-lucky bastard he once was.

Lorenzo runs his hands over his face, heaving out a long-suffering sigh. "I'm not going to lie to you, it's bad."

"How bad?"

"Gotta get our shit together, bad. While we were focused on holding ties with the Irish, Salvatore was focusing on our own backyard."

My knuckles turn white as I grasp my chrome desk, on the

verge of fucking bending it completely. "Don't talk in riddles, Lorenzo. Spit it out."

"Governor Marino."

There is a stillness to the room at his words, followed by silence.

My fist slams down on the table, cutting through the heavy tension lingering in the air. Lorenzo doesn't jump back, but he winces, aware of how thoroughly and mercilessly fucked we are.

Frank Marino, the Governor of New Jersey, has always been a thorn in my side. Ever since he rejected my proposal for port access and I had to go above him and work with the governor of New York, we have not gotten along. That, coupled by the fact I know of his past business dealings with my deceased uncle, leaves no love lost between us. But to know my cousin has anything to do with him is even worse.

"Talk."

Lorenzo shakes his head, and I know what he's about to tell me is going to be bad. There is a tenseness to his shoulders, one that's often not present. No one else would notice, but to me, Lorenzo is an open book. The same goes for him about me. It makes everything much easier in certain situations that we can speak without words.

"Governor Marino is in talks with Salvatore. If what I hear is true, and it always is, Marino is giving him port access."

"Fuck."

"Yeah." He nods.

I motion my hand to the chair. "Sit. But before you do, grab the scotch. We have a lot to discuss."

Lorenzo moves over to the side table, his hand reaching out to grab the decanter. Once in hand, he grabs two glasses.

"Should I even bother getting ice?"

"The fucking glasses are a stretch." I use the remainder of my willpower not to spit on the floor.

Normally, I would drink scotch on the rocks, but right now, I just need a drink, and I don't care if it goes down with a side of cyanide.

When both our glasses are poured, he takes a seat, and like me, I know he needs it. War may be a part of my business, but that doesn't mean I show up to battle willingly.

But the battle is a necessary evil. To win, one must be cruel.

"So, Salvatore has access to the ports, and there is nothing we can do about it," Lorenzo grumbles.

"Not necessarily," I grit out through clenched teeth.

"How do you figure? Marino hates you. He's been trying to get you out for years. We've been doing the same."

"We need to find something on him." My voice is rough, making Lorenzo tense. He places his drink down. Right before my eyes, my drinking buddy is gone, in his place is the *underboss*.

"I've tried." He straightens his back, sitting up taller. "I have everyone looking into him. The man is squeaky fucking clean."

"No one is that clean. Especially no one getting into bed with my cousin. We need to find something. Look into his family. His wife. His daughter. There must be something."

"Will do."

"Also, once you do that, I need you to call Cristian and set up a meeting. We are going to be needing a new shipment of guns, and now that Alaric Prince is retired, I need to discuss how business will proceed."

"On it. Anything else?"

"Get Marco on the phone for me as well. Maybe he knows what Salvatore is up to."

Lorenzo's face falls for a nanosecond, before he rearranges it into his usual blank stare. There is no love lost between them. Marco is another cousin of mine. He's older. Old enough that he was involved with the war between my father and Salvatore's.

His loyalty falls with me, but Lorenzo doesn't trust him. To be honest, I don't either. But like all potential enemies, I keep him close.

The closer he is, the faster I will see if he's a snake like Salvatore.

With nothing more to say, Lorenzo leaves my office.

I pick up my phone and dial a number I haven't called in a long time.

"Hello, Matteo. I wondered how long it would take."

"Cut the shit."

"If you don't want me to talk, why are you calling, Cousin?"

"You know exactly why."

"Why so serious?" He tsks like the Joker, mirth in his voice. "Maybe you need to get laid. Is that it? Get rid of all this pent-up stress. Did you need me to help you find someone . . ." My teeth clench at his words, knowing full well what he means. "Francesca is a little old now, but I bet she still can use her—"

"Shut the fuck up!" I bellow, and he chuckles on the phone.

"Did I hit a nerve?"

"Don't you want to be better than your sadistic father? Haven't you had enough war? Back off now, and I'll let you live."

"Not a chance. I want what's mine . . ." He pauses. "And I'm prepared to do what I need to get it."

"You realize this is a war declaration," I say quietly. Smoothly. There is no way back from this. Frankly, I don't want there to be.

"Guess so."

I launch the phone in the air, hurling it against the wall. The sound echoes through the air as it smashes through the drywall.

I'll have to get a new phone, but lucky for me, we go through burners so often we are basically a phone store.

It's only a few minutes later when Lorenzo walks back in. He looks at me and then at the far wall.

"Problems?" he asks as he points at the phone.

"I called my cousin."

All emotions other than anger evaporate from his eyes. It reminds me of ice spreading, hardening his features.

"Didn't go well?"

"What gave that away?" I lift a sarcastic brow.

"Could be the broken glass on the floor." Lorenzo shrugs, trying to loosen the mood. It works as I lean back in my chair.

"What did you find out?"

"Nothing yet on the Marco front. As for Cristian, I secured more guns for us. We have to meet to go over the numbers and models we want. He wants us to go to his warehouse in New York to look over his inventory. How many are you thinking?"

"Hundreds. We need both the compound and the warehouse stocked and prepared for anything. I don't just want guns; we also need tear gas and grenades."

"I'll let him know when we schedule the meet. Anything else?"

I shake my head. "Come back after you speak to Marco."

It's hours later.

I'm staring at a map of locations my men need to collect from this week, and I'm putting together who will go where. I need to call my men in to discuss what's going on, but I am reluctant to until I have more info.

As if on cue, the door opens again.

Lorenzo is back, and this time, he walks up to my desk. He's holding an iPad.

"What did you find out?"

"A lot," he answers.

"Get everyone in here." I don't specify who I mean, but Lorenzo knows who I want to hear this. My most important men. My underboss, capo, and consigliere.

Lorenzo fires off a text, and a minute later, Roberto and Luka step into the room.

"The first thing we know is this, Marino's wife has been depositing money into the bank account of Ana Checklov's family for over twelve years," Roberto says. He is, for all intents and purposes, what most would refer to as my *consigliere*. He is my advisor and one of the smartest men I know. He studied law before stepping into his role in the business. After Lorenzo, he is the closest person to me.

Lorenzo nods and then hands over the iPad, and I see the documents that Jaxson Price, the computer hacker I keep on retainer, has sent over.

"And who is Ana Checklov?"

His hand reaches out and swipes at the screen. Behind the bank transactions are documents on the woman in question.

"An affair?" I ask, and it's Luka who shakes his head.

"No, according to the records, she was Marino's daughter's nanny," he answers.

"Interesting. Why would the governor be paying the nanny for twelve years?"

"Probably an affair." Lorenzo laughs, agreeing with my earlier assessment.

"What do we have on her?" I ask.

Lorenzo keeps scrolling through the data.

"Not a whole lot." His finger swipes the screen of the iPad. "Wait. Lookie here."

He points at the document on the screen. There, in front, is a death certificate.

"Little Ana Checklov is dead."

"It appears that way. It looks like she died twelve years ago."

"And the payments. They've been going on for all these years?"

"Yeah, exactly."

"Now isn't that interesting. . ."

"Let's get to the bottom of why they are paying her family.

Luka, I want you to speak with anyone who knows them, neighbors, old staff members. Find out what Marino is hiding. I don't care what it costs. I need to know this now."

"Okay," he answers before he leaves to start the task I have thrust upon him. I turn to Roberto.

"I need you to get Marco over here."

"No problem. Also, I spoke to Cyrus."

"And? Do I still have money?" I laugh, lightening the mood. "Or has my banker stolen everything?"

"He's a pain the ass. I prefer to deal with Maxwell," he gripes, and I can't really blame him. Cyrus Reed, aka the bank to the underworld, is one of the biggest pricks out there, but he's damn good at his job.

"I'm sure you'll get your wish soon enough. It's only a matter of time until he's completely retired."

"Is there anything else we can do for you?" Lorenzo asks.

"Nope."

Both men move to leave the room as I lean back in my chair. This is going to be a long night.

Lorenzo stops at the door and turns to face me. "I forgot to tell you. You're meeting with Cristian to discuss the incoming shipment of guns this week."

I nod. "Come back when you have more information for me."

"Will do."

They leave me in my office with the iPad still on my desk.

Pulling it closer to me, I swipe the screen.

What are you hiding, Marino?

I look through the images of the governor. My teeth grind together as I stare at the man who has become a thorn in my side. His dark, soulless eyes stare back at me in each picture. He's probably in his mid-sixties, the age my father would be if he were still alive, with salt-and-pepper hair and an olive complexion. I imagine women must think him to be a handsome man, regardless of the wrinkles lining his weathered face. Power and money will do that.

I continue my perusal. The next image stops me because in this one, he's not alone.

He stares back at me, sandwiched between his wife and daughter.

His daughter is the one who gives me pause.

She's gorgeous.

An exotic beauty with long, dark brown hair that flows in loose waves past her breasts.

She's different than the women I associate with . . .

I drag my eyes away from her photo to look at the rest of the file.

Twenty-two years old.

Five feet two.

Well educated.

A whole future ahead of her.

*Pity.*

# CHAPTER TWO

## Viviana

ONLY ONE MORE WEEK LEFT UNTIL GRADUATION. I CAN'T believe the day is almost here.

Once it comes, I'll finally be able to distance myself.

I'll find a job.

I will get out from under my father's thumb.

I just need to make it through one more week.

Not true.

A job. Paying my bills.

A heavy feeling weighs on my chest. I'll never be able to escape him.

My father will use me as his pawn as he always does. Once I leave school, he'll keep me in line by making me work for him.

And I have no choice. . .

Maybe one day.

The door to my apartment swings open. I don't need to look up from my computer to know who it is.

It's obviously Julia.

She's the only person—well, besides my parents—who has a key.

"Hey, babe." I hear her say as the sound of her feet on the floor echoes through the space as she approaches me on the couch.

"Hi." I lift my gaze from the screen. "Didn't think you'd be here so early."

"Umm, you should have expected me earlier." She rolls her eyes, making me laugh. "We're going out, remember? It's pre-gaming time."

"Pre-gaming. Really, Jules, what am I, still in college?"

"For another week, you are. Don't rush me. You're not ready for the real world. I hear there are work and taxes and all kinds of bullshit out there. Please tell me you're still coming with me tonight and you didn't forget." She groans loudly, being her completely overdramatic self.

I stare at her for a moment. When she laughs, she reminds me so much of her mother. They have the same light brown hair and blue eyes, but it's the way she smiles. It's the same smile Ana had when she would play with us. When she would move the figurines around the old dollhouse with me.

My heart clenches.

"Viv, where did you go? You're off in la-la land." Jules snaps her fingers, pulling me from my memories.

What was she saying? Oh yeah, going out tonight.

"How could I forget? You reminded me every day this week." I pretend to sulk, but really, I love her.

"Well, we have to celebrate you graduating."

"I haven't graduated *yet*."

"Semantics."

I roll my eyes at my friend.

But she is right. Although, technically, I haven't gotten my diploma yet, I am officially done with school.

This is my last weekend living here, and next week, I will have to tell my father I wasn't going to be part of his plan for the future.

My father has considered me a bargaining chip for the longest time. I've been able to put him off for years by going to college, but my father comes from a traditional Sicilian family. In his mind, I should already be married.

Married to a man he's picked for me.

It's just a matter of time before the shoe drops, and he dictates my life.

As crazy as it sounds, I'm expecting a call about my impending doom at any minute.

For some time now, I've known that my father will try to marry me off to whoever he thinks will benefit him.

A future I want no part of.

"When do you go back home?" Julia asks as she walks to the kitchen attached to my living room and swings open the fridge. A minute later, Diet Coke in hand, she sits on the couch adjacent from me.

"Hopefully never," I mumble under my breath.

"Yeah, because Daddy Marino will ever go for that."

"A girl's allowed to dream." I let out a wistful sigh.

"That's not a dream, honey. That's a fantasy. Hell will freeze over before Marino will let you out of his sight. I'm surprised you haven't been summoned before. Isn't he champing at the bit to marry you off?"

"He is." There's a ball of anxiety in my voice, and it is growing impossibly large right now.

"And who is the lucky suitor?" She laughs. This has become a game. I go to dinner with my family, my father tries to arrange a marriage for me, and then I meet up with Julia and tell her all the gruesome details.

"Beats the fuck out of me. But I'm not looking forward to that fight. I need to think of a plan. Every time they do this, I'm afraid this will be the time they finally make me."

"Do you have enough money saved to break free on your own?"

"No," I admit. And that ball of anxiety? It gets bigger, making it harder to breathe.

"I wish I could help . . ."

I lean forward, placing my face in my palms. "I know, and I love you for it."

And I do. Julia and I have been friends since we were kids. Her mother was my nanny, and she and her brother were raised on the estate with me. After her mother passed, we had lost touch.

My father's doing . . .

He controlled me and who I spoke to.

But when we ended up at the same college by chance, our friendship quickly reverted to what it was before. The moment I heard from one of the staff members at my parents' house that Jules would be at NYU as well, I had a feeling I would see her. I was right. She sought me out, and when she finally found me, she basically jumped on top of me and vowed never to let me out of her sight again. Seeing her the first time was hard. I hadn't seen her since her mother died. The memories attacked me, making it hard to breathe, but then she laughed like she always did, smiled, and made me promise never to leave her again.

I did.

A promise I'll never regret.

No matter what it costs me, I need her in my life. She is my life raft. The only person who understands my family. Understands the power the "governor" has on me.

In her own way, and unbeknownst to her, she's a part of it.

My need to help her, protect her, and also atone for my past sins, keeps me under my father's thumb.

*She doesn't know that part, though. Nor will she ever.*

"When do you have to see him?" Her voice dips, her once peppy attitude turning more somber.

"Dinner is tomorrow, I'm sure. Like always," I deadpan.

As much as I wish it wasn't the case, my father insists I attend family dinner every Sunday night. He makes sure pictures are always taken, posted, and tweeted.

He wants to portray the picture of the perfect family man.

If only that was the truth.

But that's my role. To be the perfect daughter. All in the great pursuit of the ultimate goal.

My father has always made it very clear what that would be.

My father has presidential dreams. He also has very powerful friends who will get him there.

The man is cutthroat, ruthless, and to top it off, a real asshole.

There is not one good bone in his whole body.

He is the devil incarnate.

A feeling of dread always overcomes me when I know I have to see him. That I will have to acknowledge his presence at all.

But the worst part about it, the part I dread the most, is that no matter how hard I try to break away, he still has complete control over me. It's gotten worse too. Every year, it gets worse. My heart lurches again as bile travels up my throat.

I hate the man.

The feeling is mutual, I'm sure.

There is no love lost between us.

As if manifested by a higher power, my cell phone dings on the table. I know it's him before I even check who's calling.

Other than Julia, no one calls me.

Not even my mother.

She is the dutiful wife. The perfect politician's accessory.

Too bad she is an awful parent. Even awful is an understatement for what she is.

I grab my phone and look down. Just as I suspected, there on the screen is a message from dear old dad.

**Governor asshole: Dinner tomorrow. 6:00 pm. Do not be late, Viviana.**

Great. He's scolding me through the phone.

I tip it toward Jules to show her what he wrote. She laughs when she sees it.

"Governor asshole? Not Dad?"

"Lord no. That wouldn't properly depict how I feel every time he calls me. Now would it?" I smile. It's a sugary sweet smile, but one hundred percent laced with venom.

"No." She shakes her head. "It wouldn't."

Julia knows how much I hate my father, but she doesn't truly understand.

She doesn't understand that the money my family pays hers is hush money more than it is to help them. And she doesn't know the secret of why . . .

When her mother died in my house, she and her brother were orphaned, left to live with poor relatives. Everything I have ever done that my father has asked of me is to make sure he helps her and Jonathan.

I shake my head. I can't think of that now.

Especially when there is nothing I can do to get out from under his thumb.

He leverages everything on me. Always making sure I behave.

Needing to think about something else, I stand from the chair and turn to face Julia.

"I'm going to get showered. Need to look good for tonight." I smile. The truth is, I don't care what I look like, but my guilt eats away at me, so I have to leave.

"Yeah, you kind of smell too." I laugh at her words and shake my head as I walk toward my bedroom, leaving a giggling Julia behind.

Once I'm in my bathroom, I strip off my clothes, turn the shower on, and step under the water.

It's scalding hot.

Too hot.

Reminding me of a time before. A time when my whole life changed. A time that is still holding me hostage all these years later.

They say that time can heal all wounds.

But what if the wounds are still festering?

What if there is no cure?

What do you do then?

It's been twelve years, and I still have no answer to that question. It hovers over me like a black hole in the dark universe. I know it will eventually suck me in and eat me alive. The only question is when.

As I stand here, lost in my thoughts, I forget how hot the water is. The bathroom is fogged up, and I can barely see in front of me.

Quickly, I turn the shower knob. The water temperature changes fast. Now it feels like it's pouring ice over my body.

I shiver against the pellets hitting my skin.

But I welcome it. The job is done. It cools the memories, thrusting them back into the crevices of my mind where I need to keep them.

At least for now.

That maybe won't be the case soon, but until I can do something about it, I have to make it day by day. I have to survive the torture this man inflicts upon me, even if that means entertaining his friend's children. Or being paraded around like a high-priced hooker, one whose virtue is the price of the right political alliance.

I take a deep breath and continue to wash my hair until the water runs clear from the suds, then I turn it off and pull back the curtain to grab my towel.

When I'm done drying my skin, I can't help but stare at myself in the cloudy mirror.

I lean over the bathroom countertop until I'm close enough to touch my reflection. I look exhausted, weary, and above all— like I've seen too much. Although my face is what others might construe as perfect, at twenty-two, to me, it's anything but. Too much emotional weight sits on my shoulders. Eyes that always look haunted by the ghosts of my past.

Will I ever feel young and carefree again?

*You will figure it out, Viviana.*

Everything will be okay. I must tell myself that, even if it's not true.

I'm almost done with school. I'll get a job.

Yep. That's it. Once I get a job, it will be over. I won't need him anymore.

Pushing my shoulders back, I stand taller, knowing I won't let him win.

Eventually, I will be the victor.

---

Hours later, we're at the bar.

As much as I pretend I want to be here, I don't. My nerves are too shot for what tomorrow will bring. Carefree hasn't been in my vocabulary since I was ten years old and learned what I was born into.

I know I should get drunk with my friend and not think about it, but I can't.

The black cloud hangs over me. There is no pushing it away. How could I? Every time I see him, there is another demand made of me. Something he needs me to do that I don't want to.

No matter what, though, no matter what is asked, I'll do it.

I will willingly give another piece of my soul for the price of my friends.

The music blares through the space, drowning out some of my thoughts. I can barely hear anything as I feel Julia's hand on my arm.

"Let's grab a drink," she says, pulling me with her to the bar. I take a moment to let my eyes scan the room. Sleek, red velvet booths surround the space, and black crystal chandeliers hang from above.

"Sure!" I yell back.

Together, we make our way across the room. Once we are standing in front of the bartender, we order drinks.

He's quick at making them, smiling at me as he pours the liquid into the glasses.

As I lift it to my mouth, I swear I see someone staring at me from across the bar.

Yes. He's one hundred percent looking at me.

*Wow.*

He's handsome. Dangerously so. The kind of handsome you read about in romance books.

Mesmerizing eyes. Jet-black hair.

He has the perfect five o'clock shadow, and his cheekbones are so sharp my fingers itch to touch them.

Something is menacing in the way he stares at me, making my back muscles go rigid.

"Viv," I hear Julia say, but I'm transfixed by the man across the bar. "Viv…" she says again, and I finally turn to her. "Everything okay?" she asks.

"I was just … The man over there," I respond, gesturing over my shoulder with my head.

A line forms between her brows. "What man?"

"Across the bar."

"There's no one—"

"Right there . . ." I look over to where he was, and no one is there. The space is completely empty.

I shake my head in confusion.

He was there, wasn't he?

I lift the drink to my mouth and continue to look around. But there is absolutely no one who even resembles the man anywhere in the bar.

I must have been imagining him.

"Come on, let's dance," Jules shouts above the sound of the music, but I shake my head.

"Next song. I want to finish my drink." She nods with a smile, and then she is off, like her normal, crazy self.

A laugh bubbles up as I see her making her way into the throngs of people. Arms in the air, swaying her hips.

"Why don't you join her . . .?"

I pivot to face the new voice, and when our eyes lock, I freeze in place, my breath stuck in my chest.

It's him. The man from before.

And he is talking to me.

Although it's dark in the club, I can make out the outline of his features better now.

If I thought he was beautiful from across the room, that image holds no candle to what he looks like up close.

He looks familiar, but I can't place him. Hopefully, he's not someone who knows my family. That would be a shame. A dangerous shame at that. But the way he looks at me, I doubt it. He just must have one of those faces.

A completely gorgeous one.

Even this close, I still can't make out his eye color. If I had to guess, I would say blue or hazel. Either way, they are as I noted before, *mesmerizing.*

It's as though he can hear my thoughts, his lip tipping up into what I can only describe as a wicked smirk.

"I wasn't in the mood," I answer.

"Her loss is my gain." Confidence oozes in his voice, but where it might be a turn-off for some, when he speaks, my body grows warm.

It's not often I'm able to indulge in mindless flirting. Between school and my father trying to pawn me off on every successful politician's son or even worse, politician, I don't often have fun.

I pivot on my heels. Now, no longer looking over my shoulder, I can see his full build.

This man is out of my league.

I reach for my glass and down the last sip.

"Would you like another one?"

*Should I?*

The more I drink, the worse tomorrow will be.

But now that I'm thinking of tomorrow, liquid courage might be exactly what I need.

"You know what? Yeah, please," I answer, and the man next to me signals the bartender, who is quick to oblige us.

The music switches to a louder and more upbeat song. I can only imagine Jules is probably completely lost to me in the beat.

"Your friend is having fun," the stranger says as he reaches for my drink on the bar and hands it to me.

"Yes. She is good at that," I say.

"At what?"

"Having fun."

"And you?" He quirks a dark, thick eyebrow. I move my jaw back and forth.

"Not so much," I admit. "What should we drink to?"

He holds up his glass for a toast. Even his square fingernails are perfect. My stomach dips.

"You pick, Somber Girl."

"To crazy friends dragging you to a club just to ditch you." I shrug.

"To strangers at a bar playing hero," he answers.

"Are you the hero?" I ask playfully, the alcohol making my head fuzzy and freeing me of my normal inhibitions.

"Not often."

"Then what are you?"

More importantly—*who* are you?

He leans in close, very close, his mouth hovering next to my ear . . .

My body becomes hyperaware of our proximity as butterflies erupt in my stomach. This is not good. I shouldn't feel his hands on me before he even touched me.

"I'm the—" he starts to say, but then a hand is wrapped around my bicep. I'm yanked backward, my head swinging around to find a dancing Jules. "You promised the next song!" she screams, flinging her arms in the air.

I turn back to the stranger, about to apologize, about to ask him to join me, but when I do, he's gone.

Again.

And like before, I wonder if I imagined the whole thing.

---

The next day I wake with a slight headache.

Nothing too awful, but bad enough that I grab two painkillers, so glad that I keep them and a bottle of water on my bedside table, and gulp them down.

Once I have taken it, I reach for my phone to check the time.

It's already 11:00 a.m.

Wow, I must have drunk more than I thought.

In the beginning, I didn't plan to stay out too long, but after being dragged onto the dance floor by Jules, I drank more.

Now, I'm late waking up and have too much to do to catch up before my father beckons to me.

I inhale deeply and check to see if there are any phone calls. Unfortunately, there is.

**Governor asshole: Be here at 5 p.m.**

Shit.

I lost an hour.

Walking into the living room, I find a passed-out Julia on the couch. Her mouth is open, and I swear she's probably drooling all over my pillow.

"Wake up, lazy," I say as I take a seat on the opposite couch.

"What time is it?" She groans, lifting her hand and swiping at her half-closed lids.

"Eleven."

"And you wake me up. Jeez, Viv, stuck up much?" Regardless of her words, I know she is not angry with me. This is just Julia. Overly dramatic to the extreme. She wears her heart on her sleeve and lets you know all about it too. That's why we get along so well. Not only is she the family I never had, but she's the complete opposite of me. She pushes me to try to enjoy life. Even if that's hard for me. If it wasn't for her, I'd never have any glimmers of peace. "If you are going to wake me, are you at least going to feed me?"

"Of course," I answer in a mock tone. "What kind of animal do you take me for?"

"Fine. I'll wake up." She sits up, and she looks like a mess. Gorgeous but a mess nonetheless. "What are we eating?"

"What do you want?"

"Something obnoxiously greasy. Bacon, egg, and cheese on a bagel."

I pull out my phone and start to scroll through the food delivery app. "French fries too?"

"Umm, duh."

I swipe across the screen and place our orders.

"Ugh, Viv. I'm so hungover. I'm never going to drink again."

"Lies," I say flatly.

Jules laughs groggily, but stops when she realizes it results in one hell of a headache. I look over at my disheveled friend. I don't look or feel much better than her. The drink I had with the stranger was not needed.

Speaking of . . .

"For someone who wants me to go out and get laid, you certainly were a cockblock last night," I deadpan.

"What do you mean?" She tilts her head to the side, brows knit together.

"The guy I was talking to."

"You were talking to a guy?"

"Yes, dick. I was. And he was hot."

"Oops."

"Oops is right. Now I have to go to my parents' tonight and, who knows, that could have been my last chance at a torrid affair. Knowing my father, he's shipping me off to live with a long-lost family member in Sicily."

She grimaces at my words.

"I sure hope not."

"Me too."

---

I dread seeing him.

All the way into New Jersey, my stomach twists and turns.

As we approach the large monstrosity of the governor's house, it feels as though a heavy lead weighs me down.

There is no question my father is about to request. . . demand something of me.

Usually, there is a hefty price to be paid, but I fear the price will be steeper since I have pushed back this moment to go to college. It was inevitable that we would discuss my future, but now that I know it's time to pay the piper, I'm not ready.

So far in life, I have given in. I have played the dutiful daughter. Smiling and political for his campaign, but now as the car he's sent for me drives through the gates, I'm truly scared.

I'm done with college.

His requests will be more significant.

No doubt a price I'm not willing to pay.

A price I'll have to pay.

When the car stops, I wait for the driver to exit the car and open the door.

It's pretentious, and I hate it. But just in case a camera is flashing somewhere in the distance, I have no choice.

I step out of the car, then place my hand down and flatten my skirt.

My hair is perfectly coifed.

I am the perfect example of a politician's daughter.

I know my father has lofty goals, and I know he will use me to further them if he can.

I take the few steps, and as if on cue, the large mahogany door swings open.

A member of my father's staff sent to greet me.

You would think I would have the luxury of coming and going in my own house. . .

I don't.

And let's be honest, this is not my house. Nor was the one before.

I've never truly had a home.

Not true.

Ana gave me a home.

She took care of me, fed me, cleaned my cuts, and played with me for hours.

Well, at least she did before my mistake.

"The governor is in his office."

"And my mother?" I ask as I walk through the foyer.

"She's upstairs."

Not a surprise. She's always been too busy being the perfect wife to care about being a good, hell, *decent* mother.

She never came to my school plays. Nor did she even attend a curriculum night. Always too busy jet-setting. Hobnobbing with someone important, and most probably drunk.

Thankfully, Ana, for the time she was in my life, was there for me.

If only she were here now. She would hold my hand and give me strength. But since she's not, I square my own shoulders and pretend she is whispering in my ear. *"Plato said,*

*'Courage is knowing what not to fear.' You have no reason to fear your dad. He's just a man."*

At the time, I didn't know who Plato was, but I trusted that she was right. I tried to be brave and not fear him, and I'm still trying. Her voice still in my ear.

I continue toward my father's office and find the door open.

Of course it is.

He's waiting for me, drinking his scotch and ready to strike. You can see it in his eyes and with his posture. He oozes danger in quantities that should be illegal, and the ball of anxiety in my throat is back again.

"Come in, Viviana."

His voice takes me by surprise. I'm lurking and didn't think he knew I was here.

But I shouldn't be surprised.

My father sees everything

Knows everything.

I tentatively walk inside, taking small, measured steps.

"Hurry up, Viviana. I don't have all night, and I have something I need to speak to you about."

My stomach feels heavy, filled with dread.

I can feel the sweat start to bead in the back of my hair, my heart pounding in my chest as I cross the space and take a seat on the chair opposite from where he sits at his desk. His dark and angry eyes stare at me as his lips thin into a sneer.

"What did you have to talk to me about?" I ask, trying desperately to sound strong and confident.

"Your graduation."

My ears start to ring, making it hard to hear. I take a deep breath.

*Show no fear.*

Don't give him the satisfaction of seeing you squirm.

As my pulse regulates, he speaks.

"I expect now that you have finished, you will do your duty for your family."

"Duty?"

"Yes, Viviana. Your duty. Your mother and I have indulged you for way too long."

"What does that even mean?"

"We allowed you to go to college. Allowed you to get the best education. You are now a well-spoken, educated young lady. . ."

"And?"

"Now it's time to help us."

I shake my head, not understanding what he's trying to say.

"Help . . . how? Like work in your office?"

It wasn't an ideal solution, but I would work there for a bit to get him off my case while I save money to do something else. Of course, I'm stalling. I'm not dumb and optimistic enough to assume that's what he's talking about.

"Come now, Viviana. You know better than that."

"I do?" *Stalling, stalling, stalling.*

"Your place isn't in the office. You are much better served elsewhere."

"And where would that be?" My tone is clipped now.

"Making alliances."

Cold ice fills my veins as I wait for what I know is about to come.

"I think it's time we used your looks, personality, and now education to our advantage."

"Umm. I don't understand."

"As you know, I have goals. Big goals. And in order to achieve these goals, I need to have the right connections. The best way for me to achieve this is to work with certain people."

"Okay . . ."

"But to do this, I need to show a level of commitment. I need to tie myself to them. And you are the perfect way."

"I'm sorry, Father, but I don't understand what you are saying."

"I want you to marry Salvatore Amante."

My mouth drops open. And that ball of anxiety in my throat? It just blocked my air pipes.

"I ... I can't marry him. I don't know him," I somehow manage to say.

"Viviana, that wasn't a suggestion. You will marry Salvatore Amante. I need him. He will guarantee we get everything we have always desired."

"We? Don't you mean you?"

"You want this too, Viviana. This is what's best for me, for you, and also for Julia."

He slides a paper across the desk. "Read that over, and then tell me what you decide."

The weight of the paper feels like a million pounds of stones in my hand. My head tilts down as my eyes scan it. The words blur under my unshed tears. Old scars from the past open and start to fester, but my stomach bottoms out when I see what it says, and my heart starts to race. My shaking hands drop the piece of evidence that changes everything. What I just read makes no sense. How can this be? If this is true . . . Confusion and despair like I have never felt before pulses inside me.

"Is this real?"

"It is."

"You—"

"Silence!" he bellows. "You will not question me. You will not question what I did. Understand me . . . you *will* fall in line." The threat hangs heavy in the air. "And remember what happened to Ana is your fault. What happens to her children from this moment forward . . ." Is on me. He doesn't say it, but there is no need. Their lives are in my hands, and I'm not sure what that means for any of us.

My reply sticks in my throat, gravelly, heavy, making it impossible to speak.

I won't do as he says, but I can't allow him to know. But first, I need to find out if he's lying to me yet again.

My father is a monster. If he thinks I'm going against him, he will retaliate.

I need to bide my time and figure out a plan.

There has to be some way out of this mess.

I just have to figure out how.

Now, sitting at the table in the formal dining room, I try my best to get out of here unscathed. If there's no talking at dinner, I'd be a happy camper.

There is nothing to say, so I try to keep my head down the whole time.

Unfortunately, my mother doesn't agree with my sentiment because as I look down at the table, pushing my salad around the plate, she says my name.

"Viviana. When will you be moving back into the house?"

My head pops up. "What? No one said anything about me moving back in," I fire at my father. "Why can't I stay at my apartment?"

"That wouldn't be proper," she responds. My father gives me a pointed look. One that clearly says I will not give my parents a hard time about this.

"With you being done with school, I expect you back in the house."

"I still have graduation . . ." I try to argue, grasping at straws. Every day is needed to figure out a way out of this mess.

"Then I expect you home in one week, young lady. I can't have people talking."

And there it is. She doesn't care about me. She only cares about her reputation. Now that I'm done with my studies, living alone in the city would be scandalous to her religious friends.

I'm expected to be a virginal bride. Too late for that, but at least if they have me under their roof, they think they can keep the gossip low. It's funny how little they know about me. I'm not one for making a spectacle of myself. I have too much to lose already to chance it.

With a sigh, I nod. "Next week then."

A very long hour later, I'm back in the car, pulling up to my apartment.

I'm not sure what I'm going to do.

My options are limited.

Like always, my father has me. If I don't do what he wants, more than just me will suffer.

I've made too many people suffer already.

I can't do it again.

With my head down and my heart heavy, I step out of the car. Normally, I would speak to Julia about my issues with my father, but seeing as this concerns her, I can't burden her. Even though she doesn't know the truth—that he's using her future to hang over my head—if I told her, she would still tell me to tell my father to stuff it. Jules isn't one to take orders. She beats to her own drum. I guess growing up without parents, with relatives you don't know, makes you strong. Because she is. She's headstrong, the type of girl to make a rash decision regardless of the consequences.

Nope, I can't tell her. That's not an option.

I shake myself out of my thoughts and pull the keys for my apartment out of my bag.

Placing it into the lock, I turn the key and swing the door open.

The apartment is pitch-black.

Hadn't I left the light on?

The small hairs on my neck rise.

Someone is here.

I'm not alone.

The small lamp in the corner of the room flips on.

His eyes.

I know those eyes.

"Hello, Viviana," a husky voice drawls out, sending a chill down my back. "Let's pick up from where we left off. Why don't you have a seat? We have much to discuss."

# CHAPTER THREE

## Matteo

"WHY ARE YOU IN MY APARTMENT?" HER VOICE CRACKS, giving away the fear that she is trying to conceal. She holds herself tall, but there is no mistaking the way she sounds. And if that isn't enough, her eyes keep looking back at the door. She's nervous, but she tries to hide it. It makes me want to toy with her. But I'm also aware she is a corrupt politician's daughter through and through when she's not completely falling over her own feet with shock. Another woman would have cried and fainted long ago.

I lean forward in the chair I'm sitting in and place the gun I'm holding on my knee.

"Come closer. I won't bite."

She does the opposite as I say, and instead, she takes a step back, edging toward her escape.

It won't do her any good. Even if she makes it into the hall, my men are standing outside waiting for her.

Either way, the outcome will be the same.

"Why are you here?" she repeats. There is a false bravado in her voice, and it makes my lips tip up into a smile. I like the way she pretends she's not terrified. I find something intoxicating about a strong woman who shows no fear.

Regardless of what she portrays, I know the truth, and I will exploit it.

I allow her to move another step, but this time, I shake my head while tsking.

"I wouldn't do that if I were you." I lift my hand, displaying the gun that rests upon my lap.

Her eyes go wide.

She looks like a deer caught in headlights. There is no mistaking the fear and shock that crosses her face.

"Sit." This time I leave no room for objection, and much to my pleasure, she obliges me.

Slowly, she crosses into the room, and then she takes a seat. If I was one to laugh, I would because she picks the farthest chair in the room from me to finally sit.

Not that it will help her.

If I wanted to harm her, it wouldn't matter the distance between us. I would find a way.

"Viviana Marino . . ." I draw out. "It's a pleasure to meet you."

As I suspected, her body stiffens at my addressing her by her full name.

"How do you know who I am?"

That's when I decide to laugh, but it's not a real laugh. It's a sinister one.

Perfect for instilling fear in her. "I know everything about you. I know your name." I gesture around. "I know where you live, your drink of choice, what you studied, how you like your fucking eggs, and most importantly, I know you are the only daughter of Governor Marino," I finish, deadpan.

"All public knowledge. You use Google." She shrugs, but she is shaking. I can see it. "Big deal."

"You majored in English lit. Graduating with a 4.0 average, and your best friend is Julia Checklov. Should I go on? Very well. You've been to the hospital two times, once for a broken wrist at the age of fifteen, and the other time from a fire at the age of ten."

The shock on her face from before has nothing on the look

she's giving me now. Her normally large eyes are even bigger than usual. They look like they will burst from their sockets. She reminds me of a cartoon character.

I think she might pass out from how worked up she is, but instead, she nibbles on her lip and closes her eyes for a moment. When she finally opens them again, she looks calmer, stronger, with a passion that simmers beneath her surface. It's intriguing, like a perfectly wrapped gift that will be even more enjoyable to tear apart.

"This is about my dad," she states.

"Smart girl." I smirk. "Bet you didn't get that from your daddy."

"Well, then you're wasting your time. I know nothing about his work, and truth be told, he probably wouldn't give you anything for me."

"You think so little of your importance?"

"I have no importance." She tips her chin up, and I can tell she believes what she says. Unfortunately, she is an unreliable narrator in her own story.

"Don't you want to know why I'm here?" I can't help but grin. Fuck, she is gorgeous. And fuck, she'll be fun to play with.

"Honestly, not really."

Her response makes me chuckle, despite the fact that I normally don't. There is something about her. "Interesting answer. But regardless of what you want, I'm going to tell you."

She doesn't speak. Instead, she starts to nibble on her lip again. This must be her tell. She's nervous. I store this information away in my mind.

"Your father wants you to marry Salvatore Amante."

She stops chewing as her mouth drops open.

"How—"

I raise my hand up to silence her. "How do I know that? As I told you before, I know everything."

Clearly, I have shocked her again, but she will soon learn that it is not often that something gets past me. *My cousin being the exception.*

Even from where I'm sitting across the room, I can still see how her jaw shakes. "W-what do you want from me?" she stutters.

"You're not marrying him," I say flatly. And mean it. She won't.

She narrows her eyes and then shakes her head. "I don't think you understand. My father—"

"Is the one of no importance in this story. I understand more than you will ever know, Viviana."

"I don't have a choice," she whispers more to herself than to me, but I still answer.

"Yes, you do." My voice is strong, and it leaves no room for objection. Instead, she studies me, trying to understand why I'm here talking to her.

"Why do you even care?"

This is the part where I get to smile. Well, more like smirk. This is the part where I tell her the future she has yet to figure out. Her role in this chess game between my cousin and me. "I care because you are going to marry me instead."

I expect her to do something crazy and call me insane or scream at me, but instead, she narrows her eyes and gives me a look I can't understand.

"Why would I do that?"

"I think you misunderstand. I'm not giving you a choice. I'm telling you. You will marry me."

"And who are you?"

My mouth splits into a larger smile. "I'm happy you asked… I'm Matteo Amante."

Cue the shock.

Cue the fear.

"You're M-Matteo Amante?" she stutters.

"I see my name precedes me."

Of course, it does. Everyone knows who I am. Not only am I considered one of New York's most eligible bachelors, but if you travel in my circles, I'm also the deadliest.

Seeing as she's the governor of New Jersey's daughter, I'm not shocked that she knows.

"I can't marry you."

"You can, and you will. Your choice is my cousin or me. I can tell you I'm the better choice."

"I'm not marrying anyone."

"We both know you are out of options. We both know your father has been paying off your debt for years and hanging it over your head."

Her eyes go wide. "How do you—"

"Know? Again, I know everything. I know all about the accident."

If she wants to speak, she can't seem to find the words. Instead, she reminds me of a floundering fish as her mouth opens and closes.

"I know what happened. I know your father hangs it over your head, and I know the guilt."

It's a bluff. I don't know shit yet.

I know vague details but not exactly what happened.

"How could you know this?" she whispers. "No one knows."

"I'm not everyone."

"You're not my future husband, either."

"Here's where you're wrong, *Princess*."

The room goes silent around us. She's trying to figure me out. Understand my motive. I can almost hear the wheels turning in her head.

"What will you do with this knowledge? If my father finds out . . ."

"You let me worry about your father."

"And Julia, her brother. What about . . .?" she trails off.

"I will handle everything. Everything your father handles will fall on me."

"Why?"

"Do not have any preconceived notions that I am doing this for you. I'm not a good guy. I'm not the hero. I need something, and you are the key to getting it."

"And if I refuse?"

"You won't." I study her for a moment. I like her bite. I like that she thinks she can refuse me, that she thinks she has a choice.

"You're confident."

"I am. Plus, you do not want to deal with my cousin, who is a sadist. My deal will protect you. From him and your father."

"And you're not?"

"I am, but a different kind than him. I will handle your father. This will be a marriage in name only. You won't have to worry about me. You will have your life, and I will have mine. . ."

My words are clear. This is a means to an end and nothing more.

She goes back to chewing her lip. I want to take my hand and grab it. It's distracting as all fuck.

"What do you want from him?"

"Control. Revenge. Your father thought he could get in bed with my enemy. He will learn very fast that there is no going against me. My cousin will learn too. If you are his bartering chip, I'll take it from him."

"I'm the pawn."

"Yes."

"At least you're honest."

"That is one thing you will learn about me. I don't lie."

"So . . . you want to marry me?"

"No, Viviana. I don't. But this is the course of action I am taking. Have no false illusions. I will never love you. I will never care for you. But if you do this, if you help me, I will take care of you."

She goes quiet again.

Viviana Marino is beautiful when she's pensive. Her big brown eyes deep with thought.

"When?"

"As soon as possible," I answer.

I'm surprised by how fast she comes to a decision. I expected to have to threaten her or hang her secret over her head. But instead, she straightens her back and stands up.

"Okay."

It's done.

# CHAPTER FOUR

## Viviana

IT DOESN'T TAKE A ROCKET SCIENTIST TO KNOW I'M SCREWED.

Two proposals in one night. . .

None of them welcome.

My prospects of escaping unscathed are slim to none at this point.

Option number one: Fall in line with my father's wishes. Yet again.

Option number two: Get in bed with his enemy . . . literally and figuratively.

My heart begins to race. He did say it would be in name only.

But what does that really mean? I don't really know.

The saying "better the devil you know" rings through my head, but as much as that is the case in most circumstances, in mine, it's the opposite.

Anything is better than doing what my father wishes.

The man hates me.

All my life, he has gone above and beyond to hurt me.

Why would this be any different?

I might not know Matteo, but I know my father.

If I allow myself to be his victim again, he will never take his claws out of me. If I marry Salvatore as he demands, I will never get out from under his thumb.

But the option of saying no to Matteo is also out of my grasp.

*Is that really true? There is always another route.*

I'm a ping-pong ball.

Bouncing back and forth.

Better yet, my life is a tennis match . . .

Eventually, someone would get the point, but no matter who it is, I'm the one getting hit by the racket.

If I had a choice, I would escape.

Thinking of my options is not something I want to do because it feels like I'm stuck in quicksand trying to break free but can't.

No, this is different because I get to choose. Regardless of what Matteo or my father insists, the ball is in my court.

I can smile and pretend to appease this man, not fight him, and then do the opposite.

Or I can say yes and mean it.

I stare at him for a minute, realizing Matteo might very well be the first person to offer me a chance to get out from under my father's thumb. A part of me wonders if it's all an act and if he will actually help me. Normally, I would think no, but something in his stare says otherwise. As strange as it sounds, I feel like I can trust him.

Now that my eyes have adjusted to the light, I can see that they aren't as dark as I once imagined them to be.

No.

They are the opposite. Although I can't tell what color they are, a striking difference exists between the color of his pupils and irises.

Light.

His eyes are light.

But what color?

I step toward the wall, clicking the switch to illuminate the space between us.

I'm not prepared for the man sitting before me. He's leaning back in the chair.

Comfortable. It's as if I invited him in for a drink. Like we were on a date, and I asked if he wanted to come up for a nightcap.

His presence is intimidating. But it's his facial features that make me stop breathing.

When I saw him briefly at the club, he was gorgeous, but now in the light, I realize that word does him no justice.

He's devastating.

His eyes are green. Strikingly so. Like the way grass looks after a rain on the first sunny day. Lush and full.

Crisp.

Dangerous.

They make you want to lose yourself in them.

Not a good scenario to be in.

Ever.

I continue to watch him. Drinking him in. Studying. Searching. Filing things into memory.

His hair is dark, almost black, but it's his sharp jaw with the dusting of hair on his face that makes him exquisite.

Deadly. Not just physically but emotionally.

*This man would chew you up and spit you out if you allow him to.*

He has more than a five o'clock shadow but less than a beard. It's the kind of scruff that feels sexy as you kiss.

Shit. Don't think about kissing him.

He does have full lips. Dammit, they are kissable. A mouth that would worship the woman beneath him.

I can't marry this man. I can't.

If he wanted to, he would do unthinkable things to me, and I would probably let him.

Not a good combination in this situation.

It might sound backward, but wanting him will make this more challenging.

I'm under no false illusion that no matter what he says about having separate lives, I will have to be with him. At some point, his family business will dictate the need for him to have an heir to carry on his legacy. It wouldn't be a chore but . . .

I shake my head and pull my gaze up to meet his stare. I can marry this stranger. I can use him to further my goal.

Make my father pay for all he's done to me over the years.

I'll still be the pawn in their war. But what they both don't know is that I have no intention of being it any longer.

"I have stipulations." I walk farther into the room until I'm standing beside the other chair.

"Oh, of course you do, *Princess*." He sounds beyond amused as though he is talking to a toddler. Not outwardly funny, but as in the light of what we are talking about, he is not taking me seriously. I'm torn between seething and doing what I can to protect my life.

Is he so coldhearted that he doesn't see how all of this hurts me, and if he does, then he is as big of a monster as my dad and just doesn't care.

The thought has goose bumps forming on my skin. I'm abandoning one cage and willingly crawling into another.

One that very well could be more deadly.

"I want a contract," I blurt out. If I have that, I can make him honor it. It wouldn't hold up in a court of law probably, but it would give me a sense of security.

"You will get no such thing." He now sounds bored with me. As if my request is so far beneath him that he won't even humor the idea of it.

I stand my ground with my hands on my hips.

False bravado.

Inside, I'm quaking, but I throw off the vibe that I'm as tough as nails on the outside.

"You don't even know what the contract will contain," I answer, narrowing my eyes.

"It doesn't matter to me, Viviana. I will not put anything in writing."

His message comes loud and clear.

My dreams of this going easy crash and burn to the floor.

"I still have things I want from you," I respond. The chances he'll give me what I want are small, but I'm still going to try. Through my eavesdropping on Father's many secret meetings over the years, he taught me how to become a master negotiator.

Ana used to say, "You can't win a game from the sidelines," and she was right. Although, when she said it, it had more to do with trying new things and not negotiating with a mob boss, but semantics.

He leans forward, inclines his head, and then gives me what can only be described as a life-altering smirk. Not just because he's gorgeous but also because it reminds me of every damn fairy tale I have ever read, where the main character enters into a pact with the devil.

"And I'm willing to listen to your requests."

"Listening is all fine and dandy, but how can I trust you to fulfill them?" I counter.

The smirk drops, and it is replaced by a flat line. "I am a man of my word. I will never lie, and I will always be straightforward. If I give you my word, my word is god." His voice is full of conviction, and even though I know I shouldn't trust him, I trust he will honor it.

"It's a marriage in name only," I say.

"Agreed."

"After you get what you want, you will allow me to divorce you."

"That's a no."

"But—"

"There are no buts. There are no objections. Once we get married, you will be my wife."

My mouth opens and closes like a fish out of water, gulping for air. There is no way I'm going to enter into this pact without an escape plan. "But then how can it be in name only—"

"I won't love you."

"But then . . . ?"

"I expect you to be faithful. I expect you to eventually bear my children, but I will never love you."

"And you? Will you be faithful?"

He levels me with a look that makes it obvious he thinks I'm an idiot. Of course, he won't be. I know men like him. Men like my father. They are all cut from the same cloth.

My teeth grind together. There are many not so nice words sitting heavy on my tongue. Instead of shouting them out, I take a long, deep inhale and then blow the air out of my mouth. It does little to calm me. I refuse to be married to a cheating pig. "No." My head shakes back and forth. "I won't marry you and be faithful unless you agree too. That wouldn't be fair."

"Life isn't fair."

"You can't expect me to be one thing and then you don't follow by the same rules. . ."

"Again, I think you misunderstand what is happening here. There isn't a democracy. You don't get a vote. You will marry me. Regardless of your belief that you have a say in it, you don't."

"No," I say again, and now my voice is higher pitch. But he doesn't seem swayed at all. Instead, he looks like he's having fun at my expense. "You're an asshole."

"If I was an asshole, I would leave you to my cousin. Do you know the difference between my cousin and me?" I keep quiet, not wanting to hear what he has to say. "The difference is . . . I won't touch you unless you ask. I will take care of you. Once we are married, if you make me happy, I'll make you happy in return. But he . . . let's just say he will use and abuse you, and after he gets whatever he wants from your father, he'll get sick of you." He pauses for a moment. "You'll probably end up dead or worse."

He doesn't say anything more.

"I gave you time to try to make the right decision, but since you obviously can't and won't come willingly, I'm making it for you." He stands. "Let's go."

"What? Go?"

"Yes. We have to get stuff ready."

"Ready for what?" I sound like an idiot. I know this, but I can't wrap my head around what's going on.

"We're getting married."

My eyes go wide. "*Now*? Like, tonight?"

It feels like my head is spinning, as if I'm on a merry-go-round, and I've just stepped off. The world's out of focus. He's speaking, but I can't make out his words over the ringing in my ears. I shake my head, pushing the fog away.

"No, Viviana. We are not getting married today." His voice is low and condescending. I want to take off my spiked heel and throw it at him, but something, and not just the gun still pointed at me, makes me think that's a bad idea.

"When are we getting married?" My voice cracks.

"We will be getting married later this week."

The breath I didn't know I was holding escapes my lips in an audible sigh.

"Oh. Okay . . . good, and here I thought you were secretly an ordained priest, and we would be hitched by the end of the day," I murmur under my breath, but still loud enough for him to hear me.

I wait for him to make a sarcastic quip of his own, but instead, he nods, looking at me expectantly.

"Now that we have that settled. We have to leave, *Princess*."

This has me really confused. He just said I have a few days. I take a step back, distancing myself from him.

"Why would I go anywhere with you?" I ask.

"One, I'm your future husband. Two, I wouldn't put it past your father to force your hand just to spite me."

"But why? I really don't understand why everyone wants to marry me so badly. None of this makes sense at all."

He moves a step toward me.

*Two pieces on a chessboard.*

His height makes me feel small in comparison. He must be six foot two or maybe even six foot three. I'm short, less than average standing at five foot two, but compared to him, I'm tiny.

"You are the key to Salvatore getting what he wants."

"And what exactly is that?"

"Port access."

My eyebrow raises, and I place my hand on my hip, not really understanding or believing my whole future has to do with docking his boat. It seems a dumb reason to marry someone.

"Seriously?"

"Yes." Matteo's one-word answer makes me dig my nails into the fleshy part of my palm. This is my life we are talking about. I deserve more than that.

"What you are telling me is that according to my father and your cousin, I'm being bartered to dock a boat?" My teeth clench.

A large exhale leaves his mouth, and I can tell he is already done with this conversation. He looks bored with me. The sentiment is mutual. I want him to leave too.

"It's not about one boat."

"Then what more can it be? Why else do you need port access? Why else is my father attempting to pawn me off for port access?"

"Drugs."

His blunt answer is shocking. Most would tiptoe around these things, but then again, Matteo Amante isn't like most men.

The room is silent. You could hear the sound of a pin drop if I were inclined to drop it.

The only noise penetrating the space between us comes from beyond the window where the occasional horn can be heard. This time, I'm pissed. I step forward, getting closer to him. I stand tall, steeling my spine.

"Seriously, did you basically tell me my only worth to you is so you can import drugs?"

He shrugs at my attack. I'm like a little gnat he's shooing away. "Well, it's better than the alternative."

"Doubtful," I mumble back under my breath.

He laughs. But it's not a funny laugh. It's a laugh that makes my stomach tighten.

Evil and sinister.

His hand reaches out and tucks the piece of hair behind my ears. "You're so innocent, dear Viviana. Like a princess locked in a tower, never to have seen the real world for what it is."

"Hardly. You don't know me. You might think you do, but you know nothing of what I have seen."

"Not a whole lot if you think that's the worst it can be. Let me tell you something . . . Princess." He smiles as he tests the nickname on his tongue. "Many things are much worse than drugs."

He waits for me to ask, but I feel like the other shoe is about to drop, and I can't bring myself to say anything else.

There is a pregnant pause. One I fear will change everything when it ends.

"Salvatore might sell drugs, but that's not why he's desperate for access. He wants the port so he can bring in women."

It feels like my heart is about to explode. "Women as in . . .?"

"Yes. My cousin traffics women. Or at least that's the plan once he can convince your father of the alliance."

Fight or flight kicks in. The need to run out of my apartment and toward safety floods my system, but I can't. There is no safe place in my life. I have nowhere to go. Nowhere my father won't find me, so instead, I remain where I am. This is the better option. I can turn a blind eye to drugs, people choose if they want to buy them, but women, that is not something I can ever move past.

What kind of a monster could? Wait . . .

"Are you saying my father knows this? That can't be possible."

"Not only is it possible but it is exactly what is happening. My cousin has made allies with some very powerful people. Your father is hoping to leverage Salvatore's connections to get him a ticket into the White House. But your father isn't a stupid man. He knows my cousin will sell him out the first chance he gets . . . That's where you come in."

"And how exactly does marrying me off help him?"

"Then you become family. He helps your father make the connections he needs, and in return, your father will help my cousin. Having you as Salvatore's wife will help him obtain the goal."

"I can't believe my father would knowingly allow that to happen to the girls."

"Then you don't know your father very well, luckily for you. Men will do a lot of ugly things to maintain power. I assure you."

His words are no longer talking about his cousin. He's talking about our marriage. I am a power piece for him too.

"Now let's go."

He starts to walk toward the door.

"I'm not ready," I say to his back. He looks over his shoulder, his green eyes piercing.

"Pack a bag. Just what you need for tonight. I'll have my people come tomorrow and get the rest."

Before I can say anything else, he turns back around, pulling his phone from his pocket to make a call.

I head into my bedroom to grab pajamas and a change of clothes for tomorrow. Jeans and a sweater. Casual. Next, I head into my bathroom and grab the necessities for one night. When everything is packed in my bag. I walk back out of the room and find him where I left him.

Still in the foyer on the phone.

He must hear me approach because he hangs up and turns toward me. He looks arrogant and strong as he stares at me. Most of all, dangerous. Like with the snap of a finger, he could have me disappear. He very likely could. I should be scared, petrified, but I'm in too much shock to register what is happening.

"Ready?" he asks.

"That's not the word I would say."

He chuckles. "I like your fight."

"Famous last words."

"Don't worry, Viviana, as my wife, you will live a long and healthy life, whether you want to or not."

That's when it finally hits me. Smashing into my gut. All the air leaves my lungs at his presence and what that means for the future. *The future . . . will I have one?*

There is no time to think of that. Instead, I need to sharpen my claws and make it through this, no matter the cost.

I will get in the car with a man who most certainly can kill me.

And worse, I will marry him.

This is bad. Very, very bad.

But he's right. My father would stop at nothing to get the White House, and if that means aligning himself with less than reputable men, so be it.

The idea I was supposed to marry a man who would hurt women has my stomach churning.

A thought pops into my head. . .

"You don't do what your cousin does?" I blurt out. Because never in the conversation before in my apartment did it even dawn on me to ask. "You don't traffic women?"

He doesn't answer right away.

Instead, I see him turn his head toward me. He's too close in the back of the Escalade. And when his pensive stare meets mine, it feels like there is a vacuum in the car that sucks all the oxygen from it.

"Do not ask me such silly questions, Princess."

"Well, if you won't tell me, what the hell else am I supposed to believe?" I fire back.

"Viviana." The way he says my name makes the tiny hairs on my arm stand up. It's lethal. I know I have gone too far, and I'm afraid of what the consequences will be. "You are not to question me." He doesn't say anything more.

Nor does he try to lighten the mood. It's oppressive.

I can barely breathe.

With each pull of oxygen, it's as if my chest has a band around it.

It tightens until the point where I can't breathe.

"Can I open the window?"

"No."

The one-word answer echoes through the car. He is really fond of one-word answers, I realize.

Even though I can't open it, I turn to look out into the city night.

The streets are busy. But then again, it is Manhattan.

Even at ten, people walk. Bars are open. Clubs are frequented. I watch as the sea of red and yellow lights whisk by and lose myself in the view. An escape only the city can provide.

This is why I chose to go to college at NYU.

My father would never let me go far, but I fought to come here.

It's another world.

And now I realize my past few years might have been the only freedom I'll ever know.

The city flies by, and I wonder where we are going. I'm

surprised when his driver pulls up to what appears to be an abandoned warehouse.

I wait as Matteo gets out of the car once we pull into the garage, and when he steps out, I follow him.

The building isn't what I expect. There are cars, but it's not your typical garage. This one looks like a garage you see in a movie about carjackers.

There must be over ten million dollars' worth of merchandise here.

What have I gotten myself into?

All of a sudden, the door across the garage opens, and three men step out. Each tall, dark, and handsome, like they walked off a cover of a magazine, but this magazine is for criminals, with dark eyes and evil sneers on their scruffy faces.

These men are not the type of men you want to bump into while walking down an abandoned street.

They look lethal.

Again, these men appear in action movies and play the villain's role.

When they start to make their way over to me, I'm not surprised.

Scared but not shocked.

They don't say a word, but one of them takes all my bags, and while one rifles through them, another one moves to search me.

As much as I want to object, I know I can't.

I'm used to being searched. I'm used to my things being searched. It's the nature of my family, so I know what they have to do. Instead of objecting, I spread my arms out, and I kick out my legs.

Might as well make it easy for them.

It doesn't take them long. They obviously don't find anything.

One of the guys nods, and then Matteo starts to walk.

He doesn't wait for me, but I follow him regardless.

Like a lost puppy trying to find its way.

Neither of us speaks one word, and I feel as though the silence is oppressive.

Or maybe it's my nerves that are.

Either way, I feel like an athlete with asthma who ran a marathon and realized they forgot their inhaler once they got to the finish line.

My only hope is he doesn't realize how off-kilter I am.

If he does, he at least has the decency not to say anything as he stops and opens the door for me, allowing me to walk through first.

I'm surprised when I step inside.

This warehouse is a fully furnished and functioning house.

"I will show you to your room." He doesn't wait for me to answer before he starts to walk in the direction of a hallway. I watch as he strides in front of me, walking tall and with a purpose. This man is always in complete command of every situation, even something as simple as heading down the hall. I wonder if he can ever relax. Ever smile.

The smirk from the night of the club pops into my head. My cheeks start to warm as the memory of that night, of the way he looked at me, attacks my senses.

No. That was a fantasy; this is reality. Do not remember that smile.

I shut down all the thoughts running wild in my head and follow Matteo until he comes to a stop in front of an elevator.

He pushes the button, and it opens.

I'm not sure how many floors this building has. By the looks from the outside, I'd say five.

Then we get to the sixth floor, and it's bigger than I thought.

He leads me down another hallway, opening the door.

The room is large. It is much bigger than my bedroom in my apartment. It's about the same size as my bedroom in the governor's mansion. But where that room is ornate and over-the-top, this room is bare bones.

Modern.

Sterile.

Almost like an expensive jail cell for the rich and famous. White lines, white pillows, and very white, barren walls. I have never seen a room this void of color. If I didn't know better, I would think he designed this place to perform surgery. However, the 800 thread count Egyptian cotton begs to differ.

"You will be instructed tomorrow with the plans."

He then steps out and closes the door behind him.

I wait for him to lock it. My mind references every fairy tale, but then I realize there is no need when nothing happens.

He doesn't need to lock the doors. He doesn't need to forbid me to leave.

I have no place to go, and even if I did, I wouldn't be safe.

I don't know if I'll ever be safe.

With a deep inhale, I lock the door and make my way farther into the room.

I noticed on the right side is another door, so I swing it open to find the bathroom. It's fully stocked, and I wonder if it's stocked for me?

I grab a toothbrush and some toothpaste and brush my teeth, and then once I'm done, I wash my face.

When I step back into the room, I finally notice that whoever took my bag earlier must have already swept it for bugs because it now sits on top of the chair in the corner.

The blood in my veins runs cold.

The message is clear . . . a lock won't keep me safe. Not wanting to think about it, I'm quick to get out of my clothes and put my pajamas on.

I can barely keep my eyes open after the day I've had. I'm so tired, I go to sit down in the bed. But as much as I want to fall asleep, I don't know if I'll be able to.

An endless loop plays in my brain.

What will tomorrow bring?

The harder and more depressing question being, what will my future bring?

Now lying on my soft bed, nestled in big fluffy pillows, I know I should be sleeping. I'll need all my strength for tomorrow, but instead, a thought pops into my head . . .

What will my father do when he finds out I betrayed him?

What will marrying Matteo entail?

Did I make the right choice?

Did I really have any choice *at all*?

I toss and turn, both thoughts at war with each other.

The question is, which enemy is scarier?

Something tells me it's my husband-to-be.

# CHAPTER FIVE

## Matteo

I WAKE EARLY THE NEXT MORNING. THE BUILDING IS QUIET, AND the floor on which I reside is completely empty. I doubt Viviana is awake yet.

Once I head downstairs, I will be met with a team of my men who have yet to sleep.

With the war with my cousin escalating, we spend more time than I wish in the warehouse.

A full team is always on guard.

I know he doesn't know about this location, so it's not like he will launch an attack, but still, I like to be prepared.

I don't bother waiting for the elevator today. Without Viviana, there is no point in taking it. Instead, I head for the stairs, figuring it will be faster.

When I make it to the bottom floor, I find five men in the main room. Two of which are sitting in front of multiple computer monitors, manning the security system.

The other two are sitting around one table and Lorenzo sits at the other by himself. It might appear they aren't working, but they are. Their guns are always drawn, ready for a fight.

Each man reclines in their chair, coffee in front of them, and beside each of their mugs is a walkie-talkie for when they do a perimeter check.

"Hey, Boss," Lorenzo says, as I take a seat at the table.

It's early still, and I haven't had my own coffee, so I reach for the pot and pour myself some. "Where are we at today?" I ask the room. "Anything on the girl? Does her father know she's gone?"

"No one has come to her apartment," Luka answers from where he is perched in front of a computer.

"Very good. Let's hope this is all behind us before they even realize it."

"Boss?"

I look over at Lorenzo. His brow is furrowed. It's obvious from the way he looks down rather quickly to his cup and then back at me, he doesn't want to say what he is about to say. I move my chair until it's next to his. That way, whatever he needs to say can be said between us.

"Spit it out, Lorenzo."

"I understand why you took the girl . . . but why marry her?"

"It's the best move. Politically, Marino can't run the risk of being on the outs with his daughter. He'll bow down to my every whim."

"But marrying her?"

I smirk at him. The answer should be clear on my face of my real motive, but I still spell it out for him. "She was meant to marry my cousin. . . "

"So, this is all a big fuck you to him."

"Yes," I answer, and I think that's the end to this discussion, but he lets out a sigh.

"Matteo."

I shake my head. He should just stop, but I will indulge him in this. He's family and my trusted confidant. I just would prefer having this conversation in a more private location, but his voice is low, so I'm sure no one else can hear. "You're tying yourself to someone."

"I could do worse."

He nods, probably realizing he has nothing more that can convince me otherwise. He then grins at me. "Well, she is hot as fuck, so there is that."

I level him with my stare. "That's my wife you're talking about."

"Future." The stupid smile on his face spreads wider. Anyone else and my gun would be pulled out, but with Lorenzo, I allow myself to crack a smile. When it's just us, I can let my guard down, even if it's only for a moment, which is before I'm back to boss mode.

"Roberto!" I yell across the room. He turns around to look at me. Roberto gets shit done, so he is exactly who I need to take point on this. "Okay, tell me what we need to do to get this ball moving. I can't wait to see the look on the dick's face when he realizes I took away his only bargaining chip."

"One day."

"Then I need you to send in someone to get her prepared. Tomorrow, I'll marry her. Make it Giana."

Giana is my first cousin. She is the daughter of my father's sister.

With that settled, I stand from the table and head back out of the room. I need to work out before I get started with my day. It keeps my head straight, helps me work out my frustrations. Being me isn't easy, and this is my only outlet.

A shipment of drugs is coming in later this week, and I need to make sure everything is set up. I can't have one of my trucks intercepted again.

There is a lot of heat on me because of my cousin. Before he went to war with me, trying to steal my business, I didn't have to worry about the ports. Nor did I have to worry that I would lose a shipment. Now all I fucking do is deal with the remnants of his attacks. I don't want to be on the defense. I need to strike first and strike hard on the offense.

I'm hoping by marrying her, I'll keep him distracted as he tries to find another in.

Instead of heading to my room, I head to the state-of-the-art gym I have situated on this floor.

Luka is already there, waiting to spar with me.

I pull off my shirt and throw on my own gloves. When I'm ready to fight, I step into the center of the room to meet him.

Throwing all my weight and frustrations into the next thirty minutes gives me a good workout.

By the time I feel ready to start my day, I'm sweaty and hungry.

"See you in thirty," I say to Luka before I pull my gloves off and head out of the room.

Again, I bypass the elevator and walk up the stairs. When I get to the landing, I turn the corner and am met with Viviana.

She's freshly showered.

In a white cashmere sweater, soft and angelic like her, and the jeans she must have packed.

Her hair is slightly damp, and she is wearing no makeup.

She's different than most of the women I fuck, and that being said, she is completely out of place standing before me. This is my warehouse to do business. I never bring women not in the family here. Like generations of men in my position, I keep a pied-à-terre for my many indulgences.

No one knows about this location, so bringing her here is a risk but a calculated one. And one I still had to take.

"Viviana," I address her coolly.

She's gorgeous. Young and innocent. The kind of woman begging to be tempted and teased.

But I can't think that way right now.

Yes, one day, she will give in to my needs, but by the way she scowls at me, I know that's not in the foreseeable future.

Which is fine. I have too much shit on my plate to deal with a needy wife.

She continues to stare at me, not speaking.

"Is there something I can do for you?"

"No." She turns back around. It's as if she left the room to see if she could, and now that she knows she can, she is turning back to hide.

"Your breakfast will be served in thirty minutes. Floor two."

"Okay." She starts to walk, mumbling, "*Tyrant,*" under her breath.

"Did you say something, Princess?"

"Nope.

"You sure? 'Cause I could have sworn you did." I smirk, not letting her off easy.

"I said take a shower, you smell."

"That's unfortunate, seeing as one day you are going to lie beneath me and give me heirs."

"I will give you something much less pleasant if you try forcing yourself on me." Her voice barely shakes as she threatens me.

"Feisty. I like that."

"In that case, I'll stop." With that, she hurries down the hall, not allowing me to say anything else. It makes me chuckle as I watch as she makes her way into the room. Once she is out of sight, I go to my own. Throwing off my wet clothes, I turn the shower on.

Fifteen minutes later, I head down to the second floor.

My men aren't here. No one is. I start to eat, expecting Viviana to come.

But she never does. Throwing my napkin down, I storm up the stairs. My fist hitting her door.

I could open it, but that would certainly start shit off on the wrong note. So instead, I'm acting like a crazed lunatic.

The door flies open.

She stands in front of me. Eyes wide. A mix of fear and stubbornness looking back at me.

"Yes."

"I told you breakfast was being served," I grit out, annoyed with how she ignored me.

"I'm not hungry."

"It wasn't a choice."

"Well then, you should have led with that. 'Good Morning, Viviana. Your presence is ordered at the breakfast table.'"

"Viviana. You will get your ass downstairs. Now! We have things to discuss."

"Jeez. Okay. You don't have to be a *tyrant*."

"Well, it seems I do. Seeing as you have chosen not to listen to me."

"I didn't know." She rolls her eyes at me. Anyone else who did that would most likely get shot. But when she does it, it gives me the reverse feelings. I don't want to shoot her. I want to bend her over and smack her ass instead.

All thoughts I probably shouldn't be having right now. Especially about my soon-to-be wife.

I turn, telling her I'm done, and she is smart enough to follow me.

Once we are in the dining room again, she sits in the chair across from me.

"What do we need to discuss?" she asks.

"Tomorrow," I answer, knowing full well she will be confused. And I'm right as she answers.

"Tomorrow?"

"Our wedding."

Her eyes go wide. It looks like she is trying to process the new information I have thrown at her, and she can't. "Wait," she starts and then stops. "What do you mean? You expect me to marry you that soon?"

"I would do it today." I shrug. "But I have back-to-back meetings, and I have my priorities straight."

She falls silent, seemingly paralyzed. The only way I know she's still breathing is by the slight tremor in her hand that sits on top of the table.

"Viviana . . ."

As if pulled out of a hazy fog, she shakes her head, and her eyes focus on me again.

"My cousin Giana will be coming here today to help you with whatever you need. Food will be served shortly." I stand and start to leave.

"You're not staying to eat with me?" This time when she speaks, her voice sounds weaker than normal. As if it's too exhausting for her to pretend to keep her walls up.

"No."

"But I thought we had things to discuss."

"I lied."

"Seriously, Tyrant . . . you have nothing to say to me?"

"Sorry to disappoint you, *Princess*, but I don't."

Her mouth opens and shuts, mentally trying to think of a witty reply, but before she can say another word, I'm out the door.

# CHAPTER SIX

## Viviana

H E LEFT ME.
I stare at the empty chair where Matteo was just sitting.

Before I can stew about it, the door opens, and a woman I've never seen before walks in. She doesn't speak, just places a plate of food in front of me.

"Thank you," I say, but she still doesn't answer.

I shrug as my stomach growls.

Just my luck, the first woman, hell, the first person I've seen since getting here who's not one of Matteo's hitmen, and she still won't give me the time of day.

I guess I'll just eat in quiet.

Hunger hasn't been on my mind recently. I wasn't thinking about it at all, but now looking down at the plate filled with food, I realize just how starved I am.

I grab the fork and dig into the eggs in front of me. Next, I take a bite of a pancake.

It's as if Matteo didn't know what I liked to eat and had his cook make me one of every breakfast dish.

I would think it was thoughtful gesture if he wasn't such a dick.

Too bad he has to be so damn good-looking. It would be easier if he wasn't attractive.

I'd be able to come up with a plan without my blood pressure rising. Not just because of his looks but also because he's infuriating.

Earlier today when I left the room and bumped into him, I thought I would stop breathing.

He had no shirt on.

His chest had a light gleam of sweat on it.

And his abs.

Oh Lord . . .

There are no words to describe those.

I stuff another bite of food in my mouth.

Yep. This would be so much easier if he was ugly. Then I wouldn't be lusting after my soon-to-be husband in a way that just seems pathetic right now with how big of an asshole he's been.

If only I could find a way out of this mess, then I wouldn't have to worry that I'm going to melt into a puddle every time he is near me.

Even thinking about this now has my cheeks warming.

I feel warm and feverish, which definitely means I'm blushing.

At least no one is here to see me.

I'm almost done with my eggs when I hear the sound of heels.

Shit.

Looking up, I see a beautiful woman approaching me. She has long brown hair and green eyes. Eyes very familiar to Matteo's, so this must be his cousin.

"Viviana, I'm Giana." She reaches her hand out, and I shake it.

"Hi. I'm Viviana."

"I know." She laughs as she drops my hand and gestures to the table. "Are you finished?"

I look down at my plate, then back at her and nod.

There's not very much left, and truth be told, I'm stuffed.

"Okay, good, because my cousin seems to think I'm a miracle worker and can get a wedding together in one day."

Surprisingly, I laugh at that. I didn't expect her to talk like that about Matteo, but then I think about her words. I swear I actually gulp when the implication of them hits me.

"What do we have to get ready? It's just going to be him and me . . . right?"

She laughs again. "Oh, God no."

"What do you mean?"

"The whole family will be there. That's the hard part. Trying to pull off the impossible. Trying to make it look like this isn't a spur-of-the-moment event."

"Why?"

"Matteo Amante doesn't just marry anyone."

"But my family won't be there. Won't that look strange?"

"No. Most everyone of importance knows why he's marrying you."

I want to scream but know I can't. I don't know why I even care that everyone knows it's a sham marriage. I just do.

"I didn't mean that to be offensive. Sorry if it came out that way, but in this family, no one marries for love. Him marrying a governor's daughter makes sense."

My head drops, strands of hair covering my eyes. It's like a protective shield right now. One I need. "I can't marry him," I admit as I look back up at her.

She tilts her head, and her eyes soften. "I don't think you have a choice. But despite the hard exterior, he'll be good to you. There are worse men to marry."

"Like Salvatore," I mumble back.

"Yes, like Salvatore."

"Well, since I have no choice, we might as well get this over with." I move to stand, but before I do, I stop. "Can I ask you something?"

"Sure."

"Do you think Matteo would let me invite someone?"

"I don't know." She nibbles on her lower lip, unsure. "Lord knows how his mind works. I can ask, though."

For the first time since this whole debacle started, I smile. "Thanks."

———————•———————

Giana is a miracle worker. Not only did she find me a dress but she also found me shoes. Apparently, the only thing she couldn't do was convince Matteo to let me invite Julia. I know my family won't be there, but I don't care about that. All I care about is having my friend by my side.

Tears fill my eyes.

I knew it was a long shot, but still, I hoped. Dreamed. But it serves me right.

Giana promised me the location for tomorrow. But apparently, Matteo stomped on that too.

No matter how much I try to find out, I get nowhere.

Giana says he's probably afraid I would tip off my family.

I wouldn't.

I don't want them to stop this wedding.

I know the ship has sailed already, and there is no going back now. So instead of trying to think about it, I tuck myself in the bedroom on the sixth floor and close my eyes, willing sleep to come.

Fortunately for me, it does.

———————•———————

Now, I'm up and dressed. The gown Giana had picked out on my body. My hair and makeup also done. Giana is apparently a woman of many talents.

I look at myself in the mirror and am taken aback by what I see.

My hair is blown out in soft waves, and my makeup is nothing, merely a light dusting. The best version of my true self she had said as she placed the gloss on my lips earlier. I'm straight out of a fairy tale, ever the princess Matteo says I am. My eyes fill with tears. In this story, I'm not marrying the prince, and I'll never have my happy ending. From here on out, I'll be the property of a mob boss.

It feels like I'm slowly losing myself in a world I'm unfamiliar with. Like I'm walking into the unknown.

I'm scared.

Marrying Matteo is a calculated move, but what if I'm wrong? What if this is the wrong decision?

What if, in my need to rid myself from my father's grasp, I have damned myself to a worse fate?

My teeth biting into my lip has me shaking myself out of the void I've just entered. I have too much going on right now to think about this.

I head down the elevator because no way in hell am I walking down those stairs in these shoes, and before I know it, I'm being placed in a car to an unknown location.

Thirty minutes later, the car stops, and when I step out, I see Giana.

She's smiling at me, but when I walk up to her, she pulls me into a hug. I am not expecting that, but it's exactly what I need with all the nerves running through me.

There is no one here for me today, so I welcome the friendship Giana gives me.

"Welcome to your new home." My new home? This is where Matteo lives? It reminds me of an English manor. A large manicured lawn surrounded by trees keeps it cocooned in privacy, but the house itself makes my mouth drop. With large pillars and a limestone façade, it's straight out of a fairy tale. "You ready?" she asks, pulling me from my thoughts.

I nod but cannot bring myself to say yes.

"How come I don't believe you?" She laughs. Because I don't even believe me. But I don't say that. Instead, I just hug her back and pull back with a smile. "You will do great. Everything will be okay. Now, let's go. It's time."

"I don't know—" I start to admit. My vision clouds from the unshed tears.

"I wish I could say something else." The look she gives me is insecure. I know she does. "I wish I could say you don't have to do this, that we can leave . . ." She motions around us. Not only do I not know where I am but it also appears we are in a heavily guarded compound. "But you can't. You need to be strong." I nod at her words, and she does as well. "Let's go get you married."

She pulls me along with her until we are inside. I feel like I'm a little girl whose mom is forcing her to go somewhere she doesn't want. I'm a rag doll in her grasp.

You can do this.

No matter how much I try to pep talk myself, I'm not prepared.

I'm not prepared for the feeling that takes root in my belly as she leads me to where the ceremony is going to be. The wedding is taking place in the grand ballroom of Matteo's estate.

I walk toward the aisle in front of me.

I can't see him yet.

But that doesn't stop the nerves that are running through my blood. My stomach feels like butterflies are swarming inside. My hands shake.

Tremors I can't will myself to contain. My feet can barely walk, and it's not because of the shoes. Although they're high, they're not what's causing me the inability to make progress. No, it's my fear.

I take a deep breath, willing myself.

*Suck it up, Viviana.*

You need to do this.

I take the step.

There aren't many people here, no more than twenty. They line the aisle, waiting. I have to hand it to Giana. She did a very good job. You would never know she threw this together in twenty-four hours. Large calla lilies adorn the room, crystal chandeliers hang from the ceiling, and a small scattering of tea candles add a level of ambiance.

To be honest, other than the circumstance of this wedding and the groom, the room is perfect.

It's exactly what I would have picked for myself if I had been given the choice.

I wasn't.

As I take each step, I finally allow my gaze to look at the front of the room, and that's when my breath hitches.

It actually freaking hitches.

As if I am a real bride, and this isn't a sham marriage.

There he is.

Matteo Amante.

My future husband.

My hero or my demise.

The music in the background filters around us.

"Pachelbel's Canon."

I should walk, I need to walk, but instead, I'm stuck in this spot and staring at *this* man. He must sense my fear because his lip tips up into the damn smirk. The one that should come with a damn warning label. That one that secretly makes me quiver in fear. Stare too long and you'll be transported to hell.

He doesn't do it often.

Usually, there is a scowl on his face, but this look is scarier than his norm.

This one makes him look sinister.

A normal person would see him and think he's smiling at me. I don't even know him, but I'm a good judge of character.

No.

He's not smiling.

He's plotting, and I have a bad feeling about it.

We stare at each other for a bit before I continue to walk.

It's like in one of the movies where everything halts. That's what it feels like when I make my way up to him. Like the world stopped, and it's only the two of us, and my future is in his big, cold hands.

He's standing in front of a priest. Time stops then as if someone put their hand on the second hand and made it. It feels like I'm frozen.

A very long second passes. Then another and another. My chest rises and falls as I will myself not to pass out.

The sounds start to fade in and out. I know what the priest is saying, yet I can't hear the words. It's as if my mind knows I'm tying myself to this evil man, and my heart refuses to hear it.

Matteo is standing close.

Too close.

It feels like his presence is sucking all the oxygen out of the room.

Everything is happening so fast.

My brain not able to comprehend anything.

I nod my head. I whisper words back. Then before I know what's happening, the priest is proclaiming us husband and wife.

I can barely breathe.

The room around me is spinning.

Matteo steps forward, and his arm reaches out to steady me. I didn't realize, but I must have been swaying.

The next thing I know, he's wrapping me in his arms. Then he's lifting my face, his green eyes gleam at me. They are full of emotions I can't bring myself to understand.

He tilts my jaw up.

I can feel his gaze on my lips. I can feel his breath there, too, when he lowers his face to mine.

It feels like an eternity as I wait.

I know if I look up at him, he will be smirking down at me.

He wants to torture me. He wants to draw this out. He wants to make me crazy . . .

My brain screams for him to do something, and then he does.

His mouth connects with mine.

The pressure's soft at first, and when I exhale, he takes advantage of the moment. Deepening the kiss, he slips his tongue into my mouth.

My eyes close, and for a moment, I forget why I'm here.

I forget where I am.

I forget who I am.

I allow myself to get lost in the kiss.

As I fall into the dark abyss of Matteo, I know I lose a piece of me to him at the moment.

This man will ruin me.

And if I'm not careful, I'll let him.

# CHAPTER SEVEN

## Matteo

I HAVE TO HAND IT TO HER . . .

She's gorgeous. Even more so now that she's my wife. She's a shiny new trinket to display on my mantel.

*My property.*

The desire to claim her pulses through my veins.

I do just that. I yank her toward me, seal my mouth over hers, and take the breath from her lungs.

She falls into it.

Pliant in my arms as I manipulate her into giving in.

Her small hands are on my chest, holding on to me for dear life. I allow myself to indulge for a few moments.

Until I hear my family cheering me on.

I had forgotten we had an audience. Now that I remember, I pull away and look down at her. Her eyes are closed, and her mouth is swollen from my abuse.

She has the look of a woman who's been freshly fucked, and if I don't get the hell out of here now, I'll do just that, and I won't even care about an audience.

"Let's go, *Princess.*" My voice is cold, and her eyes jut open. The change in her demeanor is immediate. Her back straightens, and her eyes narrow at me.

"You are such an asshole," she grits through clenched teeth. I can tell she is about to storm away, so I grab her by the elbow and steer her out of the room.

Once we are back in the hallway, I stop. I can't have her being defiant in front of my family. Although I trust everyone in my line of work, you can never be too careful.

"We will eat dinner, and then we will talk," I command. My voice is rougher than usual, but then again, I'm more worked up than I usually allow.

She looks stunned by me, which makes me smile. She scowls in return.

"You think it's funny, you being a dick?" she hisses at me.

"Actually, I do. Now let's go." I continue to pull her until we are in the formal dining room. The table is set. Candles and flowers everywhere. It's not over-the-top.

I lead Viviana to the head of the table, where two chairs are set up. I pat the back and then pull it out for her.

Silently, she sits.

I'm surprised by how quiet she's being. But I guess there isn't much to talk about right now. What can she possibly have to say?

She's stuck.

There are no false illusions here. There was no other choice but to marry me.

I am her best option. She doesn't see it now. But with my cousin, she would have died.

I have no intentions to have her killed, nor do I plan to kill her myself. However, that's as far as this will go with her.

To me, she will always be my pawn. One I will push around my board to gather power.

I'm not that different from Salvatore.

We are both ruthless. But this is my kingdom.

I will do what I need to do to keep my position.

Even if that means using this girl until nothing is left.

Once she is seated, I take the spot beside her. Neither of us speaks as my family files into the room and sits in the empty chairs.

Lorenzo sits beside me on the opposite side of Viviana.

"Aren't you a lovely bride?" He scans her with an appreciative gaze, wearing a lazy smile on his face.

"Thank . . . you." She hesitates as if she's unsure of his sincerity.

"She is, isn't she? Quite the perfect *princess*."

Her head turns toward me at that word, eyes narrowing. She hates when I call her that, but she must think better of whatever she is about to say because instead of speaking to me, she looks back at Lorenzo.

"No date for the wedding? I would think a handsome man like you would have had one." Her eyes are soft and teasing when speaking with him, and my own harden at her tone.

"No time." He shrugs.

"Yes, the *tyrant* didn't give anyone room to plan."

At her nickname for me, Lorenzo laughs. "Tyrant. I like that. Very fitting."

"Don't even think about it," I advise him. "And don't get too familiar, either." There is no question of what I am speaking about. Viviana might be my wife now, but it's in name only. There is no reason for him to speak to her. He nods at my comment and leans forward in his chair to look at me.

"When are you going to drop the bomb on them?" he asks as he lifts his filled glass to his mouth. The liquid sloshes over the edge. He's probably been drinking all day for the celebration. I'm about to say something when, from the corner of my eye, I can see her stiffen. She's listening and waiting to hear what I'm about to say.

"Tomorrow. Viviana and I are going to visit the in-laws."

Her shock is audible as she gasps. "We are?"

"We are."

"I-I . . ." Her face is a ghostly white.

"You thought I would give you more time?" I chide, toying with her. Ever since I found out she can give as good as she gets, I enjoy our banter. I enjoy eliciting reactions from her. She's fun to play with. A new shiny toy in my collection of pretty things.

"I just—Can't we wait a few days?" she squeaks.

I turn in my chair to face her. Her beautiful lush lips are trembling. I should feel bad for her . . .

I don't.

Yes, she's gotten stuck in the crossfire of a war she didn't ask for, but that ship has sailed. There is no point in treating her with kid gloves. She is bound to me now.

Life won't be easy on her.

The faster she finds out, the better.

"No. We'll go tomorrow."

I turn back to Lorenzo, dismissing her.

Giana decides to walk in the door at that exact moment, which is good because she will keep her distracted.

"What's the plan?" Lorenzo asks me.

"I'll show up."

"Unannounced?"

I lift my own glass, take a swig, and then answer. "No better way to show up somewhere."

"And backup?"

Placing my drink down. "I won't need it."

He lifts a brow, and I understand his wanting to object. With everything going on, I know he's right, but instead of saying it, I level him with my stare. "My men will escort me. But yes, I'll be going in alone. I can handle myself. Nothing will happen to me in his house."

"I never said you couldn't. Will you tell your cousin?"

Salvatore. Will I tell him I stole his bride?

"No. He can find out with everyone else."

Lorenzo chuckles. "And when will that be?"

"We will leak the story to the press. Let him stew over it."

"He's going to be pissed."

"Probably. But he's a resourceful ass. Just because we took away this opportunity doesn't mean he won't find another way to get port access. I need a meeting with the governor of New York."

The alliance with New York has been a key component to my success over the years.

I can't afford to lose that.

As the servers begin to serve food and more beverages, I study my wife.

She seems more relaxed now. Much more than when she is talking to me. It seems she and my cousin have formed some sort of bond.

I'll allow it for now.

As long as my cousin doesn't try to interfere.

"What time will we be going?" I hear Viviana ask me.

I don't look at her. "Seven."

"Dinnertime?"

"Yes, I want to take them off guard."

I don't know why I divulge that piece of the puzzle, but she shakes her head.

"Then you'll want to do it a bit earlier. My father indulges my mother with a 'family meal'"—she air quotes—"that is before he leaves the house at eight."

"Six it is," I say.

She turns back to Giana, and I turn back to Lorenzo.

"We will go at 4:30." My voice is low to make sure she can't hear me.

"Any reason?" he asks.

"Precaution."

"Precaution? Do you not trust her?"

"Not even a little."

In the corner of my eye, I continue to look at her. Although

I made her do this, she came too willingly, so you never can be too careful.

When dinner is done, I stand from the chair. My hand reaches out to take Viviana's in mine.

She allows it, but I can feel her body stiffen at the contact. I have no plans to touch my wife tonight, but she doesn't know it. I could put her out of her misery already and tell her, but what fun would that be?

Not many things in my life bring me any semblance of joy, yet for some reason, taunting her does.

I like to see the fire in her eyes. I like to see the way she holds herself back. The strength that takes. Most would look at it as weak.

But not my wife.

I can tell there is a spine of steel in that lovely, pale back of hers.

She's biding her time.

But for what, I'm not sure.

I'm going to find out, and I'm going to have fun while I do.

# CHAPTER EIGHT

Viviana

WE WALK TOGETHER, HAND IN HAND. IT'S SURREAL BEING here with him. It's even more nerve-wracking how much my life has changed. Since I don't know my way around this, what one could only call a castle, I allow him to lead me. In my life, I have always lived in beautiful homes. The governor's mansion was my most recent. Even though it wasn't for a long time, I did live there briefly. But that mansion has nothing on Matteo's home.

Being here is like being in a palace.

Okay, maybe not quite as large, but still, this isn't a normal size home for someone.

It feels weird to walk with him, weird to have a fake smile plastered on my face. I want to drop the false pretense, but I'm not sure who knows the truth here, and I can't run the risk of creating more enemies.

It's already hard enough to try to come up with a plan. Giana seems like a good ally. But I can't be sure. For all I know, this is all part of the act.

Maybe Matteo has sent her in as the spy. A babysitter to report back to him. It's okay. Better to keep my guard up. I'm used to it. I have lived the past twelve years protecting myself.

What's another few?

The one thing I do know is I have to find a way to escape, not just from my father now.

The list keeps getting longer and longer.

If I could die of a heart attack, I probably would.

Holy crap.

What the hell am I going to do if he expects me to consummate this marriage?

Die.

I'll probably die. Because with everything going on, and the fact he very well may be the biggest asshole in the world, there is no way I'm going to have sex with him, and I will kill him if he tries.

My head is swimming at ways out of this situation.

It feels like I'm being walked to my death via the guillotine. French Revolution-style. I'm in the right type of palace for it. If I wasn't so scared right now, I might find my inner crazy funny. Hell, I'd probably roll my eyes at myself, but I am scared, and no ridiculous thoughts of the corrupt royals getting their heads chopped off will make me feel any better.

Even if that is exactly who I married.

A ruthless monarch.

A king of death.

A handsome devil who will probably kill me in the end.

The blood rushing in my ears is so loud, I wonder if he can hear. My heart thumps frantically. With each step I take, I try to act like I'm not scared.

No part of me likes to show weakness. Throughout my life, I have tried to master my emotions, but Matteo brings out the worst in me. I barely know him, and I can already tell.

All of these feelings are usually schooled, especially fear, but now they run rampant.

Like a runaway train with no brakes.

It's only a matter of time until I crash and burn.

Stop. I can do this. There is no other choice. I'll do what must be done to survive. My spine turns to steel, and I follow him.

Together, we walk up a grand staircase, down a long hallway, and to a destination I can only imagine will be his bedroom. Or maybe a torture chamber.

It's dark, there are no lights on, it could be because it's an older estate, or maybe that's on purpose. Maybe the staff was instructed to leave it dark to creep me out and scare me into being pliable. Knowing Matteo, this wouldn't surprise me.

It's like one of the estates that belongs on a Regency TV show.

And thinking of my life, apparently I belong on the show, too.

Other than myself . . . do marriages of convenience actually happen? I want to laugh at how crazy my life has become.

I'm so lost in my ridiculous train of thought that I don't even notice when he stops. My body collides with his. My front hitting his back.

Quickly, I move back, putting distance between us. Please don't turn around. Please don't make me feel like a bigger idiot.

He doesn't, though. Instead, he swings open the door.

The room, like the hall, is pitch-black. My stomach tightens, but then he does something I don't expect. He turns back around, steps around me, and begins to walk away.

"You're not—" I start and stop myself.

What the hell am I doing?

*Shut up, Viviana.*

He looks over his shoulder, and even in the dimly lit hallway, I can see that damn smirk that I swear he only uses on me, spreading across his face.

"Coming . . .?" His voice is low, purposeful, and most of all, seductive. My eyes must widen because he laughs at me, it's more like a fucking chuckle, but it still makes me feel small.

Don't let anyone make you feel this way. I stand taller and wait for the ridicule, something that, after living with my father most of my life, I'm prepared for.

Nothing comes out of his mouth, despite me expecting him to say more. Instead, he completely ignores me, looking back in the opposite direction, and resumes walking, leaving me there standing in the hallway like an idiot.

I watch as his shadow fades, and it's only then that the breath I am holding escapes.

That was close. Too close.

Then another feeling hits me. One I really don't want to read into . . . disappointment.

It's not that I wanted to be with him tonight, but he didn't even want to be with me. For some reason, even though I know I'm his pawn, a part of me liked the idea that maybe a man as dangerous and sexy as Matteo wanted me . . .

Stop.

Don't go there.

You got lucky tonight, and if you keep standing here waiting, your luck might run out.

Not wanting to give him time to change his mind, I scurry into the room, flip the light switch on, and make quick work of shutting and locking the door.

No unwanted guests allowed.

Now alone and safe, I let myself admire the room.

It's gorgeous.

Straight out of a magazine.

A large four-poster bed sits in the middle of the room. On top of it is the fluffiest pink comforter I have ever seen adorned with tiny little flowers. But it's the giant pillow and shams that make me want to jump into it and sleep my life away.

Which is exactly what I plan to do.

With the wedding out of the way, I feel more relaxed. Now

that I don't have to worry about him spending the night, I'm able to strip down and get into bed. I'm not surprised by how tired I am. It's been insane the past few days.

The problem is, now in my bed, my brain starts to scream at me.

Tomorrow.

What the hell will you do when you have to face your parents?

The scarier question is, how will my father react? He will see this as an act of war. Lines will be drawn in the sand. I have picked the side I'm on, but now the terrifying thought is, what if I chose wrong?

The endless fears of what he will say plague me, but eventually, they lead to exhaustion, my brain too tired to think anymore.

Before I know it, I'm opening my eyes, and the early morning sunlight streams in through the big window.

It illuminates the space and causes me to squint. I forgot to pull back the drapes last night. I'll have to remember for the future.

With a stretch of my arms, I let out a large yawn. After enjoying the comfort of my new bed for a beat, I pull back the blankets and kick my legs out from under them.

When I step out and onto the floor, I regret it a second later. It is cold against my bare skin. My toes curl as if that will warm them, but it won't. The only thing that will help is finding my socks or slippers.

I look around the room, trying to remember if I unpacked last night. I didn't. There in the corner is my open suitcase, and on top of it is half my clothes. Wow, I made a mess last night looking for my pajamas. After walking over to my suitcase, I take a moment to look around. It's the first time I'm able to really see anything. The room is much larger than I noticed last night. It's also much more intricate than it appeared in the darkness of the night. The walls are white with ornate, detailed molding. There's also a large chandelier over the bed. How did I not notice any of this yesterday?

*You were tired, emotionally exhausted, and frightened of your husband. Cut yourself some slack.*

This place looks like a hotel, not a residence.

Next, I walk over to the bathroom, again met with a sight I'm not prepared for. The room is large and like nothing I have ever seen. Yes, I have always lived a privileged life, but this is even over-the-top for me. Floor-to-ceiling marble. A beautiful cast-iron, claw-foot tub that beckons to me, but right now, I can't indulge in that. Instead, I make my way over to the shower, and I swing the glass door open to turn the water on. I turn toward the sink and notice that toothbrushes, soap, and shampoo sit on the counter. Obviously, he was prepared.

I'm not sure how I feel about this fact. One the one hand, it was thoughtful, but on

the other . . .

He knew you were coming way before you realized. The thought makes chills run down my spine. I hate not having control over my life, and it feels like I'll never gain control, either.

The scalding hot water steams the room. I reach my hand in and make sure it's not too warm. As much as I want out of this hell, I don't want to boil myself alive to get my goal.

I step into the shower despite the temperature, and the heat feels good on my skin. I allow the water to rinse me clean. Clearing away the fog of sleep. Halfway through, I realize I don't know what's in store for me today.

My father is often predictable, but in this case, for all intents and purposes, we are ambushing him. This fact will make him a loose cannon. I can't rely on how he's acted in the past to gauge how he will react tonight.

My nerves start to bubble up.

This could be bad.

I'm playing with fire . . . and I know from the past how bad it feels to get burned.

I hurry to finish, and then I turn off the water, grab a big fluffy towel, and step outside.

The condensation and steam make it impossible to see. With the towel now wrapped around me, I walk. I don't make it far before I step into a wall.

"Careful now, Viviana." His deep baritone voice feels like it's undressing me.

Startled, I try to step back, but the floor is slick, and I lose my footing.

His hand juts out and steadies me.

"What-what are you doing here?" I hiss as I look up at him. The fog from the steam is now starting to fade. His crisp green eyes are visible and staring down at me.

I feel unnerved by the way he looks at me, and when he smirks that damn smirk, my knees wobble.

I know I should move, but I can't help but look at this man.

Today, like yesterday, he looks angry. Even with the smirk, it doesn't reach his mossy eyes.

He stares at me like he wants to undress me, like he wants to pull the towel down and have his way with me. Yet when I look into his eyes, when I study him, all I see is hate.

Is it me he hates? The idea of me? Or my father?

It doesn't matter. He wouldn't answer if I asked him. What matters now is pretending to play along. I've always been a good actress.

"Morning, dear husband," I grit out, the sarcasm present in my words. It drips like maple syrup on a pancake. Just as decadent but neither of them very good for you.

"Wife," he answers, letting his hands linger on my skin far longer than necessary. I look down to where he grasps me. "Princess . . ."

My teeth grind together at that damn nickname I hate, and by the way he looks at me, he knows I despise it too. "Do you mind?" I ask him, my eyes narrowing at the spot where his touch sears me. Making little tiny goose bumps rise across the surface.

"Not at all," he answers in a casual and lazy voice as if he has nowhere better to be and enjoys driving me crazy. I hope he'll let me go soon, but he doesn't. Instead, he holds on to me.

This is going to be a problem.

Finally, I push him and cross my arms in front of my chest. "Why are you in my bathroom?"

"Well"—his brow lifts—"technically, it's *my* bathroom."

If he is going to play that card, so can I. "Oh, since we're now husband and wife, what's yours is mine . . . so it's mine."

"The same could be said for your belongings."

He has me there, but then not really. "I have nothing of value," I counter.

"No. That's not true . . ."

"Oh, I forget. I'm the pawn."

"That you are, and don't forget it. Now get dressed. Be ready in thirty minutes," he orders as if he wasn't just flirting with me a second earlier. This man gives me whiplash as if he's getting paid to do it, and he's aiming for the employee of the month.

"Where are we going?"

"I have a personal stylist coming to measure you and bring you some clothes. I can't have you looking the way you did when you first came to my house."

My mouth drops open. "And how exactly did I look?"

He doesn't answer, instead opting to walk out the door.

"In the closet is an outfit Giana left for you for today."

"*How did I look*?" I ask again, not letting him off the hook. Screw that. This is a terrible start for our marriage. Whatever we do right now is going to affect our dynamics for life.

He turns over his shoulder. His gaze starts at my feet and lifts until his eyes meet mine.

I feel naked, even despite the towel.

"Beneath me," he answers, and then he turns and goes.

My stomach bottoms.

I turn to look at myself in the mirror.

Catching my wounded expression staring back.

What a dick.

In my life, I have met plenty of awful people. But never have I met a man who could be a bigger asshole than my husband.

This should be fun.

# CHAPTER NINE

## Matteo

THE FIRST THING I HAVE TO DO IS MEET WITH MY MEN. THERE is a shipment coming in tonight. It's not a big shipment, but it's necessary. Extra guns. Extra ammo. I might not be able to accompany them. It all depends on how tonight goes. I find my man in the surveillance room. All the screens are on on the monitor. Unlike my warehouse in the city, acres of land surround this estate.

No one is getting in unless I want them to.

"What is the ETA on the boat?"

"Cristian says the boat should be docking around one."

"What time are you meeting the in-laws?" Lorenzo smirks. He is way too entertained by my fresh nuptials.

I give him a look, the type of look that says fuck off. He lifts his hands in surrender.

"Sorry, Boss," he says. "But, I mean, c'mon."

"It should be fun…" I trail off. That is the understatement of the year.

It should be fun. I can't think of anything in the world that sounds worse. But the shit deserves it. Fuck, if only I knew where my cousin was hiding. I love to kill two birds with one stone.

However, he'll find out soon enough. The moment the governor realizes I have him by the balls, he will call Salvatore. I'll make sure of it. To think my cousin believes he can go around me to get port access by hitting up the governor of New Jersey.

"I need you to call Tobias," I tell Lorenzo. "We need to re-schedule the drugs."

"That's not going to be a problem. With the new guns, are we going to war again?"

"I prefer not to. I prefer we find my cousin's location and kill the son of a bitch before it escalates to that. But seeing as we have no leads . . ."

"That's not necessarily true," Lorenzo says.

"What do you mean?"

"We have her."

"And you think my cousin genuinely likes her? My cousin doesn't give a shit about anyone."

"No, but your cousin cares about taking over New York. If he thinks he still has an in, it could work to flush him out."

I cross my arms and think about what he says as I start to pace.

Back and forth. Back and forth.

He might be on to something.

It might be a good idea to use her as some sort of bait. But by the looks of her this morning in her bathroom, I'm not 100% sure she would willingly help.

I can ask her, or I can tell her. I didn't find out exactly what her father was hanging over her head, but I can and then I can use that as a means to get her cooperation. I can even make it seem like she's working with her father. That she is working to take me down and then by doing that she can maybe find out the location of my cousin.

"It's a solid idea." I nod my head.

"Will you tell her?"

"I'm not sure yet. I'm going to see what happens tonight. We need to find out about her past. Figure out what happened and why her family is paying a substantial amount of money to her ex-nanny."

"I will get on it right away. I'll get in touch with Jaxson Price again. If anyone can find out, it would be him."

"Offer him double to expedite the request."

"Are you sure that's a good idea? Won't he always expect it?"

"I don't give a rat's ass what he expects. He's the best, and I want the information now. I have no problem paying if it's worth it."

That is the reason I am in charge. I don't nickel and dime anyone. I pay what something is worth, and into that equation I allocate time too. What your time is worth. My time is priceless, but that's a whole different story.

"Is there anything else you need?" Lorenzo stands up, ready to leave. He looks around, anxious to start working.

"No. Have most of the men stay here."

"Are we not going back to the city?"

I shake my head. "I'll keep a team there too. But I think with the shipment, it will be easier to transport it from here."

He pulls out his phone and starts typing into it, sending a text. "Anything else I need to tell the men?"

"Nope. We are all set. I'm going to hit the gym, then get ready. If you need anything, I'll be working out. When Giana and the stylist arrive, show them to Viviana's room."

"Do you think it's a good idea to let them spend so much time together?

"It's either that or let her talk to her friends."

"True."

I walk past him and out into the hallway. I take a few steps before looking over my shoulder. "Until we know what we are dealing with, she's not to speak to anyone outside of the family."

"I think that's a good plan. How do you think she'll take it?"

"I really don't give a flying fuck."

Hours later, I'm dressed and ready to go. I make my way to Viviana's room. This time, I knock.

I don't have to, but since I need her on her A game, I don't want to get her frazzled. My knuckles bang on the door once, twice, and on the third knock, I hear her footsteps.

"Who is it?"

Silly question. As if I would let anyone near my wife's room without my permission, as if they would even attempt.

"The fucking pope."

"Sorry, I stopped believing in God when a mobster forced me into marriage."

"You were always going to be forced into marriage with a mobster. So don't act like this marriage is coming out of left field."

Surprisingly, that makes her open the door. I expect her to give a little pushback, but she must realize she has no choice.

There she is.

Her hair is blown out, and she has a light dusting of makeup on her face. She's wearing a dress, it's black with tiny rosebuds on it, and she has boots that come above her knee.

My wife—no matter how many times I refer to her that way, it always feels little odd. But that's who she is, my wife. She's a gorgeous woman, and if she was anyone else, I would've fucked her last night.

Hell, I should have fucked her the first night I saw her at the club. But I've got big plans for Viviana. So, keeping my dick in my pants for now serves me better, then I can serve her up by dangling her on the hook.

Plan or not, it doesn't stop me from admiring how sexy she looks. When all is said and done, I'll have her, but not yet.

"Are you ready?" I ask, and the look on her face is fucking priceless. Her eyes remind me of one of the cartoon characters whose eyes pop out of their sockets. At this point, she looks so scared she might turn into the Road Runner and make a dash for it.

"Are we leaving now?" She takes a step back, now going in the wrong direction.

"Yes."

She turns, and her eyes are no longer visible. I don't like it. Viviana is easy to read because her features give everything away. Without being able to see her, I can't learn every tell of hers. I won't be able to read her lies.

"I thought I had more time."

"Well, you thought wrong."

"Shit," she mumbles under her breath before turning over her shoulder and looking at me.

The fear that was in her eyes only moments ago seems to be replaced with another look. Now her lip is a flat line, and there is a small line between her brows, but it's her shoulders that clue me in to what she is doing. She is putting up her walls.

A façade probably needed to deal with her father.

I watch her for a moment before I move to walk out the door. When I take a step, I speak over my shoulder. "Let's go."

"I'll just grab my bag." She walks over to the corner of the room and grabs her stuff and then steps closer to where I am. "Okay, I'm as ready as I'll ever be." Her back is now ramrod straight.

I like this look.

Making herself appeal regal.

She is the queen that she needs to be to stand by my side.

After silently appraising her, I start to walk down the hall. Viviana trails me. With the house quiet today, the clanking of her heels is the only indicator she's following me.

The air between us is silent as we walk to the garage, and then we get into the G-wagon. Although it is a nice car, that's not why we take it. Despite what it looks like, it's my safest car.

Bulletproof.

Built to withstand almost anything.

Roberto is in the front seat. He will be driving us tonight.

I take a seat in the back beside Viviana.

She won't look at me when I get in beside her, and as we drive, she stares out the window.

To the untrained eye, she's acting unfazed. But I see past her façade.

She's nervous.

Her finger is tapping a pattern on her thigh she doesn't even realize she's doing. I wonder what she's nervous about? Obviously telling her parents that she's married. Is she nervous her father will try something? She must know she's safe with me. But really, why would she know that? I've given her no reason to feel that way.

"Stop tapping. Everything will be okay."

"And how do you know that?" she fires back as she stares out the window.

"Because it always is." I wait for her to turn to face me, but she refuses to budge. It's infuriating talking to her back.

"Easy for you to say," she mumbles under her breath to the window.

"You are with me now, Viviana," I state by way of explanation.

"That's supposed to make me feel better?"

"Yes."

"And why is that?"

"Because he would never fuck with you."

"Didn't he fuck with you by trying to barter a deal with your cousin . . .?"

She's too smart for her own good.

"Yes. And see what happened? I married you. Your father knows better. Regardless of his alliance with Salvatore, I am not to be trifled with. Our war precedes us. Your father, if he's smart—and

I have to imagine he is—doesn't want to get caught in the crossfire. The last time there was a war like this, the collateral damage was heavy. Your father can ask the senator from Boston what the price he had to pay for going against me was. Oh wait, he can't. There is no speaking to him where he is now . . ." My words hang heavy in the space between us. You would have to be living under a rock not to have heard about the senator's untimely demise.

She finally turns away from the window and looks at me.

"So, what's the plan now?"

"Don't worry about the plan. You are just here to sit and look pretty."

She lets out a laugh. "Wow, sexist much."

"It's not sexist when it's the truth. I married you to prove a point. I married you because you benefitted me strategically. That's it. Nothing more. The only point you have to make now is sitting there."

"And if I don't."

I lean toward her, my arms reaching out to trap her against the window. Our faces are so close I can feel her breath tickling my lips as she exhales. Her jaw trembles, but it's the lip that does me in; the way she sucks it in and bites it ever so gently. If she was anyone else, I'd grab her and fuck her in this car.

"Do not mistake my kindness for weakness, Viviana. I have not hurt you . . . but I can."

My words hang in the air like the threat they are.

I have kept my distance.

I have not demanded anything of her.

"You will be obedient. Do you understand?"

She doesn't respond, just continues to nibble on her bottom lip.

"Speak, Viviana."

"Yes, I understand," she grits out through clenched teeth.

"Good."

Now that's settled, I pull my phone out of my pocket and call Lorenzo.

"How are things up ahead?" I ask.

When I travel, I usually bring an army of men. This time I only brought enough to keep us safe during the drive.

Two decoy cars, as well as one to scope out the terrain.

"Clear. No sign of anything out of the ordinary."

It takes us about one hour to leave my family's estate in New York to get to the governor's house.

He doesn't know we are coming, so this should be interesting.

"When we arrive, you are to speak to security. My men will be positioned if anything goes wrong, but we are going in relatively blind."

"Relatively?"

"I have a man inside."

"You do?"

I lift a brow. "I guess it shouldn't surprise me. You seem to know everything."

"I am always one step ahead. Remember that."

Her face pales, but she rights herself.

When we start to pull down the long drive, Roberto rolls down the window so the security guard sees her face.

"Hi." Her voice sounds friendly, and I have to hand it to her. Although she is nervous, she seems to handle herself well under pressure. "I'm here to see my dad."

He looks at her and then nods.

"He didn't seem surprised by your car or that you are being driven."

"I never drive to see them. I either Uber or they send a car service." She shrugs.

Roberto pulls the car around to the front of the circular driveway and then kills the engine, then he is out of the car, doing his job of appearing to be merely a driver.

We both exit before the door opens to the house. It swings open, and it appears that her mother is standing there.

"Vivi. I didn't expect you," her mother says, clear confusion evident in her voice as it pitches on the last word.

"I had some news I wanted to share with you and Dad."

That's when I step out from the car and into view.

Her mother stumbles, her gaze locked on me. She looks me up and down, but there is no recollection. She doesn't know who I am, which I like. Not that it matters. Regardless, I'm getting in to speak to the governor tonight, but this way, at least, she won't try to stop me.

"Hello, Mrs. Marino." I walk up to her and take her hand, kissing the knuckle, and she giggles like a schoolgirl. "I'm Matteo." It's like taking candy from a baby.

"Come, let's find your father," she says to her daughter, who rolls her eyes at her mother behind her back.

Together, we walk through the foyer and down a hallway.

In the background, I can hear a man on the phone. It's Governor Marino. I can't hear the words, but it's him.

"No. Absolutely not." I hear as his wife opens the door. He hangs up the phone abruptly. Once he's off the phone, she strolls into the room.

"I'm in the middle of something," he barks at her. When Viviana hears him yell at her mom, her body stiffens.

"I'm so sorry. But Viviana is here, and she brought a friend," she whispers, voice weak and full of fear.

Mrs. Marino steps farther into the room so that Viviana and I can walk in.

He can't see me yet, but I can see him as he scowls at his daughter.

"What is the meaning of this?" His voice is almost a shout, making Viviana's shoulders slouch forward.

I watch her and her mother, both of whom are now looking down in defeat.

An irrational urge to throttle him spreads through my limbs. My right hand clenches into a fist.

There is a strong desire to barge inside this office, grab him by the throat, and then kick the shit out of him, but I know that won't bode well for my plan.

I need to calm the fuck down. In this state, this will all be over before it begins.

Taking a deep inhale, I try to calm myself. After I count to five, my blood pressure has dropped enough that I won't do anything stupid, like shoot him.

"The meaning of this, Governor, is that she wants to introduce you to her husband," I respond, my voice bouncing in the silent room as I step out from the shadow to meet his confused stare.

Unlike his wife, Governor Marino knows exactly who I am.

"What—"

"*Husband*," I say again, allowing my lip to tip up into a smirk. "I'm sure you are familiar with the concept. You are one, too."

His face goes pale, but then he shakes himself and looks between Viviana and me.

He seems to be at a loss of words, so I step closer, pull Viviana to me, and wrap her in my arms protectively.

I'm surprised how willingly she lets me.

Her shoulders, which were once tight with fear, seem to loosen.

"We got married," I inform him smugly. My voice, cocky and condescending, the kind of tone that if ever used on me would get someone shot with a bullet in the head.

"Is this true?" he asks his daughter. His face gives away no emotion at all.

"Yes," she whispers back, tucking herself in closer to me as if she is afraid about how he will react to the news.

She's small in my arms.

Much smaller than I had imagined.

The need to protect her filters through me, and I'm not sure why or where it came from, but it's an odd feeling.

One I don't like.

But regardless of how I feel right now, I have to pretend it doesn't bother me.

"How?" He narrows his eyes at me. "Why?"

"Why?" I lift my brow. "Do I really need to tell you, Governor, the whys of marriages?"

"Humor me."

"In my line of work, I don't have the luxury to marry for love . . ." I start. My meaning very clear to him. This is a business deal. One I have made without his knowledge. One he now has to honor. "But looking at Viviana." I pull back and smile down at her. "You can see why she is the perfect bride." Again, my words are not lost on him.

Point to me.

Game. Set. Match.

"How could you?" he hisses at Viviana. Pure venom dripping from his mouth. There is no doubt in my mind that if I was any other man, he would try to kill us both for defying him.

"Easily," I taunt back, lip tipped up and all.

His face turns an unnatural red. He reminds me of a teakettle, and he is about to explode.

"You will get this marriage annulled."

"You do not give the orders here, Governor. Viviana is mine now."

His hand flies down, hitting his desk.

"Do you know what you've done, you little twit?"

I step away from Viviana and prowl over to where the governor is standing behind his desk.

Before he can even move, I pull the gun from behind my back and point it straight at his head. "Do not ever speak to my wife that way. Do you understand? Me coming here with Viviana is a courtesy. You will not address her. You will have nothing to do with her unless I deem it so." I say this more to his wife than to him. Something tells me the governor would be more than happy not to speak to his daughter at all. Especially after this. I lower my gun and give him a pointed stare.

He doesn't speak at first, seeming at an impasse of what to say.

His hand reaches for the glass on his desk. It's filled about halfway with melted ice and scotch. He lifts it to his mouth before swallowing.

We all stand in silence as he drinks before placing the glass down on the large wooden desk. The sound echoes through the quiet of the room.

"How do we move forward?" he asks, breaking the silence. I can tell by the way he clenches his fists that he wants to lash out badly but knows how disastrous that would be for him.

"You welcome me into your family. No questions asked. You cut ties with my cousin."

I expect him to argue, but instead, he lifts his glass and takes another swig before nodding his head.

"Fine," he says through gritted teeth.

"Then I guess we shall be going."

He looks from me to Viviana. "I'd like to speak to my daughter first."

"Speak."

"I meant alone."

I turn to Viviana. Her brow is furrowed, and her arms are crossed in front of her chest protectively. "Are you okay with this?" I ask.

She doesn't look okay. Her body language tells quite the opposite story. The position in which she stands screams she wants to leave with the way she's angled toward the door, fists softly clenched. "Yes," she answers, voice strong.

She's not okay with this, but she is doing her best to appear that she isn't scared.

"I will be right outside the door. If you need me—"

"She won't."

"You have two minutes."

I turn on my heel and walk toward the door. Mrs. Marino walks with me and then once we are in the hallway, she closes the door.

I refrain from allowing myself to smile.

This is exactly what I wanted.

# CHAPTER TEN

## Viviana

THIS IS BAD.

No. Beyond bad. Disastrous.

Having to be left alone with my father is basically the definition of hell.

I feel small.

Like I'm a tiny bug on the floor, and my father can smash me with his boot.

I didn't realize how much I relied on Matteo for his strength until he stepped out of the room.

The moment he did, though, I noticed it.

It became cold in the room once his arm pulled away from me.

Now, it feels like there is an arctic chill. One that starts with my father's angry gaze.

The man who raised me steps forward. His hand is clenched at his side. A fist is formed. I'm one hundred percent sure that if Matteo wasn't standing directly outside the door, my father would hit me.

It should be lucky for me, but I know my father. He's going to make me pay in other ways.

Now, I just have to hope whatever the threat is, it is one in which I can convince my new husband to help me out of.

Debatable if he'll care to help me.

"How could you, Viviana?"

I stand taller, trying my hardest to seem strong.

"He asked, and I said yes."

"You were supposed to marry Salvatore Amante."

"I was, wasn't I?" I run a hand over my hair, "I'm sure he will get over it." My father raises his hand to smack me, and I smile. "My husband wouldn't like that." I let my lip tip up to a smile.

"You like this, don't you? Oh, poor, sweet Viviana. You have no idea the monster you crawled into bed with. He makes the devil look nice. You'll regret your decision."

"I doubt that," I mutter.

"Oh, no? You don't think so? Have you thought about Julia? Have you thought about what your impetuous decision will do to her?"

"Yes, Father, I have. And I hope you can see you left me no other choice. You wanted me to marry a man I didn't love."

"Yet you still did."

"But on my terms."

He lifts a brow at my lie. But instead of cowering, I stand prouder.

"Yes, believe it or not, it was on my terms."

He narrows his eyes. "And what of your friend?"

"You won't do anything. I'm still just as important to you. I still can bring you what you need. I am married to Matteo Amante."

I hated myself for saying that, but for Julia, I would make my husband give my father what he wanted.

"So you will help me . . .?"

"What do you mean?"

"Take down Matteo. You are in the inside now. Atone for what you did. Help me take him down."

"What? No, that isn't what I said. I meant I can convince him to help *you*."

"That shit will never help me. This is the only way. You need to use your position and find his weakness. I need to take him out."

"I'm not going to do that."

Bile crawls up my throat because as much as I say I won't help him, he will make me. I have no choice. I thought I could spin this somehow in my favor, but the risk of casualties is too high. My heart hammers as I wait for him to drop the threat that I know is coming.

"You will. You know what there is to lose if you cross me."

*And there it is.*

I bite my lower lip and hear his words. I don't say anything else. Instead, I nod. Shaking my head at the same time.

I hate this man.

Hate everything he stands for.

My only way out is to hope Matteo will help me.

The thing is, I'm not sure he will.

"And once I take him out, you will marry Salvatore. That's the price you have to pay for your disobedience."

"You think he still wants me?"

"Yes."

"Are we done here?"

I need to get out of here. The air is getting more and more stale by the minute.

I can barely breathe.

"Yes."

Without waiting for him to say another word, I turn on my heel and storm toward the door. When I fling the door open, I see Matteo waiting on the far wall. His back is up against it, and his foot is kicked up and resting.

"I'm ready to leave," I say to Matteo.

He looks past me and into my father's office. I wonder if he could hear what my father said.

No. Not from where he was standing. Unless he moved right before. But by the way Matteo was relaxed, I doubt it.

"Then let's go." He motions his arm out, pointing toward the foyer. I start to walk when I feel his hand rest on my back.

My footsteps stop.

I'm not sure why, but it is like I'm frozen in place.

I know why he supported me in the office, but now that it's just us alone in the hallway, it doesn't make sense.

"Everything okay?"

"Yes, sorry. I was lost in thought."

Not wanting to say more, I continue to walk. His hand remains on the small of my back.

It feels like the longest walk of my life.

Each second an eternity stretches out.

It feels good, though.

Exactly what I need to get out of this hellhole.

As we approach the door, one of the members of my parents' staff opens it. I can't remember his name; he must be new here. *Is he the inside man?* I'm about to introduce myself when Matteo pulls me through the doorway.

Neither of us speaks, and when we get into the car and wait for Roberto to start the ignition, we still don't.

Any of the emotions or support he showed before are long gone. For a second, I was actually stupid enough to think maybe he wasn't such an asshole, but as he taps on his phone and doesn't acknowledge my presence at all, I know he really is.

It's fine.

I don't know why I thought otherwise.

"Now that I did what you asked, can I have my phone back?"

"I'll consider it."

I roll my eyes. He doesn't see it as I'm positioned looking at the window, but it still makes me feel better.

I'll take anything right now to do that.

Even if it means I'm acting like a petulant child.

# CHAPTER ELEVEN

## Matteo

I AVOID MY WIFE THE NEXT DAY. NOT FOR ANY OTHER REASON than until I find out what when down in that office, I have no reason to talk to her.

I'm sure Marino asked her to betray me. Knowing how he works, what makes him tick, it is almost unthinkable to consider he wouldn't try to take advantage of the situation.

I want to know what she said.

If she said yes, I can spoon feed her false information.

If she said no . . .

Well, I'll cross that bridge when we get there.

The plan will be easier if she said yes. Then I can seduce my wife with no feelings and feed her to the sharks.

After I get what I want, I could show her what being disloyal means. I don't revel in killing a woman, but I'll do what I have to do to keep my kingdom. I'm not sure what she's doing. I know that Giana went to visit her, and depending on what I hear, I'll give Giana better instructions on how to handle Viviana.

I find my men where I always find them, in the surveillance room.

It's their favorite place to hang out.

It is state-of-the art, and if you aren't watching the monitors, it's basically a man cave.

"Okay, what do you have for me?"

"I have the audio." He smiles.

"Is it clear?"

"As a fucking fresh fallen snow. We got both of them."

"Good."

Plot twist: What Viviana didn't know last night was that I bugged her.

Not only was I not worried about Marino doing anything to me since I have a man in his house but I also got the benefit of hearing their convo.

That was a nice treat that I hadn't anticipated. Sometimes good things do happen to bad people. In this case, spying on my wife and her dad is a good thing.

"Talk to me. Did you listen?"

"Not yet. So far, the only person who listened was Eddie, but seeing as we haven't spoken to him, he hasn't told us what was said."

That makes sense.

Eddie was my man inside.

He's newer to the outfit, so he makes an easy fit. He's invaluable. He gives me the insight I need about what goes on behind closed doors. Nothing goes on inside the governor's mansion without me hearing about it from Eddie. That includes and is not limited to the impending marriage of Viviana Marino to my dear cousin, Salvatore Amante.

We don't speak to him often, not unless something big is going down.

"What are you waiting for? Fire it up."

In the surveillance room, we have a state-of-the-art sound system, so as soon as my men activated the wire I had planted on Viviana, the room goes quiet to listen.

Her father's angry voice booms through the space. Hers seems softer, yet she's holding her own. Hearing her this strong has me smiling to myself.

They keep talking, and he does just as I expected him to do. He asks her to be his spy. Her answer isn't as obvious in the recording. She argues, she objects, she even says no, but it's the lack of words at the end that has my brow arching.

When the recording finishes and turns off, my men look at me.

"Did she agree?" Lorenzo asks.

"It sure did sound like it," I respond. Without eyes in the room, I can't be one hundred percent sure, but the audio evidence is pointing that way.

"I'm not so sure." Lorenzo rubs his chin. "It kind of sounds like she was just trying to appease him."

"No. She is working with him," Luka interjects. "It was clear as day."

"What do you want us to do about that, Boss?" Roberto asks.

"Nothing." He furrows his brow at my one-word answer.

"What do you mean, nothing?" Lorenzo asks, so I turn to him next.

"Exactly what I said. Nothing." The men all look confused now.

"Then what is the plan?"

"The plan is to give them a taste of their own medicine. No one comes into my house and thinks they can get one over on me."

"You will use her?"

My lip twists up into a dark smile. "Oh yes, I will use her. And when I'm done, I'll tuck her away, somewhere she can do no damage, and I'll only her pull her out when I need a kid."

They all nod their head, happy with my plan.

"And how do you want us to act?"

"Give her some rope. That way she will hang herself on it eventually. Give her back her phone but have software installed so we can see and hear everything she does. I want to know everything about her, so I'll install bugs everywhere. If she thinks it, I want to know."

"Got it. This will be fun." Luka laughs.

"I want her to think I'm falling for her ruse, and then . . ." I slam my hand against the table. The sound loud and bouncing off the walls.

I stand from my chair.

"Now that that's settled, I have to go."

"Where to . . .?"

"To seduce my wife." I leave behind a round of laughter as I stalk out of the room. Seducing my wife isn't something I had planned. But what better way to take her father down than to use his plan and turn it against him?

Her dad wants her to use her proximity to take me down.

I'll use mine to her.

I will make her fall for me.

Make her believe I care.

And then I'll feed her the information, not just to kill her dad but to get my cousin as well.

Once that's over, I'll decide her fate.

I head down the hall and stop in my office. When I make it inside, I open the top drawer in my desk to grab Viviana's phone & iPad to give to the team for alteration. After this is done, I'll be able to hear and see all the communications she makes.

This will be my first step.

A peace offering of sorts. She just won't know why.

Walking back into the surveillance room, I toss the merchandise to my men. Pacing the room, I wait for it to be done.

Surprisingly, it takes them no time to install the programs.

Now, with Viviana's gear in hand, I make my way to her room. I knock once, and I'm surprised to hear her tell me to enter.

When I walk in, I find her sitting on the couch in the corner. I expect her to be watching TV, but instead, she is reading.

"What are you reading?" I ask, actually interested to know. She holds up an old copy of a children's book. It's weathered around the edges, and I'm surprised we would have the book, but then I remember my mother reading it to me as a child.

"*Beauty and the Beast.*"

"Interesting choice."

"I thought so. Seemed fitting. I'm surprised you had it. It was slim pickings in this room."

I suppress a chuckle. She isn't wrong about that one. I'm not known for my outstanding literary choices.

"That was my mother's favorite story to read me as a child. Where did you find it?"

"Why are you here?" she says, changing the topic. But I don't need an answer. This is my old bedroom from when I was a child. Although most of the furniture has been changed, the chest in the corner was mine from when I was young. I don't offer that information though. I don't need her to read into why I have it here.

"I came to bring you these." I lift my hand up, and her eyes go wide.

"My stuff." The way her brow arches in speculation has me wanting to laugh. She doesn't trust me at all. Rightfully so, but still, it is rather funny. She wears her emotions on her sleeve. Something that will come in handy in the future.

"You did well with your father," I say, shocking her even more.

Her dark eyes are large, but her jaw is still tight. She is waiting for me to say more. To issue some sort of order, declaration, threat.

"And this is my reward?"

I shrug at her suggestion, trying not to give anything away. "If you would like to see it that way."

"How else can I see it?"

"A peace offering. I've been an asshole."

"Ya think?"

"You proved your loyalty the other day, and I want to make it up to you." Her eyes narrow. Clearly, she doesn't believe me.

I place her objects on the table beside her. Her hand reaches out and grabs her phone, but still, her movements are slower than usual. She's waiting for the other shoe to drop.

"And I'm allowed to use it?"

"Why else would I give it to you . . ." I lead.

"To use a GPS tracker to see where I'm going." She smiles at me, a sugary sweet smile, one I want to wipe off her face and kiss her at the same time.

"There's no need to do that."

Her lips pull back into a flat line.

"How come?" she asks, voice tight again.

"Because now that you're married to me, you will go every-where with one of my men."

"I don't really need a bodyguard."

"Unfortunately, we're going to have to agree to disagree on that fact. You do, in fact, need one. Period. I'm a very powerful man, and I have many enemies. And the moment you married me . . . they became your enemies too."

"Well, that hardly seems fair."

"Princess, haven't you learned yet?" I tsk.

"So, from now on, what you're saying is that someone will be following me?"

"Yes."

"Life might have been better under my father's thumb," she mumbles under her breath.

"Yes, if you want it to be sold to a man who would have no qualms about raping you."

Her eyes go wide as her face pales, and I realized I took this a step too far. This is not a page in the Seduction 101 handbook.

Moving a step closer, I crowd her. This time when I look down at her, I can see there are small flecks of color in her irises.

Little gold flecks.

Too bad she's a traitor. Fucking her often wouldn't be a chore. Now to just get my head out of my ass and do what I need to do.

Seduction won't be hard, seeing as she is beautiful.

The only problem is, I'm as romantic as the main character in the book she's reading.

"Have dinner with me tonight."

"Was that a question or a command?"

I inhale and refrain from barking out that she will come if she knows what's best. That is not the way to win this game.

"Please have dinner with me today."

"That wasn't so hard. Now was it?"

I look at her expectantly. She still hasn't given me her answer, but I wait for her to speak despite my impatience.

From where she's sitting, her head is craned up and looking at me. Our eyes are locked. She's doing that thing where she nibbles on her lower lip. She's thinking. Although I don't know what there is to think about. I am her husband, and at some point, she's going to have to spend time with me.

Especially since her father's plan is to use her to get to me. She can't possibly do that unless she seduces me as well. It's a game of cat and mouse. Both of us trying to be the predator. Unfortunately for her, there can only be one.

There is only ever one winner.

What Viviana doesn't know is, I never lose.

"Okay," she says.

When I reach my hand out, her eyes go wide. She's shocked by the movement. She doesn't expect this.

*Good.*

I like to keep her on her toes.

She stares at my hand, outstretched and waiting for her.

For a moment, I wonder if she'll reject it. I wonder what is stronger inside her—the fear of her father or her strength. She answers my question when she places her small and delicate palm in mine.

With our fingers interlocked, I pull her up until she's standing.

Then together, we walk out of her room. I lead her down the grand staircase. My steps are slower than normal. Seeing as I'm much taller than her, my gait is longer, so I consciously alter my own to keep pace with her.

When we arrive in the dining room, I drop her hand to pull out the chair. She takes a seat, and then I sit beside her. Looking at her, I realize the last time we sat this close to each other was at our wedding. I'm going to have to change that if I think I could use her. But how does one seduce their own wife, their wife who is attempting to do the same?

If she was any other woman, it wouldn't be this hard. Before this, I didn't really date. Sure, I had a shit ton of sex. But date? Nope.

In my line of work, there is no room for relationships. Relationships are cemented in place solely for alliances.

Which is why I now have a wife. Except, in this case, there's no alliance to be made. If this was a date, I would talk to her about what she wanted in life, what she desired, and what she likes. I'd pretend I care. So that's exactly what I'll do.

"We don't really know each other," I start.

"Well, we did get married after basically a second. That doesn't bode well for getting to know someone."

Her sass is there. Present in every sarcastic quip that leaves her mouth. I like the fire.

"Very true, but I'd like to change that."

Her eyebrows arch. "You do? Why?"

"Why do I want to know my wife?" I ask, to show her that the idea is not so farfetched.

"Yes, that is exactly what I want to find out."

Leaning forward in my chair, I place my forearms on the

table. "Believe it or not, I did not enter into this marriage without thinking of what it meant. I have no plans to divorce you. In my world, that doesn't happen. If we are to be together, if eventually you will be the mother of my children, I'd like to get to know you. I know I didn't start that way, but I want to now—"

"And this was all changed because of my father?" Her delicate features are natural, but her voice is lower, trying to determine if I'm telling the truth or feeding her a story.

The latter is the answer, but I'll sell it like a traveling salesman selling snake oil as a miracle cure.

"Yes. Seeing you with him made me realize there is no love lost between you, and because of that, because of the way he treated you, I want to protect you."

For a moment, I wonder if I've come on too strong and she will see through my lies, but the rigid line of her jaw softens.

"Okay," she answers.

"Good. Let's start with you telling me a little about yourself."

Her eyes go wide at my statement. "That's a long answer." She laughs. "Let's narrow it down. What exactly do you want to know?"

"From what I gathered, it seems you went to NYU. What were you studying?"

"You are already know *this*." She rolls her eyes. She's right I do, but I still want to hear it. "I'm studying, or I mean I studied English literature."

"Hence the reading?"

"Yes, hence the reading."

"You know, I have a library."

"Why does that not surprise me?"

"And you just graduated?" I ask. Leaning back in my chair, I lift my elbows off the table.

"I did, actually. However, with everything that happened, I didn't walk."

"What does that mean?"

"Honestly? Absolutely nothing. I still have a diploma. I still graduated from college. I just didn't have one of those moments when I stood on a podium and smiled at my parents."

"Do you wish you did?"

"You've met my parents. What do you think?" she deadpans, and I can't help but laugh. She cocks her head to the side. "I don't think I've ever heard you laugh."

"Don't get used to it. I rarely do it."

"You should do it more often. You have a nice laugh."

"In my line of work . . . well, let's just say, no one laughs in my line of work. Not often at least."

"That's sad."

"Life can be sad." We both fall silent, and just as I'm about to open my mouth and ask her more, one of the members of my staff walks into the dining room.

She has a bottle of wine in her hand and then starts to pour us both a glass.

"I hope you drink red."

"I'll drink anything." She laughs. "I've gotten used to getting drunk in order to make it through dinner with the parents."

"I hope you don't feel that way now."

She looks taken aback. Maybe I'm coming off too strong. But I don't have all the time in the world to make her trust me, and she is not stupid.

I need to convince her I'm the real deal, and then I need to take her, her family, and my cousin down.

There is no way she would believe right now that I would be reckless enough to drop confidential information in front of her. However, if I play the game right, if I lead her into a false comfort and then I drop the information, she will play right into my hands.

I'll be able not to just take down her father but also to find my

111

cousin. It is surprising how elusive he has been. I own New York, I should be able to find him, but seeing as he tried to get into bed with New Jersey, I have to assume that's where he's hiding. Although most of Jersey is mine, there are certain jurisdictions where my power is limited.

"So . . . NYU? I know you lived in an apartment, was that where you lived throughout college?"

"No. Actually, I always lived in an apartment, but the one I lived in before was like Fort Knox. My father had so much security detail on me, it was pathetic."

I find it interesting that she says that because one of the things I was shocked about was the lack of security she had.

"Obviously that changed," I comment.

"Yes, well, I had to prove myself obedient. Once I did, he let out the reins a little bit. Once he was sure I would do anything he wanted and asked . . ." she trails off, not finishing the train of thought.

"Agreeing to marry my cousin being one of them."

"Yes, that he sprung on me right before I met you. He was a tyrant—*but not like you.* One who didn't believe I needed an education or a diploma, which is why I studied English lit in the end."

"But you at least love to read?"

"I do, but since I know he would never have let me do anything else. I chose something I loved, even if it meant I'd never have a career with it."

"Well, that is a luxury most don't have. Most people go to school to learn something they hate because it makes them money."

"True. I should be happy I was able to follow my passion. I loved college. I loved learning. And in the end, I will always have the memories and the knowledge."

In front of me was the opportunity I needed. It was a perfect in to warm her up to me.

"If you could do anything, what would you do?"

"Why? It doesn't matter."

I lean forward and place my hand on hers. "It matters to me."

As the words leave my mouth, I realize there is some truth to them. It's not that I care necessarily, but I'm curious about her. I want to know all about her. Not just to use her but because something intrigues me, and I would be lying if I said otherwise.

The way she looks at me is almost unnerving; she studies me, trying to understand. With my hand still on hers, I lean forward, closer to her.

Sell the story.

Make her believe.

"I—" she stutters out. "I love to read, as you know. I've always wanted to do something in that field. Maybe be a literary agent or an editor. Opening a bookstore would be amazing too." Her voice comes out whimsical as if she's lost in a dream. "I've always wanted to find the next great book to get lost in."

"Then do it."

"You, you would let me work?"

"Believe it or not, Viviana, you are not a prisoner here. Right now, it might be hard for you to start a job, seeing as there are some complications."

"Your cousin?"

"Yeah. But it shouldn't be that long. After."

It's a lie. If she does what I think she will do, there is no working where I will put her.

"Can I start looking now . . .?" She sounds so hopeful. If I give in to her, it might help her believe more.

"I'll consider it, depending on the threat, but you would have to take a bodyguard."

"Okay." She nods while smiling.

Her lips spread clear across her face.

I never have seen her smile like this before.

It's truly the most beautiful smile I have ever seen. It's the type of smile that could start wars.

It already has.

---

When it's over, I escort her to her room. As she opens the door, she turns around and looks at me.

"Thank you for tonight."

"It was my pleasure. If you'd like, we can start having dinner together every night that I'm here."

"Are you not always here?"

"No. Sometimes, I go out."

For a second, she looks like she might ask more, but instead, she lets her lip tip up.

"I'd like that," she says.

"Good night, Viviana."

"Good night, Matteo."

After she steps into her room and closes the door, I head down the stairs. We have a shipment coming in tonight, and I need to get ready to oversee it.

Normally, I don't.

But seeing as this is a new route and new drop location, I do.

I decide to have a drink in my office before we leave.

I'm sitting alone, scotch in hand, when Lorenzo walks in.

"How was dinner?" he asks, brow lifted.

"Good."

The man still acts like we are in high school, expecting me to tell him about the cheerleader I banged under the bleachers.

"Anything else?" he asks.

I lift my brow. "Are we girls?"

"Well, no . . ."

"Sit." I pat the chair.

Lorenzo obliges. I stand and grab a second glass. "Have a drink with me."

His eyebrow lifts. "What are we drinking to?"

"Laying the groundwork." And hopefully getting laid with the wife afterward. I am no fucking saint.

"With the missus?"

"Ding, ding, ding. Correct. I anticipate having her under control within two weeks."

"And then what?" He eyes me curiously.

"Then the fun starts."

"Do you think we should finalize the details now?"

"No. Not yet. Too many variables can change. But I think we should set her up. Give her small pieces of info to tell her dad, and when we know he trusts her, we strike."

"Will you be okay killing her when all is said and done?"

"Of course."

"Interesting."

"What's that supposed to mean?"

"Nothing," he responds, but I know he has more to say. The man knows me better than anyone. He knows the kill wouldn't be easy on me, but I will do what I need to do, regardless of what he thinks.

We continue to drink, and the conversation is lighter after that. No more talk of war or killing my wife.

An hour later, it's time to leave.

Like always, we take multiple cars. This time, unlike the last time, I'm in the middle one. I like to switch things up. That way, if anything happens, it's harder to get to me. Seeing as no one knows of this location, I'm sure I'm okay, but you can never be too safe.

When we pull up to the port, we pull into the toy warehouse.

As far as warehouses, this one has never been under any scrutiny.

"Do you ever feel weird that we are stuffing drugs into a teddy bear?"

"No," I respond to Roberto. It's a lie. I hate this shit, but until my cousin is out of the picture, I need to keep dealing this crap. I can't risk my cousin taking over and becoming even more powerful than he already is.

It still sucks to have to hide it in something meant for a kid. Luckily, there is no risk of this getting into the wrong hands.

The toy factory no longer sells stuffed toys to real stores. It's one hundred percent only selling our pieces, so there is no room for confusion with shipments. It's merely a front.

"We sell a product that for all intents and purposes shouldn't even be illegal. In some states, some of the shit we sell isn't. Coke, weed, pills . . . if someone wants to get high, let them. Fuck, weed is legal in half the country, even Oregon just decriminalized heroin and cocaine."

"That better not happen here. It will kill our profit margins."

"If it does, we'll be fine." And we will. We have our hands in multiple pots. Drugs are only a small component.

Protection. Gambling. Loans. These are my moneymakers.

Drugs are something I've been trying to get out of for a long time, but until I do, I have to put up with this shit.

Soon.

"Listen, we might be stuffing a teddy with molly, but at least we don't sell women."

That is my argument to myself. I don't like the drug aspect, but it has always been a part of my family business. In order to change that, I would piss a lot of people off within the family from the loss of earnings.

I've spent the past three years since my father's death doing just that.

My goal is to be out within five more.

When the car stops, I get out. "How much longer?"

"Tobias said the boat should be coming in within fifteen minutes."

This location is prime due to its isolation and the toy company's good standing. The only issue I have is, although the governor of New York is on my side, I have to worry that the governor of Jersey would catch on. The Port Authority is headed up by both New York and Jersey.

I make a few calls as I wait, and just as Tobias has said, the boat pulls in at the exact time.

My men start to unload the crates, placing them on the concrete before they are all pried open and checked.

It takes us hours.

I'd much rather be at a club getting my dick sucked right now. But instead, I'm pulling

drugs out of a stuffed lion's head.

By the time we finish, the early morning light starts to slowly seep in from the hazy sky.

I'm back in my car now. The drugs are left behind with Roberto to sort and ship off to the distributors. It's just me, Lorenzo, and my driver on the way back to my estate.

"What did you think of the location?"

"It will work perfectly for now."

"You still want out of dealing?" he asks me.

I give him a brief nod. "I do."

"Think the men will care?"

"Maybe. But I think that when I devise a more viable solution that makes even more money, they won't give a flying fuck."

"And what will that be?"

"No clue. But don't worry, I'll figure it out."

"I know you will. You always do. You remind me of your dad."

His words have me looking over at him, stunned.

Lorenzo has been my friend, cousin, and closest confidant.

His opinion means everything to me. Knowing that I am anything like the man my dad was means everything.

I chose not to speak. Not to thank him. Not to say anything at all.

My emotions are sitting too heavy on my tongue, and I know if I open my mouth, I will say something.

In my line of work and in my family, you don't do that.

Instead, I nod once.

He knows me well enough to know I appreciate it, and then I pull out my phone and text Tobias.

Tobias is more than a business acquaintance. In my line of work, I don't have many friends, but to me, if I had one, it would be him. We met at Cyrus Reed's estate many years ago. Both of us clients of the banker. Over drinks and poker, we formed a bond of sorts, which is uncommon in this life.

Regardless of what he does for a living, I trust him with my life.

Born and raised in New York, his family is from Greece, but a family connection he wouldn't speak of has him directly connected to the Columbian cartel.

Because of that connection, he is my primary source of drugs.

I never asked questions, which is probably why he likes me so much, and since he has always honored the same code, I like him too.

**Me: I'm at the restaurant.**

It's coded obviously.

I'm here, meaning the drugs are here.

**Tobias: Good. Enjoy it.**

I place my phone back in my pocket and look out the window.

Guess I won't be sleeping anytime soon. Lucky for me, I don't require a lot. Tonight, I will decide what to do with my wife.

Something away from the house . . .

Or maybe something on the property.

I'm not sure if she will be comfortable going somewhere with me yet.

The weather is starting to get cold.

Although snow hasn't fallen yet, it's just a matter of time.

The trees are barren, so there isn't much to see on the property.

Instead of a walk, I decide I'll take her into the city tomorrow.

We can go shopping.

I can tell by the way she talked about getting a job, she's anxious to get out of the house, so that is what I'll do.

We will spend the day together.

# CHAPTER TWELVE

## Viviana

A WEEK HAS PASSED. THE DAYS HAVE BLENDED TOGETHER IN this house. The highlight being dinner with Matteo every night, as strange as that sounds.

It's surreal.

Even now as the early morning sunshine streams in from the tall windows it feels like I'm lost in a dream.

My eyes blink open, and for a moment, I almost forget where I am. *Almost.*

But when the room comes into focus, beautifully ornate and the opposite of my apartment, I remember everything, and reality crashes down on me.

This isn't a dream.

I'm still here, in this strange sense of purgatory.

No idea what my future will bring, and completely afraid of what my past will.

There is nothing I can do now. I'm at the start of a roller coaster, about to begin moving, with no clue what's in store.

I'll need to suck it up and just go with the flow because I'll have no say in the matter, anyway.

I let out a large yawn.

Now that I'm resigned to my fate in this house, I think about my father.

Even though it has been a week since I spoke to him, I still feel unnerved by the whole encounter.

His words still filter in my mind. I can still see the tightness of his jaw and the way his hand was fisted. The anger was palpable in the room. I am lucky I got out of there unscathed. However, even now, it lingers on my skin. The fear and uncertainty of what the future will bring.

I don't have many choices.

My father left me none.

Matteo is my best option.

Although I don't know if I can trust him with my secrets. If I could, it would change everything. Yesterday he showed me a different side of him, a side that made me think maybe I could. But I'm taking it one day at a time and trying to see what today brings.

For all I know, he'll be a raging asshole yet again.

Even though it's a good possibility, I really hope it's not the case.

Love is not something I expect, but an alliance of sorts could make my life a whole lot easier.

Because the other option is to fall in line with my father.

There is also the choice that I can make to escape both of them. But it is more than just me that I need to consider in this equation. Too many people rely on me, and that's the reason I can't be selfish. I need to really consider my options.

Too much is at stake not to.

So instead of worrying and dwelling, I need to get out of bed. I need to shower. I need to put makeup on, and I need to smile. I need to convince Matteo I'm not the enemy, and that I can be trusted.

As if summoned by my thoughts, there is a knock on my door.

"Viviana." I hear his voice. It's husky and deep, like always.

I imagine there is a scowl on his face. Although he's handsome with a scowl, it's when he smiles and laughs that he's truly devastating.

That side of him is scary. Because that side is the part that makes me humanize him.

Not a good thing right now.

"Hold on a second," I shout back. He can't come in. I'm barely dressed.

I jump out of bed, my feet hit the cold floor as I run to the closet to throw on clothes, but first I have to pee and brush my teeth. When I look in the mirror, my mouth drops open. I look ridiculous.

There is no saving my hair or face right now.

I have sleep lines from the pillow, and bedhead. It looks like I just had sex. Since I didn't, it's not a good look for me.

Quickly, I brush my teeth and run the brush through my hair. Since I still have to shower, I throw a robe on and head to the door. Unlocking it, I open it and poke my head out.

"Hey, I just need to get in the shower real fast."

His green eyes stare at me, and like usual, it appears there are many words hidden behind them. "I'd like to take you to the city today."

I must look shocked because he smiles at me, a little lopsided grin that makes my heart stop, even if just for a second.

A damn smile on a damn man I cannot seem to read and who is giving me mixed signals every single day.

I try to tell it to stop, but it's a damn traitorous muscle, and it won't listen to me.

Yes, he's attractive, and yes, he's my husband, but I cannot get those two things confused.

I can't catch feelings.

Not when there are so many unknown variables.

"I'd love that. How much time do I have?"

"How much time do you need?"

"Thirty minutes."

His eyes go wide at my answer. "That's fast."

I shrug. "I'm not high maintenance."

"I like that about you."

If it's not bad enough that he is gorgeous, now he has to say stuff like that. Cue the freaking butterflies in my stomach.

Great.

Just freaking great.

I'm attracted to my husband. Hell, by the way my body reacts to him, it's more than that. It feels like I'm sucker punched when I realize it's much more than that.

In the course of only a few days, I realize I actually like him.

I have a crush on my husband.

This is bad.

I need air, so walking the New York City streets might be exactly what is necessary right now. Maybe he will be a huge dick, and these insane flutters will stop.

Or maybe it will be worse.

I shake my head and decide to stop daydreaming about how the day will go and just live.

Thirty minutes later, we sit silently together in the car.

I was mildly surprised when he didn't insist that I cover my eyes while we drove out of the compound.

He didn't, but seeing as though when we were passing through the gates, I noticed the men standing with guns at the checkpoints and from lookout towers; I realize that even if I had directions, no one would make it into this place alive.

It should scare me, but it doesn't. Instead, it makes me feel safe.

I'm not sure what that means for me or about me, but I'm pretty sure it's not normal.

I also realize that, technically, if he wanted to lock me in this place, I would have no way out. Luckily for me, that's not the case.

As much of a monster as he makes himself out to be, in the grand scheme of all the men in my life, he's really not that bad.

*It's almost like he's my dark hero.*

I won't tell him that. Knowing him, he'd probably shoot one of his men just to prove me wrong.

No, that's not true. I'm being too hard on him.

As rough around the edges as he is, he has proven multiple times that he's not that bad. It's not surprising that we don't speak during the duration of our drive. But once we cross over the bridge that leads into the city, he turns to me.

"What do you want to do first?"

"I have choices?"

"All the choices in the world, sweetheart. This day is about you."

His words stun me. When he said we were going into the city, I assumed we were going to be staying at his other home.

"Can we eat?"

"I'm sorry, I forgot that you didn't eat anything this morning. You must be starving."

His brows pull together. He's clearly upset that he didn't take me into account.

"It's really not a big deal. In college, I never ate." That makes him squint at me.

"Really?"

"Yes, didn't you ever pull an all-nighter studying and forget to eat?" I ask him.

He looks at me like I'm insane, green eyes wide.

"No."

"Did you . . .?" I trail off, not knowing how to broach this topic. "Did you go to college?"

He chuckles. "Of course, I went to college, Viviana."

"Oh, I just figured . . ."

"The School of Hard Knocks."

I stop. Stare at him. He lets out a roar of a laughter that makes my chest feel fuzzy.

"Yale," he supplies. "You figured since I run the mafia that I'm an idiot."

Great, Viviana. Just great. Here he is, offering me an olive branch of peace to make our co-existence better, and I've insulted him left and right.

"That was presumptuous of me."

"No, sweetheart, it was natural of you. I'm not mad. And the truth is, it's okay. Most of the men in my family didn't go to school, my father included. But he insisted the world was changing, and I needed to be well-versed in life and books in order to adapt to the change. Adapt or die, he used to say."

"He sounds like a smart man."

"He was."

"Was?"

"Yes, he and my mother passed away a few years ago."

"I'm sorry." I nibble on my lower lip. I want to ask him so many questions, but I can't find the words in my mouth.

I'm surprised when he smiles at me. It's not a large or infectious smile, but it still makes my heart beat a little faster.

"It's okay to ask me what happened to them."

"I don't want to pry."

"You're my wife now. It is not prying."

I take a deep breath and give him a tight smile. "How did they pass?"

"They were killed."

I let out an audible gasp. Not only am I shocked that his family died in such a horrific manner but I also can't believe how easily he speaks about it. He acts as though his family went to the supermarket when, in fact, they were murdered. Or at least I think they were. He hasn't said that yet, but I can only assume in the line of business he's in, that's what happened.

"How?"

"There was a bomb . . . The fire it caused killed them."

As soon as the words leave his mouth, it feels like I've been sucker punched. It feels like a knife twisting in my back. As though I can't breathe through the pain, through my own memories.

"I-I . . ." There are no words that make it out of my mouth.

"As I said before, it's okay, Viviana. I have had three years to mourn them, and although I miss them, I have learned to move on."

"Does it hurt to talk about them?"

"Not anymore."

He turns his attention back onto the street.

New York traffic is at a standstill, our car barely moving.

"We'll get out here," Matteo says, shocking me and causing his driver to turn in his seat.

"Here, but—" Through the rearview mirror, I can see the shock on the driver's face as he speaks.

"I said here." Matteo's clipped voice leaves no room for objection.

"I'll tell the men . . ."

"No need."

"But—"

"No one knows we are here. No one followed us. We're fine. We'll walk. If I need you, I'll call."

With nothing more to add, he throws open the door and steps out. I scoot over across the center of the car to leave from the same door he does.

His hand reaches in, and he takes my hand, helping me out of the car.

I expect him to let me go, but instead, he interlocks our fingers.

His warm hand around mine.

It's chilly in the city, but with his proximity and the way he makes my heart work faster than normal, I don't feel the cold at all.

Instead, I feel my cheeks heat, and my pulse roar to life.

"Where are we going?" I squeak above the sound of the cars honking in the distance.

"It's a surprise."

"Oh. . . Okay."

My stomach chooses that moment to growl, and I'm thankful that it's noisy in the city so he can't hear. I am starving, but things are going so well that I don't want to point it out.

Fifteen minutes pass. I keep expecting him to drop my hand, but he never does.

When he finally stops walking, I see he's stopped in front of a small Italian restaurant.

"I hope you're really hungry."

Now that he said it . . .

"I'm starved," I admit.

"Good. Because they make the best brick oven pizza in the city."

He lets go of my hand, and instantly, I miss its warmth. But then he places it on the small of my back. I'm not sure why, but something feels so intimate about the move.

I don't know if it's because he looks down at me, and it's as if he can see through me, or if it's just the feeling of him touching me. I feel shaky, and I have to rid these thoughts from my head. With his free hand, he opens the door to the restaurant.

"After you," he says.

I take a step forward and walk inside.

The restaurant is not what I would expect from the man who lives in such an immaculate estate.

I notice the walls have old, faded paper on them, but then in certain spots, there's paint. There are a few tables, not many, probably around ten, but like the rest of the place, they look like they've seen better days.

"Follow me."

He starts to walk, leading me to the far wall. There is a table for two in the corner. He pulls out the chair for me, and I sit.

"As I said before, they have the best pizza, and trust me, I know."

"How did you find this place?"

"That's a long story."

"Well, I have time." He's about to open his mouth and start speaking when an older lady walks out from the door in the back of the restaurant that must lead to the kitchen.

"Matteo, it's so good to see you. It's been too long," she says, as he stands and gives the lady a hug. She pulls back, eyes on me, wearing a large smile on her face. Curiosity playing in her weathered eyes.

"Who's your friend?"

"Maria, this is actually my wife."

The lady, who I now know as Maria, lifts her hand to her mouth. "You have a wife? I didn't know."

"It all happened rather quickly."

"Franco, come out here! Matteo Amante is here, and he brought his beautiful wife!" she screams.

A gentleman with salt-and-pepper hair and a gray beard comes toward us. He shakes hands with Matteo before they both turn to me.

"Welcome. Matteo is like family," she says warmly.

They both start to speak in Italian, their voices excited. Since I don't speak Italian, I just sit there smiling at them. It's nice to see Matteo like this. He seems like a different man.

Eventually, Matteo sits back down, and Maria and Franco go back to the kitchen to grab us the pizza.

It's not a moment later when a big, giant pie is placed in front of us.

"Holy crap, that's big." I laugh.

"You didn't eat breakfast."

"I mean, I'm hungry, but that's enough to feed an army."

"Pretty sure an army would require a bit more than that."

"I mean, I don't limit what I can eat but this is ridiculous. I can't believe you bought so much. You have to take home leftovers."

"If that's what you want."

"Why, you don't?"

"I'm not much for leftovers, actually. I prefer fresh food. But it is a lot, and if you want to take it home, we can."

"Maybe Roberto will want some."

"That's kind of you to think of him."

Matteo serves us each a slice. I fold the middle in half and take a bite.

"Oh, my God. Holy crap. That's good."

He smirks and actually looks proud. "Told you."

I take another bite. The robust flavors bursting in my mouth. After I chew and swallow, I look up from my plate.

Matteo is watching me. My cheeks start to feel warm. I was moaning while I ate my slice. Is it possible to die of embarrassment?

"No."

"What?"

"You can't die of embarrassment."

I lift my hand and cover my eyes groaning. "Did I say that out loud?"

"Afraid so."

Yep. Mortified.

Kill me now.

I cough and clear my throat.

"You were going to tell me about this place?" I say, trying desperately to change the topic.

"That's right, I was."

Matteo leans back in his chair. His green eyes appear lighter, and they look off to the left as if he's pulling out the memory from a file deep in the back of his subconscious.

"I can't remember exactly the first time I came here. I must have been four or five. For as long as I remember, I've been coming here. Knowing my mother, I was probably here in a stroller. You see, Maria was my mother's childhood friend. They grew up together. They had both moved here when they were very young. Both of their parents came from the same village in Sicily. The town was called Nicolosi. It was actually my mother's maiden name. They were the best of friends, and even when my mom got married, they stayed in touch. Coming here was my mom's haven from the family and from all the drama of my father's business. Sure, my father did come with her every now and then, but this was her place. Hers and mine. I haven't been here much in the past three years. It's been too hard, but I'm happy I'm here now."

My mouth falls open, and I can feel the dampness in my eyes. I don't know why I'm so emotional. I'm not sure if it's because I can imagine him here as a little child with his mother who needed to escape. In my life, I've seen my mom feel the same way, but she didn't have any place to go that my father wasn't. I've also felt that way. I don't know how he feels coming here, but the fact that he showed me this part of him makes me want to cry.

I don't, though. I push back the tears that want to form, and instead, I reached my hand across the table and take his in mine.

"Thank you."

"For what?"

"For opening up to me. For bringing me here. For showing me a different side of you."

"It's nothing."

I give his hand a little squeeze. "No, Matteo. It's everything."

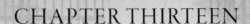

# CHAPTER THIRTEEN

## Matteo

I DIDN'T EXPECT TO OPEN UP LIKE THAT.

It just happened.

For some reason, she's easy to talk to, and that fact doesn't sit well with me. It's like she's weaved a spell, and I had no other choice but to oblige.

It's awful.

Fucking awful.

But on a more positive note, she's playing right into my hands.

Both literally and figuratively. I look down to where our fingers are now entwined.

I would be lying if I didn't admit it to myself, that sitting across from her at this table is comforting.

Her eyes are soft. They look at me as if she wants to save me.

It's a shame really, because had she not agreed to work with her father behind my back, I could see myself falling for her.

It makes no difference, though. What's done is done.

"What about you? Do you have a restaurant your parents ever took you to?"

"You mean other than making me stay home with the nanny?"

As soon as the words slip out of her mouth her shoulders tighten.

The nanny.

The family her father is still paying even now, years later.

What happened to her?

Why are they paying her off?

This is one more thing I need to get to the bottom of. This can be something I can use against the governor.

Maybe when she gets more comfortable, she will open up. Or maybe now that her phone is tapped, when she calls her father to talk about her mission, she will mention it.

Fuck, that will make my life so much easier.

"After we're done eating lunch, what do you want to do?" I ask, changing the topic.

The haunted look that is in her eyes fades away.

"I get to pick?"

"Well, I picked lunch."

"And you did such a great job. I'm not sure I can do much better."

"You don't have to do much better, you only have to tell me what will make you happy."

She cocks her head.

Still unsure.

"Viviana, we started on the wrong foot. Yes, I'm a dick. I'm controlling too. But we don't have to hate each other. We made a promise for forever. Forever is a long time."

She mulls over my words but eventually nods her head.

"I want to go ice-skating."

"Is there a rink even open? It's not cold yet."

"Yes."

Her direct and forceful response has me laughing.

"Fine. I'll take you."

"Can you skate?" she asks.

"Yes. Can you?"

"No," she admits on a sigh.

"Then why do you want to go skating so bad?"

"Because my parents never let me. I told myself when I was older, I would go by myself when I finally moved into the city, but between school and everything, I never found time."

"So you're telling me in four years of living in the city you never went ice-skating?"

"That's exactly what I'm telling you."

"Well, I guess I know the plans for later today. And here I thought we would wind up at Saks or Bergdorf to buy you a new wardrobe."

"Nope. I'm not much of a shopper."

I stare at her, transfixed by what she says. "You constantly surprise me."

"What do you mean?" Her nose wrinkles.

"You really aren't like most women I know."

"Stop generalizing then."

I smile. "Touché."

"Anyway, is that a good thing or a bad thing?"

"It's a good thing. A very good thing." The truth is, that's one of the things I begrudgingly like most about her. I like that she's not like anyone else.

It's going to fucking suck if I ever have to kill her.

I remind myself that she made a deal with her father to sell me out. No matter how cute she looks smiling at me about ice-skating, it doesn't matter. I need to always remember this is just a game, and she is merely the pawn.

———•———

I decide not to take her ice-skating, but I won't tell her now. Instead, I decided to tell her we have other plans. That we should spend the day doing other things, and that ice-skating will be the last.

I'm lying.

Normally, I don't lie.

But seeing as she agreed to sell me out to her father, there is no harm.

I walk us to Fifth Avenue. Viviana growing up, lacked for nothing, so I expect her to look at the stores, but she doesn't even glance. It's very refreshing that she doesn't seem to care very much.

In another life, I could see myself enjoying my time with her. In another life, she would make the perfect wife.

But this life isn't ours to have.

We walk all the way down Fifth Avenue until we reach the New York City Library.

This is what she gets excited about. Not the designer stores. No, Viviana gets excited about the library.

If only I had a bigger library in my house. Mine is small and unkept. I have a few books for the kids who come over who are my family members. Nothing crazy, but still, I will give her access to it after we return from the city.

It will give her something to do.

Plus, it might be my way to get her to trust me more.

I'm sure that reading the fairy tales she loves will make her more open to suggestions.

I think back to the book I found her reading in my old room, and I have to refrain from laughing. When she alluded that I was the beast in the story, she couldn't have been any further from the truth.

If this was a fairy tale, I would not be the beast.

Although I do have some redeemable qualities, none of them are aimed toward her. If anything, I'm Gaston.

The villain.

And in this fairy tale, there are no heroes.

# CHAPTER FOURTEEN

## Viviana

I'M OFFICIALLY HAVING THE BEST TIME, WHICH IS NOT something I would've thought I would be saying today. It's certainly not something I thought I'd be saying a week ago. Or two, at that. This is all unchartered territory. Feeling welcome, and interesting, and like I matter. As we step into the New York City Library, my senses go into overdrive. The smell that permeates through the air: old books. It's heaven.

It's nice to have him here. Although normally when I come here, I have Julia in tow.

She knows just how much I love the library. She's the only person who knows how badly I love to get lost in a story.

She and I are connected in that.

Neither one of us had the childhood we deserved.

Hers, however, was not her fault…

Mine.

Nope. Not going there.

I always would sit in my tree house and wish I could escape into my own world.

Now, I want to give that dream to other children. I survived by losing myself in the classics, but how amazing would it be if I could find a fantastic fantasy and bring it into the world for others to enjoy.

That dream faded a long time ago.

When my father so pointedly told me that my only place was beside my future husband as a prop.

I'm happy to have the dream again. Even if it never comes to be, I'm happy to just dream.

No matter what happens with my father or what he makes me do, this will happen.

I'm surprised when we spend an hour at the library. I assumed we would walk in, and after five minutes, Matteo would get bored and want to leave. But instead, he let me look around, sit down, and read.

Another thing that surprised me was I assumed he would play on his phone the whole time. Obviously not speak on his phone, but I expected him to text. Instead, he spent the whole time watching me.

At first, it was a bit unnerving. Then despite what I thought, I found that I liked it. I liked the way he watched me. His green eyes, usually cold and distant, had a different look to them. This time his pupils were large. They were dilated as he watched me.

But it was the way he watched. He watched me like a predator. He watched me like he wanted to jump across the table, throw me down, and have his way with me. I'd like to pretend that I had no reaction to this. But as I read each word, all I see above the book is him tracking my movements, ready to pounce.

"Are you ready to go?" I ask.

"Don't feel rushed by me. I'm enjoying myself."

"All you've been doing is staring at me."

"Case in point. This is why I've been enjoying myself."

"Well, I'm ready."

"We still have a lot of time before we go to Rockefeller Center. Is there something you want to do beforehand?"

"I was wondering . . ." I bite my lower lip.

"You can talk to me. What were you wondering, Viviana?"

"I was wondering if I could see my friend Julia."

"The same Julia you wanted to invite to the wedding?"

"The very same."

He mulls over my words, not giving away what he thinks he's going to do. I wonder if he'll say yes. Or maybe he'll say no. Maybe this whole last week of him being nice has just been an illusion in my mind. I sit and wait for him to answer. I close the cover of the book I was reading and stare up at him.

On instinct, I bite my lip harder, a small exhale bursting from my mouth when I nip too hard. I follow the movement of his eyes and can't be one hundred percent sure but, if I had to harbor a guess on what he is staring at, I would have to say my mouth.

When he still doesn't answer, I start to fidget uncomfortably in my chair. The silence of the library is deafening right now. He leans forward. His elbows resting on the surface of the table. I lean forward as well, our faces are closer, so he doesn't have to raise his voice.

"You can see your friend, Viviana. Tell her to meet us for coffee."

"Shh." I hear from a patron sitting farther up the table from us.

A laugh wants to escape my mouth. But I hold back from making a sound. Instead, I mouth to Matteo that we should go.

He gives me a nod and stands. I'm putting the book in a pile before I noticed that he's walked up to me. With one hand, he grabs my pile, and with the other, he takes me.

We return the books back to where we found them and then we walk back out the foyer of the library. Once we're back in the busy New York streets, I let out the laugh I was holding.

"We almost got in trouble."

"If you think that's trouble, then you've never seen trouble."

"Probably not."

"Don't worry, spend enough time with me and you certainly will."

"Where should I tell her we're going?"

He prattles off an address, and for some reason, I'm pretty sure that like the pizza restaurant we went to, the owner will be someone he knows. I'm okay with that. Every time he introduces me to someone, I find out a little more about my mysterious husband.

My desire for knowledge is all-encompassing. I want to gather information like one would do before a test. I send a text message to Julia, telling her where we will be, when we will be there, and asking her if she will join us. My phone vibrates in my hands.

**Julia: Wow. You're alive.**

**Me: Sorry I've been MIA.**

**Julia: MIA? More like dead. You better have a good excuse for why you have dropped off the face of the planet. I was worried SICK about you.**

**Me: I do. Promise.**

**Julia: And . . . ?**

**Me: I'll explain when I see you.**

**Julia: When/where? Talk to me.**

As soon as I put my phone back into my bag, I stop short.

"What's wrong?"

"Shit," I mutter under my breath.

"What?"

"I just realized I haven't spoken to Jules in so long. Even after I got my phone back, I didn't call her, I didn't know what to say so I avoided her. Now I realize how bad an idea that was. I haven't spoken to Julia since the night at the club. She doesn't know anything. For all she knows, I was buried in a shallow ditch, because I didn't talk to her."

"Are you worried how she'll react to the news of your marriage?"

I give him a look that says are you fucking kidding me. "Yes, Matteo." My arms start to move dramatically in an animated fashion. "Of course, I'm worried. I got married without my best friend. She's more than my best friend. She is the closest thing to family I have. And I have two parents who are alive." Matteo steps up to me and takes my frantic hands in his. My eyes go wide as he lifts them up to his mouth and places a soft kiss on top of each.

"Talk to me."

I don't know what to tell him. On the one hand, I want to tell him all about my past. All about how important Julia is to me. About her mother. But until I know if I can trust him, I need to be careful with my words. Too much is at stake.

"Her mother was my nanny. Since my family . . ." I bite my lip, nibbling it for a second as I remember all the memories that flood me. "My family was never around. My mother was too busy being a socialite, Julia and her family were my only family. At least for the first ten years of my life. I can't lose her."

"She will understand."

"Will she?"

"Yes. You say she's family. Tell her a version of the truth. She knows your life is not exactly ordinary."

"And what exactly is that?"

"That your father wanted to marry you off to a horrible man, and I was your savior." The right side of his lip curls up into a smirk.

"Do you think you're funny?"

"No one has ever accused me of being that. But yes, I think I am."

I give a little chuckle. "Believe what you want. Now, let's get going."

The walk to the coffee shop takes us about ten minutes. It's not far, and since the weather isn't too cold, it feels nice. Just as I suspected, it's a small, cozy café. From the Italian word on the banner, I have a feeling when we walk inside, Matteo will know the owner.

As the bell jingles, I am almost immediately correct. Matteo doesn't even need to take one step inside before a man, who looks to be a little older than Matteo, walks up to us. Again, they speak to each other in Italian. And again, I curse the fact I never learned. He introduces me as his wife. This time when he does, it feels as though swarms of butterflies start to dance in my belly.

My cheeks warm, and I'm sure that I'm blushing, which is stupid because I shouldn't feel this way. It wasn't long ago that I hated him, and in a matter of one week, he's basically turned my body into a traitor.

Once the introductions are made, we sit down at the table.

It's not a minute later that the same man, who he introduced to me as the owner of the small café, comes back to the table. This time, he places a white envelope on top of the linens. Matteo takes the envelope without checking what's in it and places it in his pocket. The man says nothing more and just turns and walks away, leaving me still staring at the place on the table where the envelope just sat.

"What was that?"

"Nothing to concern yourself with."

I want to say bullshit. I want to demand he tells me. For so many years, I was left in the dark. All the time I lived under my father's roof I was treated like a child, not able to make her own decisions. The thing is, as much as I want to ask him at the same time, I'm not sure I want to know.

I am under no false illusion it's about my husband, but at the same time, do I really want the gritty details?

# CHAPTER FIFTEEN

Matteo

I WATCH HER AS SHE WAITS FOR HER FRIEND TO ARRIVE. HER face is more serious than normal. There is a tiny line that forms between her brows like she is thinking really hard of how she is going to break the news to her friend that she got married.

Then there is the way she nibbles on her lip.

I'm used to seeing her do this move when she is nervous, but now as she chomps on the plump skin, I know she truly cares what her friend thinks.

When the bell on the door finally chimes and a girl who looks to be Viviana's age walks in, she jumps from her chair and barrels into her.

They both seem equally excited to see each other.

As though it's been years and not weeks.

It feels like just yesterday I waited in Viviana's apartment for her to arrive, but seeing these two together makes me understand it's been much longer than it felt.

After a few seconds, they separate.

That's when her friend finally notices me. She narrows her eyes as I stand and approach. She doesn't even need to speak for me to know that she is currently giving me the silent third degree.

Turning back to Viviana, she gives her a pointed look.

"Who is he?" she grits through her teeth. Not even pretending not to be upset.

"About that . . . How about you take a seat? I have someone to talk to you about."

"What's going on? Viviana, in my whole life of knowing you, you have never randomly shown up with a guy. You've barely dated. And here you are, missing in action for almost two weeks, then you bring him here. Tell me what is going on, now."

For some reason, I find myself stepping up to Viviana's side and getting close to her. I don't outwardly touch her, but my hand skims her hand, our fingers making contact. She straightens her back as if my touch gives her strength.

"Please, sit down, Julia, I will explain everything. I promise."

"Sounds like it's going to be one heck of a long story," she says, before striding over to the chair and sitting down. We both also take the seats that we were in before, but I pull my chair a little closer to hers, making a clear statement that we are together.

"Remember that night I went to my father's?"

"The last time we spoke?" The bitterness in her voice is heavy. Like a jilted lover left at the altar forced to talk to her ex.

"Yes, that's the night I'm talking about. As you know, it's never fun going to have dinner with my family, but this night was worse. This night, my father basically took my life away from me. He-he," she stutters, clearly still affected by his words. "He wanted me to form an alliance for him. I-I was supposed to marry a man named Salvatore Amante. He thought that by marrying me off to him, it would help him politically."

Julia's face shows signs of shock. Her mouth open, waiting.

"Matteo"—Viviana looks at me—"is Salvatore's cousin. Matteo, knowing the type of man Salvatore is, wanted to help me . . ."

"And how exactly did he help you?"

It is then that Viviana removes her hand from her lap. She

twists the ring on her finger around until it is no longer just a platinum band on her right hand, but now the diamond is showing. She removes the ring and places it on the left hand.

"You're engaged?" Julia hisses.

"No." There is a pregnant pause as Julia waits for what she will say next. I'm waiting too, but not because I don't know the answer, but because I'm curious as to how her friend will react. "I'm actually married." The silence is deafening after the statement.

Julia stares at her friend, blank and lifelessly.

Finally, Viviana leans across the table closer. "Say something. Please." Her voice cracks. There is so much emotion wrapped up in the one word. It's a plea. A frozen panic, unfathomable pain.

She needs her friend to be okay with this, but instead, Julia's jaw tightens.

"You got married without me," she states.

"It wasn't like that."

Julia stands from her chair. "Yes. It clearly was."

"Where are you going?" Viviana stands too, but unlike her friend who stands tall with strength, Viviana's shoulders slump forward. This is a much different version of the girl I saw go head-to-head with her father.

Her friend crosses her arms at her chest. "I need air. I need to think."

"Please let me explain. We needed to keep it quiet." Viviana steps closer to her and lifts her hand, but Julia shakes her head.

"Still, I'm not just anyone," Julia says, and for some unexplainable reason, I feel the need to defend her.

"I don't know you, Julia, but I know that my wife cares deeply for you. You can't blame her for this. This was done for her protection, as well as yours. I insisted that she marry me."

"That's well and good, but I still can't deal with this now."

"Please," Viviana pleads again, but she's still not deterred.

"Not now. You are supposed to be family. You are my only

143

family besides my brother, and I wasn't there with you. Listen, I'll get over this. But right now, I need to be alone."

"I understand," Viviana whispers.

Without another word, she turns back to the door and leaves. We are both quiet.

From where I'm sitting, I have my head cocked to look at her. Her head is down, facing the floor. She's staring deeply at it. It's as though there is something interesting there.

Of course, there isn't. She is just lost in a train of thought.

Standing, I walk in front of her. Blocking her gaze with my body, I grab her by her hand.

"What are you doing?"

"We're leaving."

She shakes her head. "Don't we have to pay?"

"No," I tell her.

"Okay . . . Can we just go home?"

"No."

Two thoughts pop into my head.

The first is, I don't like seeing her like this. That thought gives me pause. She's nothing to me other than a means to an end, so why do I care?

The second is, justifying why I care. It doesn't feel genuine, and that thought bothers me.

I can use this to build trust.

For some reason, that idea feels wrong. But I refuse to let that stop me. Instead, I push forward with the plan.

Use her weakness to my advantage.

"Where are we going? I don't want to ice-skate."

Good. Thank fucking God because as much as I want to lure her in, ice-skating is not something I want to do.

If this hadn't happened, I was already trying to formulate a plan on how to get out of it. This way, she thinks she decided.

Which works better for me.

I lead her outside, and then we start walking uptown.

This time, the walk is longer, and the air is getting colder. She pulls her jacket tighter against her chest.

"Do you want to grab a cab?"

"Nah. I'm good. A bit cold but not too bad."

I shrug off my own coat and place it over her shoulders. She's so tiny, it's swimming on her.

Viviana stops walking.

She turns her body, pivoting until she is facing me. Her eyes are wide. She resembles a little girl trying on her father's clothes. That's how small she is. I don't think I ever realized the size difference.

"How tall are you?" I ask, and she looks at me like I'm crazy. My question takes her completely off guard.

"Five foot two. Give or take. Why?" The moment she answers, I realize how dumb the question was. I knew the answer. I was just so preoccupied by her that I forgot all about her file.

"Because my coat is huge on you."

"Well, it's not my fault you're like a giant." She rolls her eyes at me, and I laugh.

"No. I'm definitely not a giant."

"Then how tall are you?" Her perfect brow arches.

"Me. I'm six foot two inches."

"That's still a foot taller than I am. You didn't have to give me your coat, by the way. I would have been okay."

"You were cold, and that's what a gentleman does." At my words, she sucks in her cheeks as though she is mocking me.

"And you"—she pauses—"consider yourself a gentleman?"

"What else would you consider me?"

"Not that." Her eyes look up and to the right as if she is trying to figure out the perfect insult to fling at me. "Maybe the word asshole would better fit." She grins at her words, clearly proud of herself.

"You are so funny." At that, she giggles. The sound is refreshing after the past twenty minutes of silence. We start to walk again, and I'm happy I was able to lighten the mood. Thus far, it hasn't been pleasant to see her sulk. I don't do drama, and having to watch her spar with her friend is exactly why I don't do girlfriends.

This time is different because her emotions don't play into my bigger plan. It's obvious she's upset. But I don't know how to deal with that shit.

I have never had to.

This is a relationship, and I don't do relationships. An ironic fact, seeing as I'm married now.

Now that the air around us is lighter, I pull her closer to me and wrap my arm around her.

"What are you doing?" she asks, confused.

"I figured since you were cold," I offer as my completely bullshit excuse.

"Oh. Okay."

"It's only a few more minutes anyway."

"Where are we going now? I can't possibly eat another piece of food. Or drink anything more."

"Don't worry. No more food. Well, at least no more food until dinner."

The destination is directly in front of us.

"We're going to the park?"

"Kind of."

"What do you mean kind of?"

"Well, earlier you mentioned your parents never let you go ice-skating or do any of the fun things tourists do in the city. One of the things my mom used to do with me when I was a small boy was sneak me out of school, not tell my dad, and bring me into the city. She would then take me on a carriage ride."

"Is that what we are doing?"

"I believe it is, Princess."

# CHAPTER SIXTEEN

Viviana

*P*RINCESS.

And for the first time, I feel like one. This is not a nickname to mock or belittle me.

I'm still shocked by his idea. A carriage ride.

If you had asked me if I thought my husband had any romantic bones in his body, the answer would have been no.

But each second I spend with him, I'm starting to think maybe he does after all.

Together, with his arm wrapped around me, we make our way to the horse lineup.

He walks away from me as he talks to the driver. Once they settle the fare, he's grabbing my hand and helping me up.

As we start our journey down the path and into the park, I turn my head toward Matteo. I'm still in awe of him for planning this, but what I'm mainly in shock about is that he opened up to me about his past.

Maybe there is more to him. Maybe this can be more.

I shouldn't indulge myself in these stupid fantasies, but when he looks at me, I can't help it. It is as if he can hear my inner rambling about him because he chooses that exact minute to turn his face toward mine.

Our gazes lock.

His pupils are large and dilated, and the bright streams of sunlight reflect off them. Bouncing around us like a dream come true.

Something is different about the way he looks at me. A hidden secret there. Something primal steals away in his stare, and pulls me in, wraps its tendrils around me, not allowing me to pull my own gaze away. It speaks to me of want, desperation, and most of all need.

Will he cross the imaginary divide?

My heart pounds in my chest as I wait, the passing seconds filling the tense space between.

*Kiss me.*

The voice in my head is foreign, but it begs him to close the distance. To wrap his arms around me. To bring his body to mine. In my thoughts, I can almost feel his lips. Almost taste his mouth.

They would be firm when they found me.

It would be intoxicating.

A cough brings me out of my haze, and I see Matteo staring at me still, and his eyes are locked on my lips.

While I was fantasizing about him, he had moved closer. Now we were close enough that one small bump of the carriage would have us kissing.

Hit a pothole. *Please.*

I can't believe how much I want this. How much I want him.

It's not just because he's handsome.

Hell, he's drop-dead gorgeous. But it's also because of the way he treated me today. Everything he did.

It was like he was taking care of me.

No one has ever taken care of me.

Not true.

Ana did.

She took care of me.

Look how that turned out.

"Are you okay?" his voice cuts through my thoughts.

I blink, righting myself.

That's when his hand reaches out, and his warm fingers cradle my jaw.

This is it.

This is the moment when Matteo Amante will kiss me. Really kiss me. Like a husband kisses a wife.

At the wedding, it wasn't real. I hated him too much to appreciate it. But now, here in the carriage, in New York City, this will be our first.

His body starts to move, and now his face is a mere inch from mine.

*Kiss me.*

He's about to. My eyes close of their own accord and my lips part in waiting.

Ring.

Ring.

Ring.

A phone.

My eyes jut open. No, not mine. It's Matteo's phone ringing. He's pulling away now, his hand reaching into his pocket to grab it.

The moment now lost.

I miss it instantly.

"Speak," Matteo commands, before he goes silent, a line forming between his brows.

He's not happy. I swear it looks like he's going to explode. There is a vein that is pulsating in his temple.

Suddenly the carriage feels like it's closing in.

"I will be there as soon as possible. Have Roberto pick us up at Sixtieth and Fifth. Ten minutes."

He hangs up and won't look at me. Instead, he's breathing heavily and staring off into space.

"Is everything okay?"

He turns back toward me and he doesn't need to say anything for me to know that something is seriously wrong. I don't think he will tell me, but I can't help but ask.

"No." He doesn't offer any clarification about what his answer means. I knew he wouldn't, but I still reach out my hand, place my hand on his thigh and give it a little squeeze.

"You know, if you ever want to talk about it, I'm here."

There's an awkward silence that falls into place, and I hope and pray that he breaks it, but as the carriage grinds slowly to a halt, I know it's too late.

The magical moment is gone.

The Matteo I had the pleasure of glancing at has faded away.

In his place is the ruthless monarch.

The king of the city. The monster.

He has reverted to the villain of the story.

Unlike before, he doesn't help me out of the carriage. He doesn't even acknowledge my existence.

We walk up the block where two black SUVs are waiting at the corner. Standing in front of one is Roberto.

"Go with Roberto," he says with no emotion in his voice.

"Are you not coming with me?"

"No."

"Will—"

"I'll see you later." He turns before I can press. Walking toward the other car, he opens the passenger door, climbs in, and they are driving away.

I'm left on the sidewalk with my mouth hanging open. Abandoned.

"Mrs. Amante, are you ready?"

"You don't have to call me Mrs. Amante. You don't call Matteo mister."

"It's different."

"No, it's not. Please call me Viviana."

"I'd prefer not to." He opens the back door for me, and once I'm inside, he shuts it.

Despite the heat being on in the car, I feel chilled to the bone. I still have Matteo's coat wrapped around me, so it's not the temperature that's getting to me. It's the way my husband threw up his walls and shut me out so quickly. It's the way, in the matter of a minute, he completely changed. I'm having a hard time reconciling it. Which one is the real Matteo? Is it the gentleman who helped me, who took me on a carriage ride to make me feel better, or is it the other?

The car is silent as we drive back to the estate.

Eventually, I must doze off because I hear Roberto's voice.

"Mrs. Amante, we are here." I blink open my eyes and see the large home in front of us. "I'll come around and get the door."

I know better than to argue. Instead, I wait for him to come around. My hand lifts, wiping away the remainder of sleep.

It feels like I've been hit with a sledgehammer with how tired I am.

This is why napping is never a good idea for me. I'm always cranky afterward.

Now is obviously no exception.

Julia used to say I woke up like a devil in college.

Jules . . .

I need to call her.

Make this right.

If I could explain the circumstances, she would understand I had no choice.

It's hard, though. How do you explain that you married the head of the East Coast mafia, and he's at war to keep his title?

You don't.

Not unless you want to put a target on your back.

When the door opens, I step out and walk toward the main

entrance of the house. It's already opened, one of the many people who work for my husband standing there letting me pass. I don't bother with pleasantries, nor do I bother taking my coat off and, in this case, also Matteo's coat. Instead, I had straight up to my bedroom.

Once inside, I walk straight to the bathroom, pulling off an article of clothing with each step I take. A shower is necessary, washing away the grime of the last few hours. It's funny how many ups and downs today had.

All in all, I thought I found out a lot about my husband, but now as I step into the warm water, I'm not sure what the truth is. Something tells me he's complex enough for both to be the truth. I stay in the shower until the bathroom is foggy, and my fingers become prunes. Then I step out, grabbing the big white fluffy robe hanging from the hook by the door.

A memory of that first morning when Matteo surprised me in the bathroom. That won't be happening today. I'm sure he's not coming home. I'm not sure how I feel about that. A part of me welcomes the idea of having some peace and quiet to think. Another part I don't like to acknowledge wants to see him again. Wants to pick up where we left off in the carriage. Wants to kiss him.

I decide to ignore that part. I pick up the book beside my bed and crawl in to read. It's funny how similarities between this child's fable and my own life are glaringly obvious. Maybe that's what made me reach out for a book clearly not written for me. I'm still tired, and my eyes continue to blink. It's still a little early for dinner, but I guess I could fall asleep, then wake up and eat. Maybe Matteo will be here.

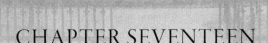

# CHAPTER SEVENTEEN

## Matteo

A FUCKING SHIPMENT.

We lost a whole fucking shipment.

One of my trucks was commandeered on the way to Upstate New York.

So now I'm in the car with Lorenzo trying to figure out who the fuck took it.

It doesn't take a rocket scientist to realize it was Salvatore. However, how Salvatore found out about it is a whole other problem. One: I'm being watched. Two: There is a mole.

Neither option is good.

The only saving grace at this point is that it's not one of the shipments that came from the warehouse. This was a shipment of goods in storage for a few weeks, and we only got around to moving it today.

This means the tight group of people who know about the toy factory are good.

I'm leaning toward the fact that I'm probably being watched.

Of course, it's not unheard of that there could be a mole, but my men have all been with me for years, and before they were my men, they or someone in their family was with my father.

Knowing we've been compromised, I choose to meet my men at the old warehouse. It could be a trap, but I'm willing to take a chance rather than lead someone to my other location.

"Be diligent," I bark at Lorenzo as we weave through traffic to get to where we need to go.

"We aren't being followed."

"That might be the case, but there's a good chance they know we're coming. There's an even a better chance they're already there."

"You think we're walking into an ambush?" His brows furrow.

"I'm one hundred percent sure we're walking into an ambush," I confirm.

"If that's the case, why are you telling the men to go there?"

"Because in this case, I can dictate the outcome. Call up the men. I want them to know to expect anything. Do we have masks in the car?"

"We do."

"Everyone is to wear a mask. We're going to fumigate the place before anyone steps inside. If anyone is there, we will knock them on their ass. If not, well, then we are one canister short, but at least we know."

"Okay. I'll make the call."

With that conversation done, I turn to look out the window. The sky is gray now, and the sun hides behind a cloud. It looks like a storm will hit soon. How different the sky is now from earlier.

Today was a good day. Then some asshole had to fuck it up for me.

Viviana was finally starting to let down her guard.

Then everything was ruined.

This could derail my plan to seduce my wife.

I could have handled it better. Not only did I lose millions but I also have to figure out if it was my cousin or someone else.

It's bad enough to fight one war.

But having to fight two fronts . . .

That never works out well.

Look at Napoleon, for example, he had a hard enough time before the Russian winter kicked his ass.

It takes forty more minutes before we are ready. Half the men pulled up from the back. The other from the side.

I'm coming in from the front.

Lorenzo is ahead of me. He opens the door and throws the tear gas in. My hand lifts as I count off. At one, my signal, we all charge.

The smoke starts to clear a minute later, and three men are on the floor, clutching their faces with machine guns beside them. They're packing some pretty heavy machinery.

"Get the rope." I turn to Lorenzo. "You get chairs."

My men get to work tying up the intruders.

It's not long before the gas wears off, and they start to realized what's happened.

"So, which one of you is going to tell me who you work for?"

None of them answer me.

"Is that how you guys are going to play it?" When no one speaks again, I shrug. "Very well, this is much more fun." I turn behind me to Lorenzo. "Do we have truth serum?"

"Not on us, Boss."

"Okay. You heard him. This is not going to be easy . . ."

I'm handed pliers, and I step up to the first man. He's older than me, probably by ten years. His hair is salt-and-pepper, and his face has a beard. I would put him in his late forties. If he works for Salvatore, he's probably a connection his father had made.

"Last chance to speak." Nothing. I give him a sardonic smile. "Let the games begin."

Lorenzo steps up beside me. This is not our first rodeo. He

holds the man's head, grips his jaw, and opens it. With the pliers in hand, I lean forward.

"You sure . . ." I trail off for emphasis. At this point in the torture, I'm not really asking if he's sure. There's nothing he could do to stop this. His front tooth will be coming out, but I love to toy with my prey first.

I put the metal around his tooth, grip it, and then twist. A bloodcurdling scream echoes through the large cavernous space of my warehouse.

I hold the tooth up to his friends. "Are you sure no one has anything interesting to say to me?"

The man in front of me is now crying. It's hard to hear exactly what he's saying since Lorenzo is still holding his jaw open.

"Let him go. I think he wants to talk." Blood fills his mouth. As he goes to close it, it drips down his chin and onto his shirt.

"Do any of you want to make this easier on yourself?"

"Fuck you," the one guy gargles through the liquid collecting in his mouth.

"Okay, another one?" I yawn, directing this question at my men.

"How about you take out his eye next?" one of my men says from behind me. I turn around to look at which one. I take my finger and point.

"Now that's a good idea. But maybe not an eye. Maybe we should start with a finger."

"No!" the man screams, but I am already moving closer to Lorenzo to grab the blade.

"Anyone want to talk? No? None of you want to save your boy's ass? Okay, well, I'm going to be honest, I don't like the loyalty here. If you're going to let your friend get tortured, I guess I should spread the wealth."

Instead of walking to the man who's bleeding all over the floor, I walk up to the man sitting next to him. He looks to be the same age. This one doesn't have a beard, but he has wrinkles around his eyes.

"You're up. Anything to say?"

"We were just hired to do the job." Well, that takes me by surprise. I didn't actually expect any of them to talk.

"By who?"

"We don't know."

"You had me. I almost let you guys go." I grab his index finger and hold it up, still smiling. I must look like a crazy fucking lunatic. Which at this point, after losing ten million, I am.

"Salvatore. We work for Salvatore Amante."

"That's what I thought . . . gun."

"But—"

"But what? You thought I would let you live? You thought that you could sneak into my warehouse, steal my drugs, and then come back to kill me, and I wouldn't be pissed? You ruined a perfect day. And now you all have to die."

I lift my gun and fire one, two, three times. And when they all slump forward in their chairs, I place my gun in the back of my pants and turn to walk out the door.

"Clean this up," I say to all my men in the warehouse. "Lorenzo, let's go."

When we make it back outside, head to the car, and start to drive, Lorenzo finally speaks.

"Where we going, Boss?"

I don't answer right away. Instead, I look down at myself. There is blood all over my white shirt.

"Should we go into the city?"

I know what he's asking. If we go into the city, as we do on most nights when I torture a man, I'd find a woman and fuck for hours. It's probably exactly what I need, but for some reason, I'm just not in the mood. Sticking my dick in some nameless whore doesn't seem that appealing.

Now sticking my dick in my wife, on the other hand . . .

Fucking Salvatore.

If he hadn't hired those guys to take my truck, I could be balls deep in Viviana by now.

I'm no idiot. It was clearly written all over her face how much she wanted me.

I could have spent a night doing her instead of going home dripping in blood and no pussy.

It's pretty late when we get home. We pull the car into the garage, and I head up the stairs. Before going to my wing, I walk up the opposite stairs, the stairs that lead to her room. Her door is closed, and I consider knocking, but the truth is, she's probably sleeping. I open the door anyway, walking inside, but what I see has my dick going hard.

There, on the pristine white linens, is brown hair splayed across the pillow.

Following the path down, her eyes are closed, her mouth soft, the hollow of her neck bare. She's naked. Her breasts are exposed, and her perky nipples are up and erect, ready for the taking.

I should wake her, finish what we never began, but I'm dripping in blood. My hands are still coated in red filth.

I turn on my heel, walking straight out of her room and down the hall until I make it to the right wing of the house.

I storm inside. I'm all worked up with no outlet. I consider having Lorenzo send a former hookup. It wouldn't be the first time I called one over just to let one suck me off.

It won't do. Only one woman currently occupies space in my mind. Not a good thing either. I walk to the bathroom, turn the knob in the shower, and strip off my clothes.

When I step under the water, the floor starts to turn red as it washes away the sins of the night. While it washes me clean, it does nothing to solve my other problem.

My cock is still ready to fuck.

I grab myself in my hand. It's either this or I wake up my wife. Since that's not going to happen, I stroke myself root to tip. The hot water flows from above, rinsing away the blood on my hands.

It drips off me, clinging to the surface of my skin.

Death and sin.

It's primal and dirty.

It's everything I need right now.

My grip tightens as I think of Viviana lying on the bed.

Naked and ready.

Waiting for me to fuck her.

And I do.

Deep and hard.

Until I fall over the edge.

# CHAPTER EIGHTEEN

## Viviana

A NOISE COMING FROM OUTSIDE MY ROOM HAS ME STARTLING awake.

What time is it?

That's when I notice that my door is ajar.

Why isn't it closed? It's supposed to be closed.

I'm about to get out of bed when I notice a cold feeling run through my chest. That's when I look down and see that I'm not wearing anything.

I threw off my clothes and fell asleep.

Now the chill that attacks me isn't from my naked body, but from the fact someone was recently inside my room and saw me like this.

I jump up from my bed and grab my robe, tying it tightly before I creep out the door.

No lights are on in the house, but regardless of that, I keep walking toward the stairs. Maybe Matteo is home? Maybe he came to see me? To apologize.

I'm not entirely sure where his room is, but I vaguely remember Giana saying it was in the other wing of the house.

When I get to the stairs, I decide not to go down them. Instead, I head toward the landing that will lead me to the other side of the house.

This side is dark, too.

I'm surprised.

I know the house has more security guards than a jail, yet no one is up here.

It's eerily quiet. Ghost-like, even.

This is how a horror movie begins . . .

The dumb girl walks in the dark to her death. It seems pretty fitting right now. But as my brain starts to run wild with how I might die tonight, I see it. At the farthest point of the hallway, a light is on.

That's where I'll go.

Making my way to the door, I knock once, but when no one answers, I peek inside.

Curiosity killed the cat and all.

There is no one in the large suite, but in the corner, another light is on, and it sounds like water is running.

Maybe Matteo is brushing his teeth.

I only have to take a few steps before I have a perfect vantage point into the bathroom.

The door is swung open, and what I see has me gasping out loud. I quickly cover my mouth, not wanting to be heard

There's Matteo.

I don't know what shocks me more.

The way he has his head thrown back, chasing his ecstasy, or the red liquid I assume is blood pooling at his feet.

Is he hurt?

Should I check on him?

No. Of course not. He's obviously not hurt if he's touching himself.

I harbor another glance at him.

My face feels hot and tingly.

That's not the only part of me that feels alive.

I have to get out of here before he catches me.

The idea of him seeing me here…

If he sees me, I'll end up jumping on top of him and kissing him. I might have wanted that earlier, but now I don't.

Who am I trying to kid? Of course, I want that, even after he left me, but I don't want him to know how affected I am by him.

Slowly, without being heard, I step backward.

When I'm finally back in the hallway, I can breathe. My body is on fire from what I just saw. It feels like I'm a burning inferno, and nothing I do can put out the flames inside me.

Tiptoeing so I'm not caught, I make it back to my room.

With the door closed, I get back in the bed and will myself to go to sleep.

Sleep, however, won't find me.

I can't get the vision of Matteo touching himself out of my head.

No matter how hard I try, I see his hand moving up and down.

I wish it was me he was touching, and I wish I was the hand holding him.

Shit.

Now I'm all hot and bothered.

My nipples harden behind the robe, taunting me to touch them.

So, I do.

I have no choice. I'm a live wire ready to explode.

It's the only thing that will calm me enough that I can find sleep.

---

The next morning, I wake up in my bed, robe now off, buck naked, and the memory of last night hits me like a tsunami.

Oh, dear God.

I saw him, and then . . .

How could I do that?

How could I touch myself while thinking of a man who left me alone in the city?

Then he was covered in blood when he got back.

Where did he go?

What did he *do*?

What happened last night?

I'm so confused.

But I'm also mortified with myself.

This is so bad.

My phone starts to ring, pulling me out of my thoughts.

I groan when I see it's my father.

Don't answer. Send him to voicemail.

But I know that's a luxury I don't have.

"Hi, Father," I answer.

"Viviana." The way he says my name makes my eyes water. There is no warmth or comfort. He hates me. If I ever wondered if that was true before, now I most certainly know.

I can't even comprehend why he ever desired to have me.

But then the obvious thing pops into my head. His political aspirations. He needed to look like a family man.

"How is it going with our goal?"

"Umm."

"Viviana, do not make me keep my promise to you. Remember what I showed you. Remember all you can lose if you don't play by my rules."

His words hit their intended mark. They stab me in the heart, making me bleed right into the comforter.

"I will do what you need, Father, but please stop."

"Only after."

"I need your reassurance," I answer with all the strength I can muster.

"And you won't get it." Then the line goes quiet, and I know he hung up.

Tears fill my eyes, making it hard for me to see. I let myself cry. I fall into the comforter and cry until I can't breathe.

I need to figure something out.

I'm not sure how.

But I do.

Maybe I can trust Matteo to help me?

Failing isn't an option.

I can't let Julia down.

No matter what happened, how mad she is, she's family.

I will protect her. I won't let anything bad happen.

Even if it means losing myself in the process.

# CHAPTER NINETEEN

Matteo

M Y PHONE STARTS TO VIBRATE. LOOKING DOWN, I NOTICE A new text has come through.

**Cyrus: Where the fuck are you?**

**Me: Meaning?**

**Cyrus: The game. Are you coming or not?**

It dawns on me then that I have been so wrapped up in my wife and her father, I haven't stopped by Cyrus's poker game for a hot minute.

*Breaking old habits. Not a good look for you, Matteo.*

Cyrus Reed might be my banker, but he also holds one of the most exclusive high-stakes poker games on the East Coast. Which also happens to be a perfect way to clean dirty money.

**Me: Busy.**

**Cyrus: Get your BUSY ass over here. I have business to discuss.**

My head shakes, knowing full well Cyrus won't stop until I agree. He's a dick, but I trust him, and outside of my men, that's a rare thing.

I turn to Lorenzo and nod.

"We're leaving. Get the helicopter ready."

His right eyebrow quirks up. "Where we off to, Boss?"

"Stop calling me Boss, Lorenzo. No one is around."

"Fine, dick. Where to?"

I chuckle at that, smiling at my cousin. "Cyrus." There is no reason to explain. Lorenzo knows all about what goes on at Cyrus's estate in Connecticut.

Thirty minutes later, the helicopter is landing on the sprawling grounds of the compound he owns.

Once the blades stop spinning, we exit and step out into the cold winter night, heading straight for the side entrance that will lead us to the room where we will play cards.

I nod to the security stationed outside, and he swings open the door.

Coming here used to be a weekly occurrence, but my trips have become fewer with everything going on with my cousin.

When I step into the room, a cloud of smoke hits me. Tobias is in his usual spot, smoking a Cuban.

I'm surprised to see everyone is here tonight. All the men who have my back in this business—Cyrus, Tobias, Alaric, James, Mathis, Trent. All men I do business with, but also men I call friends.

"I didn't think you would show," Cyrus says as I step farther into the room.

Together, we walk toward the table, Lorenzo trailing a step behind.

"You said you wanted to talk, so I'm here."

"I was lying."

I cock my head at his candid answer.

"Then why am I here?"

He takes a seat and gives me a pointed look to also sit. "Tobias told me what happened."

"Did I miss something? Are we a bunch of women who sit down and discuss shit now?"

"You're at war, Matteo. Your shit was stolen. Talking about this doesn't make us anything. I'm concerned for my bank." His voice comes out monotone as if he's trying not to seem fazed, but I know him. I went to war for him in the past. You don't go to battle without forming attachments. His battle is mine, and my battle is now his.

"I'm still going to deposit money. I'm not broke," I deadpan.

"Who's broke?" Alaric asks as he sits.

"Matteo." Tobias laughs.

"Fuck you." I chuckle back.

"Don't worry, half the money he gives Cyrus is invested with me," Trent Aldridge chimes in like the condescending, arrogant ass that he is. When I first met Trent, I thought he was a douche, but he has long since proved himself to me.

"Yes, and we all know all your shady-ass Ponzi schemes you have going on," I respond.

"Yeah, speaking of, what the fuck are you doing with my money?" Cyrus cuts in.

"I'm making you a sick investment. Do you really care how?" He gives us all a pointed look.

One drug dealer.

A corrupt banker.

The head of the mafia.

The former arms dealer.

A crooked nightclub owner.

And the man who runs London . . .

Sounds like a particularly decadent start of a joke.

Either way, no one says a word.

Instead, we all shrug as Cyrus raises his hand, and a waitress comes over with our drinks in hand. The beauty of being a regular means everyone knows what you like.

"Whatever you have going on with Salvatore, we all got your back, man," Tobias says as the cards are shuffled.

"I know."

"Just tell me where and when, and I'll come out of retirement." I turn to look at Alaric, and I know for me he would.

Who would have ever thought these crazy-ass men would end up being my brothers in arms?

As we drink our drinks and play our hands, I tell them everything that's happened and what my plan is, and it feels good.

---

The next day comes, and I still haven't seen Viviana.

It feels like my wife is avoiding me.

It's been two days since our trip to New York, and she has sequestered herself in her room.

I've been too busy with the lost shipment to deal with this, but now that time has passed, I've decided I have given her enough time.

Now I'm sick of it.

I storm up the stairs.

When I'm standing in front of her door, I hammer into it with my fist.

"What?" I hear muffled.

"I'm coming in."

"I'm-I'm . . ."

"Open the door, Viviana."

"I'm doing something."

"Open the door now, or I'm breaking it in, then the only thing you'll be doing is giving me answers."

I hear the sound of rustling and then the soft patter of footsteps. The door swings open. There she is. No makeup on, hair in a messy bun on top of her head. She's wearing leggings and a sweatshirt.

"Are you sick?"

Her eyes widen. "No . . . Do I look sick?" she asks, confused.

"If you're not sick, why are you hiding in here?"

Her gaze drops down to the floor. "I'm not."

My hand lifts and tilts her head up until her stare meets mine.

"Why are you avoiding me?" She doesn't answer. "Is this because I left you in New York?" Her cheeks turn a shade redder. "So that's not it?" No comment. "Something else then?"

Still no comment.

Her face keeps getting redder and redder until she resembles a cherry tomato.

"Just leave."

Interesting.

Wonder what has her acting like this.

"Fine. But I expect you at dinner tonight." I turn around and head straight to the surveillance room in the house. Tony is there in front of the monitors.

"Hey, Boss," he says as I enter the room.

"I need you to pull all the phone records for the last few days. Also, the surveillance from the past few days."

"Are we looking for anything in particular?"

"Look at two nights ago. The night of the warehouse."

That was the last time I spoke to her, and according to Francesca, who went to clean her room, she hasn't left since then. She has taken her meals in there as well.

He starts to go through the film, looking through everything that happened on video that night. In the hallway, you can see me entering my room. I closed the door. I know what I was doing that night.

The video switches to the next movement. It's actually outside of Viviana's room. It's dark in the hall, and the time correlates with when I was arriving home. She creeps around the house, and then surprisingly, she's now on video knocking on my door. I don't remember this, which clearly means I was in the shower. The next thing on the video is peculiar. Viviana walks inside. There's nothing for about thirty seconds, and then Viviana is seen again creeping through the hallways until she went back to her room.

This is the last time she left. Interesting, she came to my room and then went into hiding.

Suddenly, it all becomes clear. My little wife is a peeping Tom, and on top of that, she is too embarrassed to look me in the eye.

A smile spreads across my face. If she likes to watch, I'll let her.

I start to imagine what it would be like if she was in the room. I can't wait until I can watch the footage in private of her room. Although it was a giant breach of privacy, installing that camera in there is now looking like the best idea I have ever had in a long time. I'm about to kick everyone out to watch it now, but then Tony interrupts my thoughts.

"I found something."

"What is it?"

"A call came through to her cell phone."

*"And?"* I hate that my pulse kicks up at that.

"It was less than a minute long." His fingers continue to type on the monitor. "The number is registered to Governor Marino."

"Pull up sound from her phone."

"That might take me a few minutes."

"Well, I sure as shit am not going anywhere right now, am I?"

*First, you see me naked, then you speak to your father.*

*What are you up to, little wife?*

I pace the room as I wait. It only takes about ten minutes before Tony has the audio playing through the room of her phone call.

My fists form as I listen. It's not that I like my wife, but a part of me enjoyed spending time with her. Part of me hoped that her father would call, and she would tell him where to stuff it. But apparently, I was wrong, and this all is just one big ruse.

This doesn't change my plan. I will still go ahead with seducing her and then feeding her false information. Viviana is fire. Burning hot but not easily controlled.

I don't care why she's choosing to work with him. She didn't come to me. Regardless of her reasons, a traitor is a traitor.

"Do not tell anyone what you heard on this tape."

"Obviously, Boss."

"I plan to deal with this in my own way."

"You don't have to explain anything to me."

"I know that, but I wanted you to know anyway that I will not let this go unanswered."

"Sounds good."

I walk out of the room and go find Lorenzo. He's in one of the offices on the phones screaming about God knows what. It seems he's still looking for the missing cargo. Even though we killed the three men, we found nothing on their bodies to indicate where the drugs went.

Knowing Lorenzo, he won't stop until he finds it, which is okay by me. At the price it fetches on the black market, I appreciate him looking.

When he hangs up the phone, he looks up at me.

His brows are knitted together, and frown marks line his forehead.

"What's going on?"

"No one knows where our fucking drugs are. Which I find really hard to fucking believe."

"Breathe."

"How can you be so fucking calm?"

"I'm not so fucking calm. I just know we have other things that are important, and while we already lost one shipment, we need this war to stop before we lose another."

"And how are we going to do that?"

"Through my wife."

"What good is she?"

"She is working with her father."

"This, we know."

"But she's also very much attracted to me, which means I have her right where we want her. As soon as I fuck her, I'm going to start feeding her intel. She won't know what hit her until it's too late."

"Think it will work?"

"How can it not? She's trying to get info from me. She's already ready for it. When her father asks how she got it, if she tells him about our relationship, he will eat that shit up. Everyone knows when someone is in love, they get complacent."

"You want her to think you love her . . ."

"It's the only way it will work."

"And then what?"

My lip tips up.

"Then I ruin her."

# CHAPTER TWENTY

## Viviana

I DREAD GOING TO DINNER.

Dread seeing him.

Dread *seeing* him.

How can I possibly look into his eyes after what I saw?

This morning when he came storming into my bedroom, I thought I would die from embarrassment. I didn't die, but I came close.

Now, I'm in my bathroom. Dressed in a pair of black leggings and an off-the-shoulder blouse. I'm not sure if I'm too casual or if I'm overdressed.

I have to assume I'm just right. Matteo always looks well put together. I just feel stupid going downstairs, having not left the room in two days, and wearing this top, especially since it's snowing outside.

Yep, it's officially winter, and now with the impending cold, I feel like I'm really stuck in this house.

I can't imagine any impromptu trips to the city anytime soon.

I put a light dusting of makeup on. Nothing over the top. Then when I'm finished, I complete the look with a light pink lip gloss.

My hair. Blown out in beachy waves.

I'm not sure why I'm putting such effort into my looks. It's not like anything will happen between us.

*But you want it to.*

I want to scold myself in the mirror reflection to stop this insanity. To tell myself not to care, but that would be a giant lie.

Pull yourself together.

Also, it's time to leave the room and stop hiding.

For the next ten minutes, I berate myself with reasons to face the music and stop hiding, and then after one final check in the mirror, I gather all my strength and leave my room.

I'm not late, but it appears Matteo is early. He's already sitting at the head of the table. His large presence occupies all the space in the room, and just as I suspected, he dressed in pants, a sport coat, and a button-down. He makes it appear casual by the way he leaves the two top buttons open. Seeing his skin peeking out from the crisp white shirt has me, yet again, ready to blush.

Calm down.

No need to get all hot and bothered.

He's just a man . . .

An insanely hot one who touches—

"Everything okay over there, Viviana?" His voice cuts through the graphic image playing through my mind.

"What-what do you mean?" I croak.

"You're staring, and you seem a bit flushed. Is something wrong?"

He gives me a look that I find strange. It's almost wicked the way his lip curls up across the side of his face. It's almost as if he knew I saw him pleasuring himself, but that's not possible.

Or is it?

"What's wrong?" he asks again, his smile spreading farther across his flawless face.

"Nothing."

"It looks like you saw something."

Shit.

No.

How could he know? How could he read me so thoroughly? Like an open book?

But it's obvious.

By the way he stares at me, it's so very obvious that he knows what I saw, and what's more obvious is that he likes it.

I want to crawl into a hole.

However, since that's not the kind of person I am, I throw my shoulders back, hold my head high, and school my features.

Then when I'm one hundred percent sure my façade is down, I make my way over to my chair. He stands, surprising me, and pulls it out for me.

"You look beautiful tonight," he says as he sits in the chair directly in front of me, looking into my eyes as he speaks.

Francesca brings the food out. It's as if they have surveillance cameras telling the staff when we are ready.

And that's when it hits me.

They do.

There are probably cameras all over the house, and if that's the case, he knows I saw him.

It had never dawned on me that that could be the case. Which, in hindsight, seems rather naïve, seeing as what he does for a living.

I can play this one of two ways. I can act like a child and hide in my room another day, or I can pretend I'm not bothered by it.

I choose option two.

"So, bringing up the elephant in the room . . ." I say, and his eyes go wide because he thinks I'm going to mention it.

"Where did you go when you left me in the city?"

"I had business to attend to."

"Business so important that you cut our date short?"

"Unfortunately, Viviana, that will happen from time to time. I could apologize. I could lie to you and say it would never happen again, but that's not the kind of man I am. It will happen again, probably more than you would like, but that's what you signed on for when you decided to marry me."

"Decided? As if I had a choice," I grit out through clenched teeth.

"There are always choices, Viviana. No matter what you think the consequences will be, there are always other options." His words feel weighted as if he can see into the blackness of my soul, but he's wrong. Sometimes, we have no choices. Sometimes, we have to do things we're not proud of, and I'm sure Matteo, more than others, knows that.

"Have you never done something just because you had to?"

"Everything I've ever done is because I chose to. Every deal. Every death."

The words he speaks leave me speechless. They make my tongue feel heavy. They make my heart hammer. He's openly talking about his work, admitting he's killed. I know it should make me scared, but for some reason, it does the opposite.

I don't feel scared.

For the first time in a long time, I feel like there could be another way.

My husband could be the solution to all my problems.

But would he help me?

He already has.

---

Dinner is like the last few times. We speak of mundane topics, nothing important. At some point, we even talk about the weather, which seems ridiculous in the grand scheme, but what else are we supposed to talk about?

I'm not going to ask him if he's put a hit on anybody, and I'm certainly not going to ask him whose blood was on his body. He's not going to talk to me about my father, so we are resigned to speaking about the weather.

"The snow is really coming down."

"It is."

"I didn't expect it to happen so fast. Just the other day was cold but not like this."

"They're calling for a massive snowstorm."

"Really?" I ask. I didn't know that, but seeing as I don't watch the news or read a newspaper here, I guess it makes sense I wouldn't know.

"Yes, while you were sequestered in your room, it was all over the news." There is a hint of sarcasm in his voice.

"You watch the news?"

"Why wouldn't I?"

"You just don't seem the type. I can't imagine you comfortable on a couch with a remote in your hand."

"Truth?" He smirks.

"Yeah."

"I don't watch TV, nor did I watch the news. However, I have my men keep me apprised."

That makes me smile. I wasn't wrong about my assessment of him. I rarely am about people. It comes with the territory of growing up in a dangerous environment.

"Now, that makes a lot more sense."

He leans forward in his chair, his fingers drumming on the surface of the table.

"Why do you not see me as the type of person who can relax?"

Even now as he asks that question, he's not relaxing. Case in point: the drumming.

"I don't think you could relax if your life depended on it," I answer.

"I almost feel like that's a challenge."

"Take it any way you want, but you would lose." He chuckles at my comment, and I think he's going to accept it when all of a sudden, the lights in the room start to flicker.

"Are we losing power?"

"Probably. The winds are very strong, and this is an old house."

And then, as if on cue, they go off.

"Shit," Matteo says as he stands.

"Don't you have a generator?"

The room around us is pitch-black. There are no lights on anywhere in the large estate.

"I do. But it only has enough power to light up certain parts of this place."

"The dining room isn't one of them?"

He lets out a sigh. "No. Unfortunately, not."

"Then what is?"

"Well, we don't really need to have the dining room with lights if we have the kitchen lit up. Now do we?"

"You have the kitchen lit?" My voice rises. Clearly, the idea of sitting in the dark with Matteo has my tone rising.

"No."

"Let me get this straight, you have this big giant generator, and it lights up what? Obviously not the house?"

"The surveillance room. The security system. This place is Fort Knox with or without power." Now that makes sense. "There's no generator powerful enough to light up this whole place, but if God forbid something like this happened, the house would be protected, and the people inside the house would be protected."

"Okay, so we have no lights, but we are safe, but that doesn't answer the question of what do we do?"

He steps closer to me. It might be dark, but I can feel his presence.

"I'm sure that my staff will light the candles and pass out flashlights."

"And we wait where?"

"If you're afraid to be alone, you can stay with me."

"As in your bedroom?" I squeak.

I feel his hand before I see it. He takes mine in his, pulling me up and closer to him.

I can barely see anything. It's so dark in the room. The giant windows allow very little of the moonlight to stream in and other than that, nothing.

I can see the reflection in his eyes. They appear darker in this light, reminding me of the first time I saw him watching me.

A shiver runs down my spine.

"Cold?"

"No," I respond as he pulls me into his side, wrapping his hands around my waist.

He leads us out of the room. There is no question that if I was by myself in these pitch-black hallways, I would fall headfirst onto the ground. Despite the moonlight streaming in through the windows, there is no visibility.

I can hear the branches snapping against the frame of the house. The storm is crazy, and I can't imagine it letting up anytime soon.

As he pulls me along, I almost feel like a rag doll. The only difference is, in truth, I don't hate it. I feel safer this way.

We step foot into a room, and he leads me farther inside, then lets go of me. I'm not sure what he's doing, but then he pulls a lighter out of his pocket and lights a candle. We are in a room that is probably considered his den or, because this is an estate, maybe a parlor.

"Take a seat. I'll light a few more, and then I'll start a fire."

"No." My voice comes out too forceful, and Matteo stops what he's doing to turn in my direction. I can't see him clearly in the dark, but there is no question he's perplexed by my reaction.

His hand reaches out and touches my shaky limb.

"Shh." It's almost like he's cooing a baby. Soft and strategic, it pools in my chest like warm honey. "There's nothing to be afraid of."

*You'd be surprised.*

"I-I don't like fires." The wobble in my voice is unmistakable, and I hate myself for it.

"Sit on the couch. I won't light one if you're scared. But Viviana . . ."

"Yes."

"There is nothing to be afraid of. It's merely a spark burst into a flame."

"It can't be controlled," I whisper, my voice raspy and tight.

"And that's the beautiful part," he says. "Sit. Nothing will happen."

I can see the shape of the couch, so I make my way over and take a seat. Once Matteo has lit up two more candles, he sits beside me.

"The candles don't bother you?" He's close. Very close.

Too damn close if you ask me. If the candles weren't flickering in the distance, I would think that he robbed the room of oxygen.

"No. Just the—" I can't go on. I can't explain it to him without telling him everything. "Now what do we do?" I ask, changing the topic. He turns to face me, the shadows of the light playing across his features.

His brow lifts. "What did you have in mind?" Even in the dark, I can hear the sexual innuendo in his words.

"We can play a game," I offer lamely.

"What kind of game can we play in the dark?" He smirks, and what a smirk it is.

I'm not sure if it's from the lighting or the baritone of his voice, but I swear my pulse is racing.

"We can play Twenty Questions," I blurt out, and he laughs. I guess it did sound funny how fast I said it. Like I'm excited and completely nervous and tripping all over my words.

This man turns me into a mess when he looks at me the way he does.

"You want to play Twenty Questions?"

"Yes."

"Really?"

*"Mm-hmm."*

"Okay. Let's play. But first some ground rules."

"Don't ask anything about the business," I say in my best Al Pacino accent. Like I'm some mafia tough guy.

"Exactly. I would hate to have to put—"

"Stop." I raise my hand. "I hate that part."

He laughs again, and the sound is magical. Matteo Amante should laugh more often.

"Okay. You go first. Ask away."

I lean back on the couch and try to think of something. "What's your favorite color?"

"That's the big question you got?"

I shrug.

"Black."

"That's not really a color. More like the absence of light."

"Hence, why I like it." His voice sounds like warm honey as he speaks. I want to spread it all over and lick it.

Where the hell did that come from?

Jeez.

This is crazy.

"Your turn."

"What did you want to be when you were a child? I know now you want to be an agent or editor or something to do with books, but what about when you were a child?"

It takes me aback when I realize he remembers what I said to him. It's like he stored it away, and that thought warms my heart.

"I wanted to be a vet."

"Did you have pets growing up?"

"No."

"Why not?"

I look down at my hands. "I wasn't allowed."

"If you could have any pet, what would you have?"

"It's my turn to ask the questions."

"Answer the damn question, Viviana."

The way he says my name so aggressively should scare me, but it does the opposite. Instead, I can't help but look at his mouth, wishing I had the courage to cross the space between us and kiss him.

"Viviana . . ." He says it again. I think he must know what it does to me.

"I always hoped my parents would surprise me with a puppy." I look off to the other side of the room. "Every year, I thought this would be the year they did it, but as each year passed, I eventually gave up on the dream."

"I'm sorry."

I turn back to him. "I thought you don't apologize."

"For my actions, no. But for this . . . yes."

"But-but you had nothing to do with it."

"I'm still sorry your parents suck."

I look at him again.

Looking for a lie. Looking for anything to make me think he's disingenuous, but I see nothing but the truth in his green eyes.

"You're a better man than you let on, Matteo."

"Don't tell my enemies," he says, and it feels like he hit me in the stomach.

"Next question," he says before I can think any more about the pain spreading throughout my body.

"What about you?"

"Me?"

"Yes, you. What did you want to be? Did you always know you wanted to do this?" I gesture my hand around the room, not that it really implicates "run the mafia," but I think he understands my point.

"Yes and no."

"Elaborate, please."

"When I was a boy, I looked up to my father. I thought he was a very important man, and I wanted to be just like him. Then, when I was around eleven, I realized what exactly he did . . ." He stops speaking for a minute, his hand reaching up and running through his hair. "At the time, my uncle, Salvatore's dad, was in charge. Things were different then. The business was different."

He doesn't need to say more. He made a comment once implying what Salvatore believed in, and although he's not saying it, I have to imagine the old saying holds true "like father, like son." His eyes are downcast as if the memory hurts him still twenty-seven years later.

For some reason, I want to comfort him. I want to take away the pain he feels. I want him to know he can talk to me. It's strange this feeling that weaves its way through my blood as if I want to protect him, which is ironic.

I don't listen to the objections screaming inside me. Instead, I move closer until our legs touch. I take one hand in mine, holding it, and then I lift it to my mouth, placing a kiss on his knuckle.

"What-what happened?" I stutter, scared to ask, scared of the answer, and most of all, scared of what it will mean if he does tell me.

"It wasn't exactly what happened, but what I saw."

"You can talk to me, Matteo."

His eyes narrow ever so slightly, but then they go back to normal, still hard with the emotions waging inside him.

"I wasn't supposed to go to the basement . . ." he starts. "My father always told me not to go to the basement. You see, I grew up in this house. Even when my uncle was in charge. The room you stay in, that was my room. The room I grew up in."

My chest feels constricted under his words. He gave me his childhood room. Why would he do that?

"I couldn't sleep, so I went down to the kitchen. The door to the basement is there. I thought I saw a light . . ." His voice seems to drop, and I'm afraid of what he will say.

"You don't have to tell me."

But he doesn't listen to my plea. Instead, he continues, and even though I want to stop him because I don't want to hear the nightmare he lived, I allow this of him.

"I walked down the stairs . . . There were sounds. Horrible sounds. Crying and wailing. I kept walking until I was in the back, and that's when I saw them."

"Who's them?"

"The girls."

A tear slips down my face. I can't hear any more. More tears come out.

"Why are you crying?" he asks.

"Because you were only a boy. You didn't need to see that."

He reaches his hand out and swipes away a tear that must have landed on my nose.

"What did you do?" I ask.

"I told my dad. That was the day that, for a minute, I didn't want to be my dad, and then it was also the day I did."

"I don't understand."

"When I told him what I saw, I hated him. I thought that he knew. I thought he was the one keeping them like animals, but his rage was palpable. Pure venom poured out of him. He didn't know. He told me to wait, but I followed. I followed him as he crossed the landing and barged into his brother's room. I saw what his brother was doing and who he was doing it to. She was so young, only a few years older than me. She didn't want—" He shakes his head, locked in a horrible memory. I understand all too well what that is like. "My father took out his gun and shot him in the head. Then one by one, he freed the girls. Some of them had no place to go, so he employed them."

"They worked here for your dad after everything?"

"He saved them."

"Do they work for you?"

"Some." He breathes a deep breath. "He single-handedly stopped all the trafficking that was connected to our family. It's actually something that I helped with as well. That's how I became friends with Cyrus."

"Cyrus?"

"He was at the wedding. You probably don't remember him."

I try to think back, but the whole day and night are a blur. "I don't remember much."

"That's okay."

He smiles at me, a small smile, a soft one.

"That's why you want to be like your father? He's a hero to you."

"He was, and yes, I have no false illusion that he didn't do illegal things, but his argument was that people buy drugs regardless, but at least with him running it, he could make sure it never went too far."

My brow arches. "Murder is not too far?"

"We never killed the innocent."

# CHAPTER TWENTY-ONE

## Matteo

I FEEL DRAINED AFTER WHAT I JUST SAID. I DON'T USUALLY talk about such things. I keep my past where it belongs, buried in the backyard with all my emotions and a few bones. But there's something about Viviana.

She's like my own brand of kryptonite. My very own truth serum. No matter how much I try, she finds a way to creep up and install herself in my life. I'm so fucked I don't even need fucking lube.

She's making me feel all kinds of crazy things. She's making me remember even more. It's not good. I know she's part of the plan, but each second that I know her . . . No, I can't think of that.

Salvatore is out there. Salvatore wants his place. And she is the means of getting it.

No matter how she bats her eyelashes at me, she's also lied to me, and that can't go unpunished.

It doesn't matter right now. That's a long-term plan. Right now, there is only one thing I need to concentrate on, and by the way she looks at me, I know it worked.

Allowing myself to open up like that and telling her everything was a calculated risk, but a risk worth taking. She now thinks I trust her.

The room is silent again, the air heavy with my past.

Our faces are close. So close, I can feel the way she exhales.

Her eyes are still glistening with unshed tears. I lift my hand again, and this time, I cradle her jaw.

Tilting her head up.

She watches me intently, her chest heaving as I swipe my thumb across her skin. Trailing it up to her lips. And when she parts her mouth on an exhale, I take it as an invitation and close the distance.

My mouth finds her. As my tongue seeks entry, she moans into my mouth.

My arms pull her tighter to me and then grip her close.

Out of nowhere, her hands press against my chest.

"Stop." She pulls away. "I can't do this."

I stare down at her, confused, not really understanding what just happened. I thought I read the situation. I thought she wanted me. I lift my hand, attempting to back away from her, but she grabs me by my wrist. "Stop," she says again.

"That's what I'm doing."

"That's not what I meant . . ."

"You do want to do this?" It might be dark in here, but I can still see her cheeks are red.

"Yes. Yes, Matteo. I want you, but I can't do this without talking to you first."

Talking to me about what? We're already married. It makes no sense.

"I need to tell you something first."

I narrow my eyes confused.

"Okay."

"You have to promise to hear me out and listen to everything I say before you do anything."

Now I'm really confused. I nod my head.

"Matteo . . ." she starts, but then she shakes her head, taking a deep breath. "Saying this is so much harder than I thought it would be."

"Just go on with it. I find that works best."

"My father wants me to be his spy." And although I know this already, I'm still shocked she just said it.

"When we went to his house, remember how he asked me to be in the room alone with him to talk?"

Of course, I did. I had her bugged, but I don't say any of it. Instead, I just nod again.

"He wanted me to find out information about you. And-and then to tell him," she stutters.

"And did you?"

"No."

Not a lie.

"But then he called again."

"Why are you telling me this? You do know that by telling me this—"

"You'll probably kill me. I know that, and it's worth the risk. I never wanted to betray you. I was always looking for a way out, but I can't kiss you, I can't be with you unless I tell you."

"Because—"

"Because, Matteo, no matter how much I tried, you've gotten under my skin, and I don't want to hurt you."

"If you don't tell your father, what will he do?"

I know he has something on her. I just don't know what.

"He'll hurt me."

"And still you tell me."

She nibbles her lip.

"Yes," she whispers, and I do the only thing I can think of. I grab her by her face, pull her to me, and seal my mouth over hers. This time, she kisses me with reckless abandon. She's pliable in my arms, desperate for my touch, and as the kiss deepens, she claws at my back.

It's as if she wants to fuse herself to me, and at this moment, under the weight of her confession, I want her to.

I don't know what that means for us. I don't know what that means for her father or what it means in my war with Salvatore. All I know is that right now, my wife just passed a test. A test I didn't even know I was giving.

I need her.

I need her like I need air to breathe. I need to feel her warmth, be inside her. I need to ingrain myself in her until I don't know where she ends, and I begin.

Tomorrow, the future will probably look different.

Tomorrow, we will both have to deal with the consequences of our actions.

But tonight, I'll have my wife.

# CHAPTER TWENTY-TWO

## Viviana

"Here, or in the bedroom?" he asks. "Pick fast, or I'll pick for you." The way he speaks is husky. Desire laced in each word.

But the look in his eyes has me coming undone.

I thought when I told him the truth that he would throw me out, but this . . .

He looks at me like I have given him the most precious gift. He looks at me like I'm everything, like he needs to consume me.

It's primal, and it ignites an ember inside me, making me want to allow him to.

With need coursing through my body, I answer his question by reaching out my arms and pulling him toward me again.

"Here," I say against his lips.

"Good, because I can't wait another second to be inside you." He then shuts me up by placing his mouth on mine and kissing me again. With each swipe of the tongue, the kiss becomes more heated.

"Right here. Right now," he says. "Undress," he demands, and I follow his order.

Looking at Matteo right now is like looking at the dark king in all the fables. He's filled with evil but passion too.

I stand from the couch and lift my shirt off, and then start to remove my pants. The whole time I undress, he watches me. Trailing his gaze over my now exposed skin.

No one has ever looked at me like this before.

Now fully naked, standing before him, the hunger in the air is palpable. His eyes are dark and ominous in the soft candlelight of the living room.

I watch through hooded lids as he strips out of his own clothes. Even though I saw him in the shower the other day, this is different. Seeing him naked has my mouth opening, and my tongue going dry.

He's beautiful.

Devastatingly beautiful.

He's cut from marble. Ripped and chiseled to perfection.

He is everything and more. A perfect specimen of a man.

He's a Titan.

"On the couch, Princess," he orders.

I don't hesitate to lie on the couch, waiting as he moves closer to me.

A predator stalking his prey. A lion about to pounce.

As he descends on me, he takes himself in his hand, stroking himself.

"Do you have a condom?" I croak.

His eyes narrow. "You are my wife. I'm not wearing a condom." The gravelly way he says wife has my insides melting. He crawls up over my body, his free hand pushing my thighs apart.

Then I feel him rub himself against me.

He's teasing me.

Toying with me.

He's attempting to drive me insane, and it works. He is.

I thrust my hips up. Trying desperately to put myself out of my misery and get him inside me, already.

With one hard thrust, he gives me what I want. He pushes all the way inside me until he has completely bottomed out.

His grip on my body tightens.

Neither of us moves for a beat.

He allows me to adjust to his size, and when I lean up and kiss his lips, he retracts.

I miss him instantly, kissing him harder, digging my nails into his back to tell him what I want.

He chuckles against my lips, but he gives me what I need. Pushing back until he's fully engulfed again.

He keeps up a slow and steady tempo.

Pulling out and then pushing back in.

His strokes are leisurely.

Each one sending more and more pleasure rippling through my body.

It feels too good.

Intense.

A sensation starts to take root inside me. It's almost there. Close, but not close enough. It's like it's hovering above me, and I can't reach it.

"Harder," I plead. "Faster."

Again, he chuckles but regardless of the humor he finds, he listens and gives in to me.

His slow movements become harder. Until he is fucking me with quick, deep thrusts.

This feeling is beyond anything I have felt before.

We claw at each other.

Both desperate to make the climb.

Our kissing becomes more frenzied, his movements erratic. My nails scrape down his back.

I can feel myself falling over the edge.

My body grips his.

He continues to move inside me, thrusting a few more times before he groans out his own release.

We are both panting heavily as we come down from our own highs.

A few minutes pass before I realize what we just did.

Now what happens?

Yes, obviously we are married, but did that just change everything?

"What are you thinking about?" He lifts his head out of the crook of my neck and looks down at me.

There is a line forming between his brows.

"Nothing," I lie.

He moves to get off me, and I instantly want to pull him closer. I'm not ready for this to be over. When he stands, he walks a few steps to pick up my clothes.

I feel weird and awkward as I place my shirt on.

What does one say to their husband after what we just did, when they barely know them?

It feels like the end of a one-night stand.

Do I just get dressed and go home or, in this case, go to my room?

Once I'm fully dressed, I look at him as he places his own clothes on.

He really is the most stunning man I have ever seen.

I take a deep breath, and when he looks over at me, I speak.

"I'm going to—"

"Like hell you are." He walks over to me, more like stalks, and then before I can ask what he means, he's lifting me bridal style in his arms.

I gasp at the movement. "What are you doing?"

"Something I should have done the day we got married."

He starts to walk toward the door, and then we are in the hallway, making our way to the stairs.

"And what is that?"

"Carry you over the threshold."

I'm shocked when he moves toward the stairs and starts to ascend.

He carries me like I'm a bag of feathers, and to him, I probably am. Once we reach the top of the stairs, he heads in the direction of his bedroom.

I don't say anything. I pretend as though I've never been here before. He knows I have, and I know I have, but at least this way, I can keep a little of my own dignity intact.

When he opens the door, I think he's going to leave me on the bed, but instead, he walks us into the bathroom. My gaze finds the shower. The elusive shower that once ran blood clean. Now, today, the marble is pristine.

He's still holding me in his arms when he turns the water on, and then he sets me down on my feet. I'm a little stunned by everything, but I'm even more stunned when he lifts my shirt above my head, removes my bra, and then bends down in front of me to remove my pants.

It feels like only a moment ago when we did this. The lights are still off in the estate; the candles flickering around us. Someone from his staff must have lit them.

He takes my hand, and with the other, he opens the door to the shower, and he leads me in.

I've never showered with a man before.

I find that he's staring at me with a look of confusion on his face.

"What?" I ask him as he pulls me under the warm water. It cascades down like rainfall.

"You're blushing."

"I'm not." But my high and nervous pitch gives me away.

"Have you never showered with someone before?"

"No," I squeak.

A sensual smile spreads across his face. He's the cat who ate the canary over there.

"What?"

"Wait and see."

The next thing I know, Matteo is dropping to his knees in front of me.

"What are you doing?"

Matteo's strong hands spread my legs apart, and then he grins up at me like a Cheshire cat.

"I want to taste you, Wifey."

"I-I..." It's hard to find words the closer he gets to my bare skin. I'm standing, spread open before him. I've never been looked at like this.

Yes. I've had sex before Matteo, but this is different.

It's decadent.

My legs start to shake with anticipation for the promise of what is to come.

With one hand, he steadies my trembling limbs, and with the other, he opens me for his assault.

Then he leans in and swipes his tongue against my needy body.

His mouth latches on to me as if I'm a banquet ready for him to feast on.

Even with his hand trying to keep me steady, my body shakes against him.

"I could do this all day." His mouth vibrates around me as he speaks. He continues to suck me into his mouth, the pressure building with each pass of his tongue. The feeling is heaven.

I have died and gone to heaven.

My eyes flutter closed. Tingles run down my spine, and I know I'm about to fall over the edge. My muscles tighten and tremble. But just then, as I'm about to come undone, I feel him pull away, leaving me hot and extremely bothered.

"Only with me inside you. Now that I've felt you come, nothing else will do."

He lifts his body to a standing position.

The water is still raining down on us.

He turns me around and then bends me at the hip.

"Hold onto the bench."

I do as he says and hold on to the marble bench in the shower. His body is pressed behind me, but I'm too short, so I lift onto my tiptoes so he can position himself perfectly between my legs.

I feel the head teasing me.

With a slow and steady thrust of his hips, he's inside me. Fully seated to the hilt.

He braces me at the hip and tilts my back farther down. At this angle, he can fuck me deeper. And boy does he ever, slamming into me again and entering me fully, reaching deeper than I thought possible.

His strokes grow harder, more desperate, and with each new thrust of his hips, his pace quickens. He's fucking me at a punishing speed.

Over and over again.

With a long and almost painful shiver, I fall over the edge.

Matteo gives me one, two, three more thrusts, and on the last, he pours himself into me.

"You're amazing," he grits out as he pulls himself out of me. Then he helps me to a standing position.

Once I'm standing, he lets go of me. The room is spinning. The blood must have rushed to my head in the position I was in, and I must wobble because he lets his hands hold me up again.

"You okay?" His voice is laced with concern.

"I'm good. The heat must have gotten to me."

"Here, let me wash you."

It's such a sweet gesture. He grabs the shampoo and lathers it in his hand before putting it on my scalp. It feels amazing as he works it into the threads, and when he's done, he rinses my hair and goes about washing my body. He's careful with me, not something I would have assumed, but he is. He takes care of me.

Not many people in my life have done that for me. There certainly haven't been any men. I find if I'm not careful, Matteo Amante, my husband, is exactly the kind of man I could fall for.

Hell, the more I get to know him, and the more time I spend with him, the more I see and the more I realize I think I might have already fallen for him.

# CHAPTER TWENTY-THREE

## Matteo

I FUCKED MY WIFE TWICE, AND NOW THAT I'VE HAD A TASTE, I fear I'll never get enough.

Fuck kryptonite, the woman is pure crack, the kind I'd like to get my hands on and distribute to achieve world domination.

Even now that we just finished round two in the shower, seeing her bundled up in my robe has my dick springing to action.

*Down, boy.*

It's not like she's going anywhere.

Not anymore, at least.

The moment she confessed to me was like a light switch was turned on.

This whole time I've been fighting back my attraction for her. Yes, of course, I wanted to have sex with her, but I wasn't allowing myself to think about it. It was mainly a way to get her to fall into my plans. It was almost like I thought of sex with her in a clinical way, but then she told me everything.

Now that I know, everything will change.

*All the plans will change.*

I can't be using her.

Tomorrow, I'll need to speak to my men. We'll need to brainstorm what this means. Tonight, I do no such thing.

Tonight, I'm going to lie next to this woman and probably continue to have my way with her.

She seems to be as insatiable as I am. Innocent but insatiable.

Which, in my opinion, is the perfect combination.

"Come on, let's go to bed."

"You . . ." she trails off, and she has this cute little face. I lift my brow and wait for her to continue, although I know what she's going to say. She's like an open book, which is surprising that I didn't realize she would tell me about her father, but maybe she changed her mind, and that's why. She made it sound like it was more than that, but I'm too tired to dwell on it.

"You want me to sleep in here?" In all the weeks I have known her, I have never seen her eyes grow so large.

"Viviana. As my wife, this is your room now."

Her eyes drift across the space in front of her. Then she shakes her head.

"What about the room I was staying in?"

"That was never your room."

"Then why did I stay there?"

"I was waiting for you." My comment makes her smile, not a regular smile though, this one is contagious, and it spreads across her face, touching her eyes.

"You did wait, didn't you?" Her voice is soft.

"I was never going to take you by force. Not in the ways that mattered."

"Do you have something for me to wear? All of my pajamas are in my room . . . My old room."

"You won't be wearing pajamas in our bed."

If she's shocked by my declaration, she tries to school her features. However, it's the way she nibbles her lips that I know.

"Drop the robe, Viviana."

Now she lets her mouth open, but I'll give her some credit. She does it.

The big, white, fluffy robe falls to the ground, and a very naked, beautiful, and extremely nervous Viviana gets into the bed.

As soon as she does, she lets out a tiny little moan. My bed is much more comfortable than hers.

"You like that, right?"

"Oh my God, this is the most amazing bed ever."

"You're welcome."

She giggles. "You are such a dick."

"What did you say?" I drop the towel from around my waist and get into the bed, lying on top of her. "Did you say you want my dick?"

"That's not what I said." Her voice hitches as I use my knee to spread her legs.

My cock is now resting on her bare skin.

"I think it's exactly what you wanted to say." I lean forward, trailing kisses along her jaw. She squirms under me, but I keep up my ministrations, my hand snaking between our bodies and opening her to my attack.

She lets out a moan of pleasure, and I take that as an invitation.

This woman will be the death of me.

---

When I wake up the next morning, I almost forget where I am, which is strange since this is my bedroom, but I see brown hair fanning the pillow. There's an arm lying across my stomach. Normally, if I'm going to sleep with a woman, I'll do it in my apartment in the city, not the one that Viviana has been to.

No, I have an apartment that the sole purpose of is just to get me laid. I normally don't trust women enough. They are a liability.

Fuck, until last night, I didn't trust her as well.

Everything looks different in the light of day.

I stretch my arms out and stifle a yawn. I don't want to wake her. She looks too peaceful, and as much as a certain part of my body wants to, she needs to rest.

I barely let her sleep last night. Once we started, I couldn't stop.

I'll leave her here tucked in my bed and go find my men. I need to apprise them of the change in our situation.

Slowly and carefully, I get up. I walk into my closet and throw on gray sweatpants and a white T-shirt, putting on socks and shoes as well. Then I'm out the door. Because of the time, I know I'll find Lorenzo in the kitchen.

"Boss," he says as I walk in.

"What time did the power kick back on?" I ask gruffly.

"It came back on around five."

"Huh. I slept through it."

"Yeah, about that, I heard from Francesca that you had company."

"That's what we need to discuss. I'm going to grab a cup of coffee, and then we can talk in my office."

I make my way to the cabinet and grab a mug, and after I fill it, I head down the hall, open the door, and sit down behind my desk. Lorenzo is quick to follow.

"Do you want me to call Roberto?"

"Yes."

"Anyone else?"

"No." Although I trust my men, the only two I trust one hundred percent with my life are Roberto and Lorenzo. Luka being a close third.

Lorenzo types out something on his phone, which I imagine is a text to Roberto because within three minutes, the door is opening, and Roberto steps in. He takes his usual seat.

"We were wrong about Viviana."

"How do you mean? We heard her," Roberto says.

"Yes, we heard her say what she *had* to. But last night, she told me everything."

"And you think she was genuine?" This time, it's Lorenzo who speaks.

"She couldn't have hidden the lie from me. Not just because I can read people but also . . . you should have seen her. She was scared. She knew I would kill her. She thought I would."

"What did you do?" he asks.

"Well, I fucked her, of course."

Both my men burst out laughing.

"Of course, you did. And how was it?" Lorenzo falls back into friend mode, the strict underboss disappearing before my eyes.

"I'm not going to talk about fucking my wife. The point is, she wasn't lying."

Both men look at me for details, but I'm not going to humor them with that. What I do with my wife is my business. The idea of them knowing more doesn't sit well with me.

"What do we do now?" Roberto says, breaking through the room. Sending us back to our meeting instead of the coffee date we apparently were on, like a bunch of fucking pussies.

"That's what I wanted to talk to you about. We need a new plan."

Lorenzo inclines his head down. "Should we get her involved?"

"You think we should ask her to sell her dad down the river?"

"You did say she appeared scared. There is obviously something he's holding over her. If we can fix her problem, maybe we can use her against him still, just in a different capacity. Also, from what we can see, it has something to do with her friend's mother. Maybe it's about the money? The governor is paying them off, so maybe if we can cover the debt, Viviana will be more apt to help us."

"It could work."

"How much are you going to tell her, Boss?"

"I'm not sure yet. I don't want to spook her. It's still so new."

I don't want her to think I am using her. Even though a day ago it was true, it no longer sits well in my stomach.

"I'm thinking I'm going to spend the next few days with her. Then I'll broach the topic."

"And if she says no?"

"If she says no, it won't change anything. We will have to come up with a new plan, but I'm not going to leave her out to dry. I'll still fix her problem, whatever that problem may be. It's obvious her father has been manipulating her for years. Even if nothing comes of it, knowing I stopped that, knowing it'll piss off the governor, is worth it."

"What do you need us to do?"

"I only want to keep a skeleton crew here, so up the men at the warehouse. Call Tobias. Set up another order. I want you to run point and make all the collections for next month. Normally, you're the one to pick up the money."

He was right. Normally for intimidation, I went to every one of our clients that we provided protection for, and I collected the money, but this time will be different.

"I'm going to be busy for the next week," I say again more forcefully. "You two will step in for me. If anyone asks, say I have other business to attend to."

"Aren't you worried they might not take it seriously? They might not feel pressure to pay?"

"No. You are my eyes and ears. You are an extension of me. Anyone who dares to fuck with you will see the full force of my power. The future is never certain, Lorenzo, as underboss, you need to make these men fear you the way they fear me."

He nods at my words, knowing my intention. I'm at war with my cousin, I could die, and Lorenzo will take over if that day comes. It's imperative he has their respect. "Also, it will keep them on their toes. You can use whatever force is necessary, but only if you have to. You know I don't condone the killing of an innocent."

"No problem. Do you want Francesca to stay?"

"She can take a vacation as well."

"You're going to cook and clean?"

"I'm capable of doing both. I only want surveillance workers in the house, but I only want them to be watching the grounds."

"Damn, what do you have planned?"

I smile at him, but I don't tell him I plan to fuck my wife in every single room in the house multiple times.

"Now that we have that settled, I'm going to grab some breakfast and go back to my room. You can access me via text message, but only for emergencies. Understand?"

"Perfectly clear."

I stand from my chair, head out the door, and make my way into the kitchen. Francesca is there mixing something in a bowl.

"I was preparing breakfast. Pancakes and eggs."

"Very well. Thank you. As soon as they're done, I'll take them up to Viviana."

I take a seat at the island and wait for her to cook. Then she places the plates on a tray and hands it to me as I stand.

"You can have the rest of the week off, Francesca."

"What?"

"I'm giving the staff a vacation."

Her eyes are wide, but she smiles. "I don't know what to say . . . I . . . thank you."

Not used to being thanked or showing anyone mercy, I give her a tight smile and walk out the door.

When I walk into the room, I'm not surprised that she is still sleeping in the same place I left her.

The sheets are draped over her, but it doesn't cover the top of her chest and face. Placing the tray down on the bedside table, I take a seat on the bed.

"Viviana." I place a kiss on her forehead. Her nose wiggles in her sleep.

I lean down and kiss her lips.

"Viviana," I say again as I move to sit back up.

"Mmmm." Her hand lifts to rub at her eyes. Then she starts to blink as the room comes into focus for her, she looks toward my voice.

"Morning," she groans.

"It is, indeed."

She snuggles in closer to me. "What time is it? How late did I sleep?"

"It's not late at all. It's only eight thirty."

She stares at me like I have something on my face.

"And you woke me . . ." she trails off, feigning shock.

"I did."

"But it's so early." She's pretending to whine now, and where normally I wouldn't like this banter, with her I do.

"You're lucky I didn't wake you when I first wanted to."

"I don't even want to know what time that was. I would have beat you up."

"Is that so . . ."

I watch as her eyes dilate at my words. Her tongue licks the top of her lip, which she then bites.

"What would you have done about it?" she asks, her voice sexy and sultry.

"I would have tortured you, of course."

Her chest heaves, and I know if I place my hand between her legs, I'll find her desperate for me.

"First, I have to feed you."

That makes her cheeks go red.

"Food, Viviana. I have to feed you food," I clarify as if she's a little girl who wants to eat a bar of chocolate.

"Oh."

I move from where I'm sitting and stand to get the tray. That's when she finally notices it, and a giant smile spreads across her face.

"You brought me breakfast in bed."

"I did."

"Who are you, and what did you do to my husband?"

I inhale deeply, and then I exhale. She's right. My behavior is not just foreign to her, but it's foreign to me. It's like I've done a complete one-eighty, and I don't even recognize myself. That being said, I know our alone time is limited, and I want to enjoy every minute of it, including feeding her. This woman makes me do crazy things.

It's something about the way she looks, the way she speaks, and how honest she is. Even though I'm sure it's bad for me, I indulge in it anyway.

"I brought pancakes. I'd like to take credit for making them, but I can't."

"Francesca?"

"Who else?" I shrug, and she laughs.

"She's kind of amazing."

"Yes, she's been with me a long time." I don't need to say what I mean. I'm sure that my wife can read between the lines. Francesca was one of the girls my uncle kept.

I take the tray and place it on her lap.

"All this is for me? Aren't you going to have any?"

"I don't eat very much breakfast, not until after I've worked out."

"You didn't work out this morning?"

"No, someone kept me up too late."

"I think you have it backward. You're the one who kept me up."

"Let's agree to disagree."

"Do you have to work today?" Her voice is soft and tentative.

I shake my head. "Actually, I've taken the week off."

"You *have*?" Her eyes flare with shock.

"Don't act so surprised."

"And what are you planning to do?"

My lip tips into a smirk. "You, of course, all day, every day, for the next seven days." The sound of her fork dropping on the tray is almost comical.

"Don't worry, I'll give you a few breaks."

"You'll kill me if we don't have breaks."

"I don't think you give yourself enough credit. I think you could handle me."

"So this is our honeymoon of sorts?"

"We aren't going anywhere. It's too much of a logistical nightmare, especially with the snow, so instead, I'm sending everyone away. Only the security I need will be staying behind."

"What will we do?"

"Cook, clean, fuck."

"You're incorrigible."

"But that's what you like about me."

"It truly is." She laughs before bringing the fork back up to her mouth and taking another bite. When she does, she closes her eyes and enjoys the taste and aroma that waft up from the pancakes.

"Are you sure you don't want any? You said you weren't going to work out again, so you can share my pancakes with me."

"I'll only share your pancakes if you let me feed you," I say to her.

"Okay."

# CHAPTER TWENTY-FOUR

## Viviana

WE SPEND THE BETTER PART OF THE DAY GETTING acquainted with each other's bodies. I know we did that last night, but yesterday the lights were off. Today, they aren't.

Which means there's a lot more to explore. For a man who touched every inch of my body, it's like he's never done it before to me.

He savors every minute.

It's like he can't get enough of me, but that's okay, because I can't get enough of him either.

It's funny, I don't think I've ever been so comfortable with anyone in my whole life. Obviously, I'm not including Julia in the sentiment, seeing as I'm not having sex with her, but surprisingly enough, I am at ease with Matteo.

It's not just that I feel safe with him. It's not just that he plays my body like an instrument that he adores. It's the fact that even with our differences, even with the manner in which I've come to be here, I feel like he listens to me when I speak.

No man I've ever known in the past has ever really heard me. I mean, it is pretty obvious I have daddy issues, and in the past, I've always picked a bad boy because of said "daddy issues," but this feels different.

I'm not ignorant. I'm not stupid. I know that he is unlike any other man in the world. I know what he does for a living. Hell, I know he's not a good man. But it's like, at this very moment as he trails kisses down my spine, and I can barely comprehend what I'm even thinking, I know he's a good man for me. And isn't that what's important? How I feel when I'm with him.

He kisses a trail, and then he stops right above my shoulder blade.

"Are you hungry?" he asks, hovering over my body.

"That depends on what you're offering," I joke.

"I'm talking about food, Viviana." It doesn't matter how many times he says my name. It always brings a fresh wave of butterflies to take flight in my belly.

"In that case, it depends on what you can cook. Because I guess I should tell you this now . . ." I grimace. "I don't cook. Like at all. I can't even make a peanut butter and jelly sandwich."

Matteo lets out a boisterous laugh.

"Well, then it's your lucky day. Because not only can I cook but I very well may make the best sandwiches ever, and I have a specialty of making peanut butter and jelly sandwiches."

I look over my shoulder, and I can't help the smile that spreads across my face.

This man is the complete opposite of how he is with everyone else. He's different when he's with me. He's playful and funny. It's hard to reconcile the two versions of him. I have a strong feeling that he doesn't show this side to that many people. Maybe he shows it to Lorenzo.

Maybe he laughs and jokes. But it wouldn't surprise me if he didn't. There are too many variables in his work life for him to show this side. Too many enemies, all eager to take his position. In the little time I've known him, I can tell this. Also after speaking to my father about him, the way my father guns after him, I know, but if my father had a moment in which he could pull the trigger and take out Matteo without any consequences, he would.

That doesn't sit well for me. I do need to start thinking about how I'm going to handle my dad. Seeing as this is my impromptu honeymoon, although more like a staycation, I don't want to ruin this moment. I don't want to tarnish it by bringing up the big elephant in the room.

Instead of saying anything, I don't.

"Is that what we're going to have for dinner?" I ask, staring into his big green eyes. Eyes that I can most certainly get lost in. Actually drowning.

"Since I'm trying to impress you."

"Impress me? Why would you possibly need to impress me? You already married me."

"That is true. Well, as I was saying, I am obviously not going to make a peanut butter and jelly sandwich tonight."

"Okay, so then what are you going to make, big shot?" I joke with him.

"Well, since I'm Italian and since you are obviously a failure."

"Not nice."

"Just speaking the truth. An Italian who can't cook Italian food is a failure." I'm about to argue when he places a kiss on my neck.

"I'll just stop talking. I'm going to make us lasagna."

"I can help you do that."

"We have to get up now though, if I'm going to make the noodles."

"When you say make the noodles, what exactly do you mean by that?"

"Viviana. I'm not eating noodles out of a box."

"Someone's fancy." At that, he laughs as he stands from the bed, walks over to the chair, and grabs my robe. Yep, it's my robe now. I have officially stolen it. He comes back to the bed where I am and hands it to me. I stand and place it around me, tying it tight.

"Let me get dressed, and I'll be right down."

"No getting dressed. Wear the robe, and if you complain, I'll make you cook with me naked."

"That doesn't sound so horrible."

"Only if the oil splatters." My mouth opens and shuts like a little fish.

"Yeah, let's not do that." I grimace.

"Good idea."

Once my robe is on, we head down to the kitchen.

I'm not used to how quiet the house is. Usually, somebody is walking around or at least Francesca's in the kitchen. And although I know the security team is here, it's as if we are the only people in the world, and at this very moment, we are.

It's only a few minutes before I hear the sounds of pots and pans. Clanking and banging together.

"What are you starting on first?"

He turns to look over his shoulder. Unlike me, who is in a robe, Matteo after our morning romp has opted to have no shirt on and is now wearing only a pair of the infamous gray sweatpants.

The type of sweatpants that all women have deemed should be illegal because of how damn hot some men look in them. None of these women have probably seen Matteo in gray sweatpants, and I hope they never do because this is more than illegal.

He is actually like heaven dropped down to earth. From the back, I can see his muscles as he works with his arms flexing, but it's when he turns around that I literally can't collect enough of the drool that's pouring out of my mouth. The damn V is present.

Mouthwatering, tempting, and everything I have always imagined it would be.

"I have to start with the sauce first."

"As in you make it?"

"Of course, I make it. I believe my mother would've considered it sacrilegious if I didn't. My father would've grabbed the nearest broom and hit me with it. 'Real Italians don't use canned sauce, Matteo,' he would say."

"Seriously, so nothing from a can at all?"

"The only can you can use is tomato paste, and that's only if you need to."

"This is so fascinating. Obviously, in my family we've always had someone cook for us, so I've never learned. My old nanny, well, the extent of her cooking for me was cookies, so unless you want me to make cookies, I really can't contribute very much. Also, when I say make cookies, I won't be able to make it from scratch, but I can open the container."

He laughs at my joke.

"First thing, we need to grab the meat we are going to use for our sauce. Do you know what kind of meat we use, Viviana?"

"I didn't realize this was a lesson. Am I going to fail? What's the punishment?" He smirks at my comment.

"Would you like me to punish you?"

His words do their job seducing me and making me hot. My lip sucks in as soon as I start to nibble it.

"Maybe," I answer.

"Well, that can be arranged . . ." His offer, or better yet threat, hangs in the air, making it hard to breathe for a second. What would that entail? I'd like to find out.

"Well then, you better continue with your lesson."

"Maybe I shouldn't."

I incline my head and then roll my eyes. "Just tell me what's in the damn sauce."

"It's a combination of pork and beef. That's what makes the flavor so robust."

"Fancy."

"It's like you want me to throw you over my knee."

My eyes go wide. Even though I'm shocked, I kind of want him to.

He chuckles before going on.

"Next, you can use crushed tomatoes. Normally, we would have to do this, but Francesca usually keeps some in the fridge for me, just in case the urge to cook hits me."

"Does it often hit you?"

"Often? No. Sometimes."

"Like when you're trying to impress a girl?"

"I don't try to impress anyone. And no women come to my home."

"What? But then . . ."

"Do you really want to talk about this?"

Red-hot jealousy pours through my veins, and I realize that no, I don't. I shake my head back and forth adamantly. But still, I'm curious if he doesn't bring women here. I mean, I hope there are no women at this point since he's with me, but I never did ask him that. Shit, here I am having crazy sex with my husband, yet we never had the talk.

"What's wrong?" he asks, and I see he's staring at me from where he's perched at the stove.

"I mean, I know we're married and all, but we never discussed things."

"What kind of things did you want to discuss?"

"We didn't use protection."

"One, I trust if you were not clean, you wouldn't let me. Two, I won't use protection when I fuck you. You're different. You're my wife, and as I said when we first got married, we will eventually need to have children."

"I had the shot—"

"Oh."

It's almost as if he's disappointed.

"The point is, we're both clean. I'm not fucking you with a condom."

"You can't sleep with anyone else."

"Viviana. I haven't so much as looked at another woman since I married you."

My mouth opens and shuts. Is what he says true? I want him to turn back around so that I can see if he's telling the truth, but then I remember what he once said to me. He won't lie. If that's the case, and I believe it is, why lie now? He wouldn't.

"Okay," I croak. I start to fiddle in my seat as I watch him. He's back to stirring the sauce. I stand from the chair and start to pace.

"Do you want a glass of wine or something?"

"Yeah, you can grab an open bottle in the fridge. The glasses are in the far cabinet." I realize I've been living here for a few weeks, and I don't know where anything is.

I've never had to since Francesca has always been here. And it's nice to be alone with him to just see what it is like to be domestic with him, see what it's like to have a life with him. I walk across the room and open the fridge, finding a bottle of Sauvignon Blanc.

"If you want red, it's in the back right behind this room in that door, and then there's some more in the cellar in the basement."

"Red would go better with tomato sauce, but since we're not eating for a while, right? I'd like a glass of white."

"Normally, when I make sauce, I let it simmer all day, but this time, we're going to do an abbreviated version and only let it simmer for forty minutes."

"And what will we do while we wait? Are we going to start the lasagna?"

"Francesca left noodles in the fridge, so I'll just use those. I guess I will have to think of something else to kill time."

He turns back to the pot, and then he covers it.

"What can we do then . . ." he trails off.

I'm about to answer, but then he's stalking over to me. The

moment he approaches, he pulls the string of my robe, and then it's open and gaping at the front. Before I can say anything else, he lifts me up under my underarms and places me on the kitchen island. And he's pushing me back down. Everything is happening so fast I barely can comprehend it before I feel the swipe of his tongue.

He has his face buried between my thighs, and he's worshiping me. He thrusts his fingers into me. One, two, and three and then he's fucking me with his hand.

I'm so close.

I try to grip the cold marble under my back, but I can't find anything to hold as I rush toward my high. I think I'm about to crash, but then his tongue stops moving, and his fingers pull out.

I whimper at the empty feeling.

But I don't have to for long as before I can fully comprehend it, he's lining himself up with my core and thrusting inside. His hand's now wrapped around my waist, holding me steady.

Is this slow?

This isn't slow.

No, this is fast and hard.

An unquenchable appetite.

He can't get enough of me, and I can't get enough of him. I lift my hands and wrap them around his neck, bringing his mouth to mine.

He starts to kiss me with reckless abandon, and I kiss him back. Telling him without words how much I want this. How much I need him.

As he thrusts in and out, his tongue mimics his pattern fucking me at the same time.

It starts to build.

The feeling inside me rising to a crescendo.

His movements become more erratic.

The force of his hips is more punishing.

He pulses inside me, and then I fall. We both fall over into a crazy abyss we can only find in each other's arms.

Matteo's head is cradled in my neck as we both try to catch our breath. After a few minutes, we do.

Then he is standing and walking over to the sink to grab a towel. He wets it with warm water, and then he's back to clean me.

That's a sweet gesture I wouldn't expect from him. But I like it. Once I'm clean, I put my robe back on, tying it at my waist, and then I excuse myself to the bathroom. After I do my business, I stare at my reflection in the mirror. My cheeks are rosy, and my hair a disheveled mess. I look like I just had sex on the kitchen island.

I can't help but laugh. Who would've thought that I'd be this girl? I walk back to the kitchen, and I see that although he was going to wait to prepare the lasagna, he started to heat the noodles.

"You never did tell me where you learned this."

"My mother taught me a little, but really, my father taught me everything. He told me the way to my mom's heart is through his stomach."

"That's cute," I tease.

"Not exactly what I was going for, but okay."

"So were you gonna tell me why you sometimes like to cook?"

He stops his movements, and I can tell even by watching the muscles in his back that he tenses. Then he turns around and looks at me. His eyes are soft. Softer than I thought they would be. The color like moss after the rain.

"When I cook, I think of them. I think of my family. Spending time together . . ."

He leaves it at that. Not saying more. But I can read between the lines, or maybe in my heart, I'm hoping these are the lines. But in my head, his answer is as follows: I am his family now. And that's why he wants to cook for me.

# CHAPTER TWENTY-FIVE

## Matteo

I DON'T KNOW WHY I TELL HER THAT. I DON'T KNOW WHY I open up to her at all. It's crazy. I'm letting her in when I probably shouldn't. The truth is, she's proven her worth to me. She's proven her loyalty, but still, I need to keep a little distance.

Fucking her on the kitchen island was not exactly how I planned my evening, but I have to admit, I thoroughly enjoyed it.

Now I'm back to cooking, and she is sitting down drinking wine and enjoying herself. I think she's enjoying the view too because every time I turn around, I catch her gawking at me. It's kind of cute.

It's a good thing Lorenzo and Roberto are nowhere to be found because they would yell that I've given up my man card. I haven't, of course. When the time comes, and I need to be the enforcer, the boss, and the murderer, I will.

But I would be lying if I didn't enjoy this right here, the quiet of it, the peace.

I probably shouldn't have mentioned my family, but she asked, and I found I can't withhold from her for some strange reason. Maybe it's because she didn't withhold from me.

Once the sauce is prepared, I make the lasagna. It doesn't take very long, seeing as most of the food prep was already accomplished, but still, it'll taste just as good. I sit next to her on the island and grab a glass of red wine instead.

Normally, I drink scotch, but tonight, wine will work.

"If you wanted red, why didn't you tell me? I could've drunk some."

"I remember that you liked white," I say.

"Did you have that bottle in the fridge for me?"

"I did, actually."

She lifts the glass to her mouth and takes a sip.

"Well, it's delicious, so thank you."

We sit in silence for a few minutes before she opens her mouth.

"Well, we never did finish our game of Twenty Questions, so maybe we should do that. We didn't have a typical relationship where we got to know each other before we got married, so this could help."

"Ask away."

"You said you never brought a girl here . . ." She nibbles on her lip.

"Is there a question, Viviana? Or do you just want to know about my history?"

"Does that mean you've never been serious with anyone?"

"Yes, Viviana. Before you, I was never serious with anyone." I stress the word anyone. Throughout my life, I have never wanted to marry at all. Even now, my marriage serves a purpose. Yes, Viviana is beautiful. Yes, I love to have sex with her, and eventually, she will be the mother of my children, but as much as I see these things in her, it doesn't mean I will ever love her.

Love is something I can't do in my profession. There is no place for love in the mafia.

"But there were women . . ."

That makes me chuckle.

"Of course, there were women, but I don't think you want to know just how many."

She shakes her head. I know the feeling. Of wanting to know, but not wanting to, too.

"Nope, don't wanna know that."

"And you?"

"Never anything serious. I've dated men, but there was never a point in getting serious, none of them would've been good enough for my father, and I knew eventually he would try to force my hand onto some political ally. I guess, in this case, he was going to try to force my hand onto your cousin."

I take a deep breath. My anger is palpable. I can feel it rising up like bile in my chest. Her fucking father. You would think that a man would want to protect his daughter. But he's a monster just like my cousin, just like my cousin's father. I'm not a good man, but I would never do what he was trying to do with her. Not to my own flesh and blood.

Needing to change the subject because I'm afraid I'm going to snap, I lift my drink and take a swig. When I'm done, I place it back down on the table and look up at Viviana.

"What's your favorite movie?"

"Seriously, that's your next question?"

"If I ask anything else, anything having to do with your father, I'm gonna fucking blow. I refuse for that piece of fucking shit to ruin our night."

"*Roman Holiday*."

"Even though it's not a happy ending?" I ask.

"Not all stories have happy endings."

"You're very right."

"I'm surprised you've seen it."

For some reason, this girl gets me to say things that I don't say to anyone, yet here I am, opening my mouth.

"I watched it with my parents growing up."

"Really?"

"I wouldn't lie to you."

*Not about this, anyway.*

"Tell me about how that happened."

"Well, to begin with, *Roman Holiday* takes place in Italy, and my parents, missing their homeland, made it a ritual that we would have to watch any and every movie that took place in Italy. My father also, well, I think he loved old movies. They were classic movies he grew up with. Movies he cherished, and he wanted me to experience them with him. It's kind of funny knowing the type of man he was, but regardless of everything, he was a family man. In this business, people claim to be a family man, people claim that the family is the most important but often, like with my uncle and my cousin, it only goes so far, it's only as deep as their wallet."

"What about you? What is your favorite movie?"

"Would it be too cliché to say *The Godfather*?" She giggles at that, and I can tell she wants to ask more. She wants to ask exactly what I mean—if it's not really my favorite movie and I'm just messing with her. She probably wants to know if my family's history is anything like it. She probably wants to know if growing up, when I was a kid, if it resembled a world we watched at the cinema.

Not wanting to divulge any more about my past or my family at this very moment, I grab the glass and finish it off before standing and making my way to the bottle and pouring myself another. Viviana's glass is still full so I sit down next to her.

"Twenty Questions isn't really working."

"Well, I guess we don't have to speak, but I do wanna get to know you."

"Ask, and I'll try to answer anything I can."

"I know I'm not supposed to—" She holds her hands up in air quotes. "The family."

"That's only in movies. You're my wife. This is now your family. I can't promise I can tell you very much, but I can try."

220

"Do you think you will get out?"

"I'm not sure. I think there is a misconception that all we do is sell drugs and kill people. We also help people. We help businesses flourish. We protect the people we care about. I'm sure maybe one day we will get out of the drug trade, but the rest . . ."

She nods as if she understands, and a part of me thinks she does.

Although this is all new to her, it's not as though she lived a life of ignorance. Men like her father are the reason that men like me are in business. Corrupt fucking politicians. And as long as they're around, I will probably be around too. I let out a long sigh. This night is getting heavier than I hoped.

"I'm gonna check the lasagna." I stand from the chair and make my way over to the oven. It's ready, so I pull it out and set it on the stove. Viviana is standing beside me now. She grabs two plates and silverware and waits for me to serve us.

It's not often that we're home alone, and I get to do this. Actually, I can't remember ever doing this. Well, not since my parents died. That was another thing we did, but I don't tell Viviana that. Some things are better kept to oneself.

Some things make you weak.

I can't ever show weakness.

I've made an exception for Viviana not just because she's my wife but because I need her to let me in. The plan might have changed. I might not kill her in the end. Since she showed me her loyalty, she can stay untouched, unharmed, safe, and protected, but that doesn't change the fact I still need her.

This way, though, she will know what she's getting into, and in order for her to agree to my plan, I need to humanize myself to her. It might sound cold and calculated, but it's the only way to get what I want.

Maybe she would readily agree without any provocation.

But this way is easier. If she considers me to be softer than I am, if she feels a sense of loyalty to me that she doesn't feel for her father, she should be more apt to do what is necessary to bring him down.

That might make me sound like a coldhearted snake, but in my world, there are two types. There's a mouse in the fields, and then there is the serpent that eats it.

That is the only way.

# CHAPTER TWENTY-SIX

Viviana

WE SPEND DINNER IN COMPANIONABLE SILENCE. THE FOOD is so good I don't mind the silence, even if it means my thoughts are loud and clear and sometimes overwhelming. The truth is, as much time as we've recently been spending together, it's still odd. We're barely more than strangers, but now we are married, intimate, and getting to know each other. We are doing everything backward.

When I take my last bite, I place my fork down.

"That was the most delicious thing I've ever tasted."

Matteo places his silverware down on the plate and then turns his head to look at me. He seems happy with my assessment. It's not a large smile that lines his face, but it's a genuine one. It's funny. I haven't known him long, but I can recognize his gestures now. His different smiles. His body language. I've been watching him and studying him, and he has small tells. I don't think he realizes he does. Occasionally, he drums his fingers on the table. He does that when he's uncomfortable or when he wants to talk about something else. Then there is the way he silently clenches his fist on his lap. That's when he's angry. I noticed it the first time before we were married, and then I noticed it during the carriage ride. I'm still trying to figure out if he lies, is there a tell for that? He claims he doesn't, and that there is no need, and a part of me thinks he might be telling the truth about it. Why would a man in his position ever need to lie?

There's no need. If he doesn't like something, he kills it. If you want something, he takes it.

Look at me, case in point.

I'm not stupid. I know why this marriage happened, but I still want to get to know him. I'm not sure what the future will bring. I'm not sure if I could ever give my heart fully to him. I know for a fact he'll never give his heart to me. He says he's not capable, but I listen to the way he talks about his parents. Matteo is capable of love. I just don't think he's capable of allowing himself to love.

He sees it as a weakness.

Which is ridiculous; it's a strength.

"What's going through that pretty head of yours?" he asks, cutting through my inner rambling.

"Just how good this tastes."

"Well, I'm happy you are so impressed because I have other tricks up my sleeve."

I know he's talking about food, but for some reason, it sounds like there's a sexual innuendo wrapped up in that comment. I playfully narrow my eyes at him.

He laughs, then holds up his hands in surrender. "I was talking about dessert."

That makes me give him another playful look. This one includes an eye roll, telling him I'm not buying what he's selling.

"Okay, I'll bite . . ." Now it's my turn to be playful. "What's dessert?" I place my index finger on my lower lip and seductively trace the fleshy skin.

Matteo's pupils dilate, and I know I'm about to win this game.

His gaze traces my movement, and I'm sure he's about to strike. Instead, he stands from the chair.

I'm about to ask where he's going, but he turns to face me.

There is no hiding the desire swimming in his eyes.

His hand is on his gray sweats.

Those damn gray sweats that if I don't throw out will end up being the death of me.

"Open your mouth," he orders, taking a step closer. With where I'm sitting, there is only one reason he wants me to open my mouth.

I'm directly in front of him.

Directly in front of my favorite part of him.

I do as he says, opening my mouth, and I swear as he lowers his sweats, drool collects on my lips.

There is something so sexy about this man.

He fists himself, and then when he's hard and ready, he feeds me my dessert.

---

I can get used to waking up beside Matteo.

Yesterday morning, he was gone before I woke up. Today, I'm snuggled into his chest. My hair is fanning across his skin.

His soft breathing echoes through the room. It's like a soft, calming fan. This is the first time since I've met Matteo that I've seen him so peaceful. Normally, even when he's laughing, there's a sense that he's holding something back. His jaw is still tight. Or sometimes his eyes don't match his smile. But right here as he quietly snores, he truly looks at peace.

He looks younger.

Without the small wrinkles that line his eyes and the tiny line that forms when he frowns, he looks younger.

He's a beautiful man. Complicated, though.

It's so very hard to figure him out. Last night again, he was insatiable. Like no matter how many times he took me, it was never enough.

Over and over again, he ravished me as if when he stopped, I would disappear.

It's a strange feeling to be wanted by a man like Matteo.

I could see how someone could get greedy from the way he looks, greedy for the way he touches, greedy for more of him.

It's going to take everything inside me not to give in to it. Not to allow myself to fall into the trap.

Because that's what it is.

It's a trap.

How else can you describe it?

If I give my heart to him, I'll get nothing in return. I'll be stuck in the cage without a way out. But if I don't . . . if I accept a loveless marriage, how is my life different from my mother's?

He stirs in his sleep, and then his eyes start to open.

"How long have you been up?" he asks, his voice rough and gravelly.

"Only a minute or so."

"Are you hungry?"

That makes me smile. He's always concerned about my appetite. This time when he says it, I don't think there's any other meaning. I think he truly wants to feed me.

"I can always eat."

"You wouldn't be able to tell."

"What's that supposed to mean?"

"Nothing. You're just tiny."

"Or maybe you're big."

He laughs. "Touché."

He lifts his hands to his face and rubs away the remaining sleep.

Then he's standing from the bed with his naked body on full display. I'm surprised when he doesn't attack me.

We have spent the past three days all over each other. He must notice my confusion because he leans down and kisses my lips.

"I see that look you're giving me, Viviana. If you don't stop,

I will take you up on your silent offer. But I imagine you're sore, and you might need a little bit of a rest."

I pout.

"I'm not sore."

His hand reaches out, pulls the blanket back, and then spreads my thighs.

The cold air feels heavenly against my heated skin.

He stares at me for a minute. A war rages inside him as he looks down at where I want him to touch me.

"Viviana, what am I going to do with you?"

"Fuck me," I say, my upper teeth biting my lower lip.

"You will be the death of me," he says as he moves closer to the bed, fingers parting me.

I grimace at the contact, and he laughs.

"I told you."

"I'm fine," I say like a petulant child who thought she was getting ice cream but was just told the store was closed.

"You're not. But I know something that will make you feel better."

I raise my eyebrow in question, and he answers by leaning in and swiping my sensitive skin with his tongue.

Yep.

That will work just fine.

# CHAPTER TWENTY-SEVEN

## Viviana

THE NEXT FEW DAYS PASS IN BLISS.

We don't do much. We take walks in the snow, cook a lot of meals, and indulge in each other's bodies in what must be every single room in the house.

It's been the most perfect week.

I truly never thought Matteo could be this affectionate, nor did I think he would be willing to spend so much time with me.

Unfortunately, though, our alone time has come to an end.

Lorenzo, Roberto, and a few of his other men are due back within the hour. Matteo is downstairs in the basement working out, and I'm in our room showering and getting ready for the day.

I hate that it has to end, but I know it's necessary.

We cannot live in a bubble forever.

Regardless of how fun that bubble is.

Because bubbles, I've learned, are fragile, thin things. Designed to burst and explode.

As I lather my hair, the glass door swings open. I hadn't heard him come in, but here he is, naked and stepping into the shower.

I move a step back, giving him room, and then he closes the door, encasing us in the steam.

I can feel him hardening beside me, and I have to admit I'm happy about it because when I woke up this morning, he was gone, and I miss waking up to his teasing my body.

"Did you have a good workout?" I ask him.

His eyes appear darker than normal, hungry with lust.

"You really wanna talk about my workout . . .?" he drawls.

"No, not really."

"Then what is it you want, Viviana? You'll have to tell me in order for me to give it to you."

"Your mouth."

He leans in and kisses me.

A hungry kiss that tells me he missed our morning session as much as I did.

"What else?"

"Your hands."

He reaches out and starts to touch me. His hands wrap softly around my throat, then down the hollow of my neck, down between my breasts.

"Here?" he asks, smirk present.

I shake my head.

"Here?" His fingers trace a line around my belly button.

I shake my head again.

His hands lower, tracing across my hip bones.

He stops his movements. "Here?"

Too worked up to care, I grab him and thrust his hand between my thighs.

"There," I scream above the water, and he laughs. A loud and boisterous one.

One that is only for my ears.

And I love it.

I love every minute of it.

After we take the longest shower in history, we both leave the bathroom dressed and completely satisfied.

He's dressed in a more formal outfit than I'm used to. A gray sport jacket, white button-down, and slacks.

If I hadn't just been completely wrecked by him in the shower, I would ask for round two, so instead, I cock my head. "Where're you off to?"

"I have a meeting in Albany."

"You're going all the way to Albany?"

My heart starts to pound that I won't see him for a few days. I am also concerned about what his business is about. If it has something to do with Dad.

"Just for a few hours. I'm flying up to talk to the governor about some business."

"I'll miss you," I say, my voice weaker than I want it to be.

"I'll be back for dinner . . . *and* dessert."

I knew this day was coming. Again, I don't expect we were going to be alone forever, but still, it bothers me.

What am I going to do?

Should I ask about getting a job again?

I can't imagine the timing is any better. He's still at war.

"What's wrong?"

"Nothing."

"Don't lie to me."

I sometimes forget that he can read me so well.

"I was just wondering what I was going to do."

"Would you like me to call Giana over?"

"I'd rather try to see if Julia will see me."

"Has she called you?"

"No," I admit.

"Then why bother?"

"She means a lot to me. She's my family."

He watches me for a moment before nodding his head.

"Call her, then. If she answers, if she says yes, I'll have Luka arrange it."

"I can go to the city?"

"I would rather her come here. Where I know you are safe."

"Okay. Thank you." I lean on my tiptoes and kiss his lips. Once he's gone, I fish out my phone from where I placed it a few days ago.

I haven't used my phone this past week.

Not wanting anything to tarnish it.

I check to see if I have any missed calls.

There is nothing.

Not even a text message.

It's a sobering feeling to know no one misses you.

At least I have Matteo.

My thoughts shock me.

How did that happen so fast?

How is it in the course of only a few weeks this man has burrowed himself inside me?

Despite all my efforts, I realize I'm freaking falling for him.

This isn't good.

I pick up the phone and dial Julia. I'm hoping she answers, praying more like it.

The phone rings once, twice, and on the third ring, I hear her voice.

"Hello." It's hard to hear her. She's speaking low, or maybe her mouth is far from the phone.

"Hey, Jules." She doesn't say anything. She stays quiet. "I know you're mad at me, but I'm sorry. Believe it or not, I wanted to tell you, but there were things beyond my control."

"I know."

"You know? Yes . . . Jonathan heard your father speaking." Jonathan, her twin brother, works for my father. I'm actually surprised he has said anything about me that could help me. He hates everything about me.

Not an unfounded hate.

He actually hates everyone in my family.

I'm shocked he even works for my father, but I guess even he couldn't turn down a cushy job in the governor's office. Couple that with the complete makeover he apparently decided to give himself and no part of him is recognizable from the little boy I used to play with as a girl.

"What did he hear?"

"That you were forced."

"It wasn't exactly like that."

Again, she is quiet, and I hate that I said that. Now I've made it awkward again.

"Julia, I miss you. I wanted to know if you wanted to come over."

"To where you live with Matteo Amante. The gangster."

"To where I live, yes."

"Yeah, I'll come, but not because of anything more than curiosity," she says through the phone.

"Curious of what?"

"Oh, the reason you would fight to get out of one cage just to thrust yourself into a different one."

"It's not like that."

"Oh, no . . .?" she trails off for emphasis. I could argue this all day with her, but when I don't respond to her taunt, I can hear her let out a sigh. "Tell me where and when."

"It's actually outside the city. I'll send a car for you."

"Umm. That works."

I can hear the judgment in her voice. It's there clear as day, ringing in each second in which we don't speak.

"He'll be there soon. See you soon."

I hang up before she can say anything else. Knowing I need to tell Matteo, I head down the stairs to look for him. There is a good chance he is already gone, but someone will be able to relay the message.

That's when it dawns on me that I don't even have my husband's cell phone number.

I find Luka in the office I know from my "staycation escapades."

"Hi, Luka. My friend Julia needs to be picked up."

"On it, Mrs. Amante."

Hearing him call me by my married name still sounds strange in my ears.

It feels odd to me, yet feels right.

After I'm done with that, I head to the kitchen to grab some coffee and breakfast.

I find Francesca inside. She freezes at my footsteps.

"Oh. Mrs. Amante. I didn't know you were up for the day. Please accept my apology. If you go to the dining room—"

"No need to set the table and make it formal. I can eat here."

Since I've spent so much time in this room with Matteo, it would feel weird to be in the formal dining room.

She looks confused and shaken by my decision.

"Mr—"

"It's fine. I don't want to get you in trouble. I just didn't want to be alone," I admit.

She gives me a small smile and nods. "Okay, I'll set you up right over there."

She moves around the room and grabs everything I'll need, then she sets off to grab my coffee. "What would you like to eat?"

"Whatever is easy. Also, I have a friend coming soon."

"I'll make sure to make a nice lunch for two."

A few minutes later, she brings me over a bowl of Chia pudding with fresh fruits and coconut. It's perfect.

"Thank you so much. . ." She goes to turn around, but I don't want her to leave quite yet. "Francesca."

She looks back at me. "Matteo said you've been with him for years." Her eyes widen a smidge, and I realize my mistake right away. She's afraid I know about her past. "I just wanted to know about Matteo."

"I can't speak of him." Her answer is firm.

"No. You misunderstand me. He did a lot for me this past week, and I want to do something nice for him. I figured if anyone knows what he likes."

"I'm not sure I can help." I nod and look down. "But I'll think about it."

"Thank you."

Francesca then leaves the room, and I'm alone.

The same outcome as if I ate in the dining room, but here I have great memories. Memories that make me blush, but still, they keep me company.

I do want to do something nice for him. Hopefully, she will be able to help. If not, maybe Giana can.

I'll need to call her one of these days.

Matteo mentioned giving me her number.

She could be a good person to have in my corner. Plus, I need to expand my social circle if I want to make this work here.

Time passes slowly as I eat alone. Soon I'm placing my dish in the sink and heading back into the main part of the house. I can't wait to show Julia around.

This house is gigantic. Larger than the governor's house, and then the estate I grew up in before my father traded our Georgian colonial for an even larger one. One with giant pillars, he can only hope will lead him to the largest one.

---

It's good to see her. I didn't realize how much I missed Julia until she was standing in front of me again. I throw my arms around her neck; she lets out a tiny giggle.

As soon as we stop hugging, she finally pulls back, and that's when she looks around.

"This is where you've been living?"

"Yes. This is Matteo's house, and I guess it's now mine."

The foyer around us grows silent. Like a pregnant pause, as I wait for her to say more, but when she doesn't, I decide to speak instead.

"Come on, let's go to the living room. We can talk there, and you can fill me in on what's going on in your life, and I'll do the same."

It must be shock from how big this place is or something because she still has a weird look in her eyes. But when I start to walk, she snaps out of it, following me out of the foyer, down the hall, and into the living room.

"This living room is giant," she finally blurts out, looking wide-eyed. "The whole house is, actually. He's like a billionaire, huh?"

I don't know what to say to that.

The only thing I can do is shrug, not feeling comfortable talking about my husband's finances.

"I think it's a family home. Passed down from generation to generation. I never really asked Matteo. He told me a little bit about it, but I'm not really sure."

"Well, it's magnificent, no matter what. It seems your impromptu decision to marry a mob boss paid off."

My eyes go wide at what she says.

The bite and bitterness to her tone not lost on me.

I have no idea what's crawled up her ass, but I don't like it.

"Listen, I know you are upset with me, but don't you think it's gone too far? Yes. I married Matteo without telling you.

"Yes, I didn't invite you. But there are things you don't understand about the circumstances. I had no choice to do it the way I did. I'm so sorry I hurt you, but I couldn't not . . ."

"What aren't you telling me?"

"My father . . . he threatened." I shake my head back and forth. Not able to say more.

Although so much of this concerns her, she doesn't know a lot of it, and I don't even know how to tell her. I don't even know where to begin.

"And what of me, you can't trust me?"

"I'm sorry, can we please talk about something else?"

I think she's going to argue. I think she might even sit up, stand, and then demand to be driven somewhere else, but she doesn't, which is slightly shocking to me.

"Can you at least tell me if he's horrible to you? Would you at least be honest about that?"

"Truth?"

"I always want the truth from you." Again, her words hang in the air. The air that now feels oppressive with my lies. But am I really lying? Is withholding information a lie?

Many, many years ago as a little girl too young to understand the ramifications of my actions, I made a promise to a very bad man.

At the time, I didn't realize what I was getting myself into. Had I known then what I know now, I would've dealt with the consequences of my actions instead of making a deal with the devil.

My father.

It's funny how twelve years later, I made a different deal with a different devil. I can only hope this one will turn out better.

"Believe it or not, he's actually been good to me."

*Great, if you consider him in bed.*

"So is it real now, is it a real marriage? Are you ever coming back to the city?"

"I'm not sure," I admit, running a hand through my dark locks.

"Does he even have a residence in the city?"

"He does. It's nothing like this place."

"What do you mean?"

For some reason, I feel as though I'm not supposed to talk about his apartment in the city. He didn't specifically say anything, but I also didn't tell him I would. I've vaguely remembered him saying people don't know where it is, but telling her where it is and what it looks like are two different entities. We're already fighting so much I can feel the tension in the air. What's the harm?

"He actually owns a warehouse. It's really cool. From the outside, you would think it's a dump, but inside, it's state-of-the-art. The rooms are beautiful. Nothing like this, it's modern contemporary, a bit sterile, but beautiful nonetheless."

"Must be nice."

I lift a brow. "What do you mean?"

"Nothing, I just mean it must be nice to have two beautiful homes. That's all."

She gives me a smile . . . but it doesn't quite reach her eyes. A part of me thinks she's jealous.

And from her point of view, I can understand how this all sounds a bit crazy.

Hell, to me, it sounds crazy, and I have all the information.

To her, she has so little of it.

*You could tell her.*

The dumb insistent voice in my head cuts through, demanding I give it voice.

I can't, though.

That was the stipulation.

Never tell Julia.

Never tell Jonathan.

The money would stop.

I have done all that I have to take care of the family, all to get so close to finding a way out.

"Tell me what you've been up to," I ask, trying to steer the conversation away from Matteo and me.

By the way she smiles, it appears she's okay with this segue.

"I met a guy."

"Oh!" I perk up, happy for the distraction—and for her. "Does he have a name?"

"Nope. I'm going to be as shady as you are. He's gorgeous. Sexy. He's got brown hair, green eyes. He's got that swagger."

"Okay, where did you meet mystery man?"

"At a club."

"Think it can get serious?"

"Maybe. You can never tell. Maybe he'll move me into a great big mansion like this one day." She laughs.

Hearing her laughter makes me laugh too.

"Other than the hot man you're banging . . . how are you?"

"Who said anything about sex?" Her lip tips up, and I know she's joking with me. "Of course, we are fucking."

I like to see her smile. Lord knows she's had it rough. She deserves it.

All of it.

# CHAPTER TWENTY-EIGHT

Matteo

WE TOUCH DOWN IN ALBANY A LITTLE AFTER ONE IN THE afternoon.

This will be a fast trip.

A late lunch with the governor of New York at his mansion.

On the books, I own many companies. I'm a respectable businessman who owns waterfront properties everywhere, so it isn't unheard of for me to meet with him.

But off the record, he was the one who originally tipped me off to Marino on my ass.

As many times in the past as Marino tried to do business with me, I never had to with Governor Thomas. I am able to get most of what I need done.

But my dismissal of the Jersey prick ended up costing me.

I misjudged Salvatore.

It never dawned on me that he would connect with an overly ambitious governor from the neighboring state and convince him that he was the better option.

Marino has tied his political aspirations to the wrong man.

Out of principale, I won't help him.

Not even if he is hanging off the side of a mountain needing a hand.

I'd still walk away.

Now in the car, we make the drive from the private airplane to the governor's mansion. It's not a long trip, and as we pull up to the sprawling estate, not unlike the one in Jersey, I can't help but think of my wife.

Pulling out my phone, I fire off a text.

**Me: Are you enjoying your day?**

**Viviana: Who is this?**

That makes me smile. My wife is too feisty for her own good.

**Me: Your husband**

**Viviana: Oh . . . sorry. You never gave me your number. So I didn't know.**

**Me: Who did you think it was?**

**Viviana: I wasn't sure.**

I look down at my phone. Did she think it was an old boyfriend?

The idea of one reaching out to her has my hands clenching into a tight fist.

I won't share my wife with anyone.

**Me: No one better be texting you.**

**Me: You're mine and only mine.**

I type before I can stop myself, letting my possessiveness show in my words.

I probably shouldn't have typed it, but it's true.

**Viviana: Does that go the same for you?**

And there it is. The question she asked the first night in her apartment. One I wasn't prepared to answer, but after all these weeks, and knowing now what it feels like to sink inside her, to get lost in her abyss, the answer isn't so hard.

**Me: Yes.**

I put my phone back in my pocket. Not wanting to say anything else. It's at the same time as I do that the car rolls to a stop. We're here.

We exit the car, and then my man and I go to the front door, where we are greeted by Governor Thomas's security team. Two of his men search for guns. They know that my security detail has one, my man does have his piece on him, but they all stand close. This isn't my first time coming here, and it won't be my last.

Governor Thomas walks over to me, reaches his hand out, and we shake.

He then leads me to the dining room, where we will eat and speak. As soon as I sit down, a poured glass of scotch is already in front of me. His staff knows me well.

"We have a problem."

"Yes. Marino is always a thorn in my side. However, I thought that by marrying his daughter, you'd've crushed the opposition."

"It would seem not yet. My plan is to take him down—" Governor Thomas holds up his hand.

"I don't want to hear about it."

He takes a deep breath. He looks tired and worn, as though this whole thing is too much for him to handle. I know the feeling. Sometimes I wonder why I bother. But then I think of what a monster my uncle was. I think about what a monster Salvatore will become if given the opportunity. Governor Thomas knows this as well, which is why he's agreed to help me. Doesn't make it any better. I'm sure he wishes he could throw me out, but it behooves him to have me in his corner and to have me in New York.

"I don't have a lot of information for you," he says. "What I can tell you is that you're on everybody's radar. Governor Marino, is really out to get you. You can't use any of the original routes."

"This I know."

"My best advice is don't store anything in the new one either."

I lift my brow.

"Marino has been speaking one-on-one to everyone at the Port Authority. He's also been taking meetings with the dockhands, Coast Guard, etcetera."

"Busy man."

"He's determined to take you down."

"And get in bed with my cousin," I grit out.

"We can't allow that to happen, Matteo."

"I concur. On both matters, actually."

He knows as well as I do, if that happens, no one is safe.

Salvatore won't be happy dealing with just pills and blow.

He only has one thing he wants to deal with . . .

A billion-dollar trafficking enterprise left wide open when Cyrus Reed got involved and shut it all down.

No one wants the Italians to take up the void the Russians left.

"My advice, if you choose to take it, is bring it in and transport it right away. Place it someplace no one would think . . . until it's ready for transport again. I don't want to know anything. I don't want my name brought up. I don't like—"

"That part of the business is being phased out. Unfortunately, until my cousin is out of the picture, I can't jeopardize my men being angry."

"Move it fast. Off the radar. I'll do what I can to get Marino off your back."

I stand from my chair and shake his hand.

"Thank you."

"You can't lose, Matteo."

"I won't."

Losing isn't an option. I will burn everything down to the ground, burn it all if I have to, before I let a sadistic man like Salvatore lead.

Now back on the plane, I face Lorenzo and Roberto.

They're sitting directly across from me.

"He wants us to move the cargo as soon as it comes into port. He doesn't think the docks are safe. Governor Marino has been on a rampage ever since I married Viviana. The man will do anything in his power to right the wrong he thinks we did him. Governor Thomas believes the best plan is an obscure location, one with enough storage space but not obvious."

Each of us goes quiet. Finding a close location that no one will think of is the hard part.

"What about Marco's family restaurant?"

"You want to store our drugs in a restaurant? Do you plan on putting it with the sugar? Maybe the herbs are more like it?"

I shake my head at the banter between Roberto and Lorenzo.

But that has me thinking. If Lorenzo thinks it's a silly idea, then maybe it actually holds some merit.

"Okay, when we get back to the compound, I want to talk to Marco. We will give his family a nice incentive if they agree. The bottom level has a tunnel."

"That's why I suggested it. It was used to smuggle in booze back in the Prohibition days."

"That's right. Roberto, I think you are onto something. The location is perfect and the tunnel is a bonus. We can bring the drugs in and out without anyone being the wiser. Also, I can check in often. It's a restaurant. It wouldn't be unheard of for me to take my wife there . . . often."

The more I think about this, the better it sounds. Now that this is settled, I turn my attention away from my men and stare out the window for the remainder of the forty-five-minute flight back to my home.

I have a lot to work on once back.

It's time I talk to Viviana about her father. It's time we find the location of Salvatore.

I need to see where my next shipment of guns is as well. It feels like my work is endless, and all I want to do is take another day off and have my way with my wife.

I'm not sure when it happened, but I realize Viviana has gotten under my skin despite my best efforts.

She's like an addiction.

One taste will never be enough.

# CHAPTER TWENTY-NINE

Viviana

WITH JULIA GONE, THERE ISN'T MUCH TO DO. MY LIFE HAS become rather boring. I need to talk to Matteo about it. I need a job and a purpose. I want to make a difference.

There is no way I can spend another day doing nothing.

Without thinking about it, I head down the stairs, all the way to the bottom floor. To the floor where I know Matteo goes to when he is not with me.

I'm not sure if I'm allowed here, but I'm doing it anyway. Flinging open the door to the surveillance room, Luka and Tony look up at me.

They're not shocked that I'm here. How can they be? Right on the giant screen in front of me is the hallway I just came down.

"You shouldn't be in here," Luka says.

I shrug. "I'm bored."

"Boss wouldn't like it." Tony's back is to me again, his hands hitting the keyboard.

"I'll handle Matteo."

"I'm sure you will," Luka laughs. "You certainly have him wrapped around your little finger."

"This one." I hold up my pinky.

"Yep, that's the one."

"I promise to tell him, and I promise he won't get mad. I'm

just lonely. Francesca has gone missing and I have nothing to do. Put me to work."

"Not a good idea," Tony says to Luka, and I roll my eyes.

"As much as I'm sure we would enjoy your company, I have to agree with Tony. After we get permission from the boss, it's a different story."

"Call him."

Luka looks amused by me. Tony, however, is visibly pissed.

A minute later and with a smile on his face, Luka motions for me to sit down in the chair next to him.

"I'm allowed to only show you certain things."

"Like what?"

"Like a few of the cameras we have in the house."

Tony starts to type, and then there in front of me is my old room and my old bed. My face turns warm, and I'm sure I'm beet red.

"I actually have something I need to do," I say as I rush to leave the room with the very little dignity I have left.

Well played, Matteo. Well played.

After my embarrassing run-in, I hit the gym and worked out. Then I read a little from a book, but now, there is nothing to do as I sit in the living room like a pathetic girl and wait.

The truth is, it's time I make money anyway. I have debts I'll need to pay soon.

I'm sitting in the chair, reading, when I hear footsteps. I don't look up until they are directly in front of me. I crane my neck to see who it is, but by the way my skin pebbles, hyperaware of his presence, I know it's him.

Our gazes lock, and his eyes are darker than normal.

Neither of us says anything.

Unable to take it anymore, I stand and move until my chest touches him, and then I swear I climb him like a monkey climbing a tree.

My arms wrap around his neck, and my legs wrap around his waist.

Our lips collide next, and his mouth is heaven.

I could kiss him forever.

That thought should scare me, and it actually does a bit, but not for the reasons it did at first.

I'm not scared of my desire for him.

I'm scared for our future and what it brings.

What will I do if I lose him?

It hit me today when we were texting that not only do I not want anyone else, but I don't want him to be with anyone but me.

When he got possessive, so did I.

Our kiss intensifies until he throws me on the couch, and our mouths separate.

"Did you miss me?" He laughs.

"Yes. Even if you're an ass," I hiss back as I swat him lightly on the arm.

There is no point in lying after that display. I might as well own it.

"Good. Because I missed you too."

If my mouth could drop open from shock, it would.

"Did everyone see me?" He leans forward, hovering over me, balancing his weight on his arms.

"No. Only me, I gave him permission to pull up the feed, but only for today."

"But you saw me?"

"Yes, and you saw me. We're even." His mouth grazes my jaw. "I missed this." He kisses me again on the lips. Then he moves to my neck. His tongue trails down my throat and over my collarbone until he reaches the hollow of my neck.

He then leans up and pulls my shirt open. The buttons rip away from the fabric with a popping sound.

"The door—"

"I don't care if they see. Let them see me worship you."

I'm about to object, but then his mouth and tongue shut me up.

No objections left in me.

Sometime later, and after two orgasms, I'm spent.

Still entwined in each other's arms, I take a deep satisfying breath before speaking.

"Did you have a good trip?" I ask.

He moves to lift his weight off my body before he sits up, leaving me still naked on a couch in his living room. "I got done what I needed to do."

"What's that?"

"I was with the governor of New York."

"Was this about my father?"

"It was."

I move to sit up, and I rearrange my blouse, although it's hard to do with half the buttons now missing.

"Is there anything you need to tell me?"

His head tilts down and then back up as he shakes his head.

"Not right now. I'm working on a few things . . ."

"You can trust me."

He leans forward, sucking my lower lip into his. I moan into his mouth like a wanton hussy who didn't just get laid.

When he pulls back, I groan. This elicits a chuckle from him.

"I need to go work now."

I want to pout and ask him not to, but I refuse to do that. We aren't there yet. I'm not even sure where we are.

It was only today that he agreed not to be with other women.

I don't want to seem needy, which normally I'm not. In the past, I never cared to be in a relationship.

But for some reason with Matteo, I do care.

And I'm not sure how I feel about it.

Matteo stands from the couch and fixes his pants, zipping and buttoning them up.

With him busy for God knows how long, I make my way back to our bedroom. I need to shower and clean myself off after our impromptu romp.

When I'm out of the shower and clean, my phone chimes.

I walk across the room to where I left my phone on the side table.

There on the screen is a text from Julia.

**Julia: I had a lot of fun today. I missed you. I'm sorry if I came off strange. This whole thing has been weird, but I'm happy for you.**

I stare at the phone, and an audible exhale escapes my mouth. I didn't realize how badly I needed her to say that.

**Me: Thank you! I missed you too. You will always be family to me.**

**Julia: Can we see each other again?**

**Me: How about next week?**

**Julia: I'd love that.**

**Me: Me too. <3**

I place the phone back down and go to get dressed.

Matteo is still not back, but I assume once he is, he'll be hungry, and we'll eat. However, with him, you never can tell. He's just as likely to tell me we are forgoing dinner and moving straight to dessert.

Either way, I'm happy.

And that's the craziest thing about everything . . .

How damn happy I am.

The thought is petrifying.

# CHAPTER THIRTY

## Matteo

MARCO SITS IN FRONT OF ME AND NODS HIS HEAD AS I speak, but he doesn't say anything.

I can't imagine that he will say no to me, but he could. I highlight all the details, being completely candid about the whole thing. He needs to know all the risks involved, but he also needs to know the rewards.

If he opens the Prohibition room to me to store the drugs, I will pay him a very handsome fee. His loyalty will not be forgotten either.

If he gets caught and something happens to him, his family will always be protected by me.

When I'm done speaking, I signal for him to talk.

"Yes."

"Are there any questions?" I ask, since this is a lot to take in.

"I trust you, Boss."

"I promise you, if anything—"

"I know," he says with a smile. I stand and shake his hand. Marco has been with me for a long time. Before me, he was with my father. He's been out of most of the business these days, but from what Lorenzo told me, his family has been struggling without the extra money working more for me would have brought in.

With that done, I leave my men and go in search of Viviana. After looking in all the rooms on the main floor, I find her in our bedroom.

The word "our" coming so naturally, it makes my feet stop.

You're getting too comfortable, Matteo.

She's in the corner, sitting in front of a vanity that my staff moved into the room for her. She's placing lipstick on.

"Hi," she says to me. She doesn't turn around. Instead, she talks to me through the mirror.

I walk closer until I'm standing behind her and then lean down and place a kiss on her forehead. "Are you ready to go to dinner?"

"Go? Are we leaving?"

Tonight, I have decided to take us to Marco's restaurant to check out the space.

With Viviana in tow, we head out. This time, to stay under the radar, we go out the back drive.

I can see that Viviana is confused. She's peering out the window in the back seat. Her whole body isn't turned, just her face, but as we drive out of the secret back gate, she looks in my direction.

"It's our secret way out."

"I can see that, but why do we need to go out this way?" Sometimes, I forget that Viviana isn't like any other woman I have ever met. She's well-versed in a public life. And although she probably understands going out the back door because of her father, I can understand why she seems worried.

"Did something happen that I don't know about?"

I debate whether I should tell her the truth now or if I should wait until another time. I opt to wait. A small part of me still wonders if I can trust her.

"No. Nothing happened. But we can't be too safe. My cousin has been quiet, but I wouldn't put it past him to have someone watching the gates. Normally, I wouldn't care, but since I have you with me, I'd prefer to be more careful."

Viviana must like my answer because she turns her body fully toward me, unbuckles her seat belt, and scoots over. Now sitting in the middle seat, she refastens and then lays her head on my shoulder.

"So, we're going to dinner?" she asks.

"We are."

"Where're we going?"

I can either tell her or not tell her, but for some reason, toying with her doesn't hold merit. Maybe it's because I know she is a dog with a bone when she wants information.

"I have an employee. I'm not sure if you met him. His name is Marco, and his family owns a restaurant. It's quite good, and I wanted to take you there."

"That sounds nice." For the rest of the trip, we don't speak of anything important. She asks me little questions, not about anything life-changing, and I ask her little questions back. By the time we reach the parking lot, I found out that while living in the city, she volunteered what little spare time she had walking the dogs at a shelter and teaching children how to read.

My wife is a saint. I don't deserve her, but fuck if I won't try to keep her.

The car stops, and I swing the door open, reaching my hand out to help her from the car. Marco's restaurant is the perfect location from the outside. It's off the beaten path, set higher on a hill but with a view of the water.

I'm surprised I've never been here before. It's quiet and quaint, and knowing it has the cellar gives it a bonus.

No one would think of this place, and since it's close to the ocean, it's not a far drive from the port. The less time in transit, the better.

Holding Viviana's hand, I lead us into the restaurant. The sun is starting to set in the distance, and when Viviana steps inside, the view from the windows makes her gasp. I had no idea it would be like this, but now seeing it, I can see why she's staring at me with stars in her eyes.

This place is romantic as fuck. The restaurant is relatively empty. There are a few tables in which people sit. Marco is there to greet us. He leads us to a table right by the large bay window that overlooks the water.

There's a scattering of tea lights already lit. The table is set, and it looks as though I had pre-planned this. I'm going to have to throw in some extra money to thank him.

"Marco, this is my wife, Viviana. Viviana, this is Marco."

I introduce them. Marco reaches his hand out and takes Viviana's small one in his. He places one kiss on the top of her hand. If he wasn't so old, old enough to be my father's age, I would probably kick his teeth in for touching my wife, but I can tell there's no desire there, just respect.

"It is a pleasure to meet you, Viviana." His thick Italian accent rolls her name off his tongue like pearls.

She smiles warmly at him. "The pleasure is all mine."

We take our seats, our chairs sitting beside each other. As soon as we are no longer standing, I place my hand on her leg. She's staring out the window, enjoying the view.

"This place is perfect."

"Well, it's the least I can do for leaving you home alone so much."

"About that . . ." She sounds . . . different. There's an edge to her voice.

"About what?"

"I'm bored." She pouts. "Without you there to distract me, I need something to do."

"Okay."

"Okay?"

"Yes. I don't think getting a job in the city right now is that doable, but maybe we can find something that will make you happy for the time being."

"Such as?" Her brow furrows.

"You can help Giana."

"Help her with what?"

"The family runs many different operations."

"I don't think—"

"Not those kinds of operations. Nothing with that part of the business. One of the things that Giana works on is our charity work."

"You do charity?"

"Of course, I do charity. What kind of man do you think I am? Strike that, don't answer."

Viviana reaches across the table and takes my hand in hers.

"I think you are a good man. I think to most people you pretend to be different, but I see you. You aren't the villain most people say you are."

"While I appreciate the sentiment, I'm every bit the monster they say I am."

Her head tilts to the side as if she's assessing what I've said, but instead of appearing shocked or scared, she looks at me with adoring eyes. Eyes that make me think I can tell her everything. Show her everything. Talk to her about everything.

"What is it?" she asks, and it seems she can read me more than I knew. "There's something you aren't saying."

"I need your help."

"Okay."

"You don't know what I'm asking yet."

"I don't care. The answer is still okay."

"I need your help taking down your father."

There, I've said it. The gauntlet has been thrown, so now to see how she responds.

"Whatever you need, Matteo." She leans forward, placing her lips on mine. "I'm yours."

# CHAPTER THIRTY-ONE

Viviana

I'M TAKEN ABACK BY HIS WORDS, BUT MOST OF ALL, I'M SHOCKED by how willingly I offer to help him.

He hasn't even told me what anything entails, but I don't even care.

I'm all in.

I'll do anything for Matteo.

The thought is eye-opening to me.

I'm not sure when it happened, but somewhere in the last two months, I began to feel a connection to him. A loyalty to him that I've never felt for anyone else. Of course, I feel a loyalty to Julia, but this is different. This feels different.

I'm not ready to put a word to how this feels. I'm still too scared to admit that what is going on here is more than I ever thought would, and I'm too worried something will go wrong.

"Are you sure? Because once you agree, I'm going to start telling you things that I probably shouldn't, and if you ever go against me—"

I lift my hand, knowing full well there's a threat coming next. I would never go against him. He doesn't need to tell me he will kill me because regardless, even if that's the consequence, I wouldn't do it.

"I won't."

"I know you won't, which is why I'm telling you this."

"Do you think we should wait until we're home?"

"There aren't many details. When we have more details, we'll talk about it at home. For now, I want you to speak to your father. I want you to make him think that you are agreeing with his plan. I want you to feed him false information."

His plan is not that different than my original plan. Originally, I had hoped to use Matteo as a means of taking down my father, and now he is offering me the same.

I lean closer to him.

"When I first agreed to marry you," I say, "I was hoping you could help me with my problem."

"And what problem is that, per se?"

"Like you, my problem is my father."

At the mention of my father, Matteo's jaw tightens. "I'm listening."

"He's able to control me."

"Okay."

"And I don't want him to anymore."

He stares at me for a minute before his features soften. "Do you want to tell me so I can help you . . .?"

Tears start to fill my eyes. But I refuse to ruin our night.

"Not today."

He nods in agreement.

"Soon, though," I say.

"Tell me about what you like to read."

"Besides fairy tales?"

Matteo laughs. "Besides them." He smiles at me. "Do you like any other genres?"

"I like all of them. You have to understand that growing up in the family that I grew up in, that's all I had."

"Tell me about your family."

"My mother has always been the woman you met, a sad and

lonely woman chasing love, who drank too much. My father has resented me since the day I was born."

"Why do you say that?"

"As I told you once before, I don't think he ever wanted me. He knew politically, though, for his aspirations, he had to be a family man. And in public, he's the perfect husband, the perfect family man, but when the doors close, he's anything but."

"Did he hurt you?"

"Physically?"

He nods.

"Not really. Emotionally . . . yes."

"What did he do?"

"Emotional blackmail. Everything had a price. Some more steep than others."

Matteo leans forward and swipes away a lone tear that must have slipped out.

"So remember when I told you how my parents never got me a puppy . . ."

"Yeah."

"There was more to the story. I didn't tell you all of it."

"You can tell me now."

"One year, after I had stopped dreaming and hoping for a dog, my mother bought a puppy for me. I was supposed to be well behaved all the time, but it turns out that was hard for me to do. Apparently it was hard for me to not talk back and act like a proper young lady."

Matteo laughs. "I never realized," he deadpans, and I roll my eyes.

"Well, I embarrassed him. And when I came home, the price was obvious."

"What happened?"

"He gave the puppy back to the dog shelter."

"That's awful."

"It was, but I was happy that the puppy wasn't hurt. Later, I found out my nanny, Ana, heard what happened and had a friend of hers adopt the puppy. Ana used to bring me pictures."

Another tear falls, but this wasn't for the dog. This one is for Ana.

"Look at me. I'm a mess. Here you are, taking me to this amazing restaurant, and I'm ruining it. Quick, tell me something, anything, so I take my mind off the past."

"This place used to be used during Prohibition to store bootleg booze," he says, gesturing around the restaurant. The bottom floor is an old cellar."

I lean forward in my chair, elbows on the table. "That's so cool."

"Isn't it?"

"I'd love to see it."

"After dinner."

I nod, excited about the prospect of seeing something like that.

We never order. Instead, Marco tells us he will bring us all the house specials. And like the other places we have visited, Matteo never has to pay.

When the food is done, Matteo stands and takes my hand in his. Together, we make the descent to the hidden basement.

It's the coolest thing I have ever seen. It's like every old movie, where there is a lever in the closet that opens to a secret room.

It's amazing.

They still store the liquor in there because of the temperature.

I feel like I'm transported back in time.

When we are finally ready to leave, I throw my arms around him.

"Thank you."

He smiles down at me as I pull back.

"You never need to thank me, Viviana."

"It doesn't matter that I don't need to. I want to."

And with that last statement, he pulls me close and kisses me firmly, fiercely, and like he will never let me go.

---

A few weeks have passed.

They've been amazing.

Matteo showed me his library, and although it's not as big and beautiful as the New York Public Library, it's still larger than anything I could have ever hoped for.

It hasn't been touched in years. That much is obvious from the dust collection on the top shelves.

I need a ladder to even see the books up on some of the shelves.

Which is what I'm doing now. I'm on the top rung of one, looking to see what classic novel I'll read as I wait for Julia to arrive.

"Hey." I hear from behind me. I carefully turn my head over my shoulder at the sound of her voice.

"You're here."

"Well, you did send a car to get me."

I giggle at that. It was a pretty silly statement since she's right. Roberto did pick her up today to bring her here to spend time with me.

"Give me one minute. I'll be right down."

I take the book I found out of the wall and then carefully climb back down the rungs until I'm back on solid ground.

"What do you have there?" Julia asks as I step off the ladder and cross the space until I'm standing in front of her in the center of the room.

I lift the book up, turning it in her direction so that she can see the cover.

"*Jane Eyre*."

"Interesting choice."

I look from her to the weathered book. Mr. Rochester is a little like Matteo when I first got here, but the more I stare at it, the more I think of Ana, Julia's mom.

A shiver runs up my back.

I'm quick to put the book down on the small table. Needing to get it as far away from me now that I have made a connection.

It's stupid, really.

There are no similarities.

Other than Ana was a modern-day governess.

"What do you want to do today?" I ask her.

"We can choose?"

"Of course, we can choose."

"Oh, and here I thought we were locked away in a castle. What book would that be?" She chides, clearly making fun of my love of literature and the situation I'm in.

There's a clip to her voice, one that I've never heard before.

I wonder what that's about. Recently, I've noticed a different side of her. Since she's here, it's obviously not about me. I wonder what's going on in her life.

"Well, of course not, we would just need to take one of the drivers."

"Where would we go?"

"Well, there's this great restaurant Matteo and I have been going to on the water. It used to be like a speakeasy, I think. Maybe we can go there. Or we can sit here and talk. Francesca can bring us lunch."

"Let's stay here."

"Oh, okay."

I take a seat and gesture for her to join me. "What's new? I feel like something is going on with you."

"Nothing really. I'm still looking for a job," she says. Her brother works for my father, and she can too, but she knows how I feel about him. The idea of that makes me sick.

"I think I will work at the governor's office."

I try to school my features and not show how much I hate her life being dictated by my father.

"Do you think that's smart?"

"Well, there isn't anyone hiring, plus we're already so dependent on him." Her voice is clipped, and there it is.

The unspoken topic neither of us broaches.

The accident that changed all our lives twelve years ago.

The accident that took Ana from me and her mom from her.

"You don't need to work for him."

She shakes her head. "The experience and jobs on our résumés are worth it for us."

Her words are clear. She and her twin brother don't have the same prospects as I did in life.

She doesn't realize her imagination is better than the truth.

I never had it. My father's blackmail, never allowing me the freedom.

A deal made with the devil.

She thinks the grass is greener. She thinks all doors are open to me. She doesn't realize that for her to have the doors open, mine must be shut.

I'm not sure what my father's angle is. Why he's hired both of Ana's children. It's almost as if it's another thing to hang over my head. Another way to control me.

It would've worked too. Especially had I never met Matteo.

But when I come clean to him, when I tell him everything, every sordid detail, he will help me figure out a plan.

I know he will.

There's no other way out for them or for me unless he does.

"Please don't do anything rash. I know it sounds like a dream job, but working for my father, it's never a good idea."

"Some of us don't have the luxury of anything else."

"I-I . . ."

"If the bills are to be paid . . ."

"Don't worry about that. The bills will be paid."

"And how would you know? You're not there anymore to know."

"Julia." I cross the space and sit on the same couch as her. I grab her hand. "I promise, I will not let anything bad happen."

She stares at me, but her gaze, although on me, appears vacant like she doesn't see me. Like she is not even there.

It takes a second, but eventually, she shakes her head and snaps out of it.

She stands from the couch and gestures toward the door.

"Let's get something to eat. I am famished."

Even though I'm the farthest thing from hungry, I welcome the idea of getting out of this room and away from this conversation.

Standing, I walk past her, then open the shut door and gesture for her to step out.

Once we are both out of the room, I shut the door.

Enclosing Mr. Rochester, Jane, and the ghosts in the room.

# CHAPTER THIRTY-TWO

## Matteo

WE HAVE FALLEN INTO A ROUTINE.
A quite pleasant one at that.

I work during the days, and at night, I indulge in my wife.

Twice a week, we go to Marco's.

I like to go to make sure everything is in place for the shipment. When we arrive, they unpack it, and by the time we leave, it's done.

Tonight.

"You really love Marco's," she says as she buttons up her blouse and then sits in front of her vanity to apply her makeup.

I nod my head, but from her reflection in the mirror, I can see a line on her brow form.

"What is that look for?"

"What look?"

She places her makeup brush down and swivels in her chair to face me.

"Believe it or not, Matteo, I know we've only been married a short time, but I've gotten to know you, and I can tell when you are withholding something from me. What is it?"

"Oh . . . you wanna do this? Do you want to exchange secrets?"

"What does that mean?"

"You know exactly what I'm talking about."

"I really don't," she mumbles.

"Yes, you do, but very well, I'll go first. I told you about my meeting with the governor."

"New York."

"Yes."

"He wanted me to store my shipment someplace else."

"And . . .?"

"The Prohibition room." It's like a light bulb goes off in her pretty little head. "That's why we went." My lip turns up. "Isn't it perfect?"

"I never would have guessed."

"That's what makes it perfect." I smile broadly.

"And we always drive out the back gate."

Understanding present now.

"Your turn."

Her eyes go wide. "Do I have to?" I arch my brow. "My story isn't as fun as yours. If I tell you before dinner . . ."

She doesn't want to ruin the night.

"You promise to tell me all your secrets after?"

"As soon as we get home."

"Okay. You're off the hook." I lean in and kiss her mouth. "For now."

She drops her head back down, turns in her chair, and goes back to her makeup.

I'm at the mirror by my sink when her phone rings.

I look over at her in question. She turns to face me.

"Julia," she mouths.

"Hello." I hear her say as I go about getting ready.

"Yeah. We're just getting ready."

It's quiet.

"Yep. Dinner again."

Quiet. Julia must be speaking.

"Yes. Twice a week like an old married couple. Always the same." She laughs. "Matteo is a creature of habit, I guess."

"Umm. Okay, I'll talk to you later."

I walk back up to her. "Everything good?"

"Yeah, she had to go. She's kind of acting weird. I wonder if she's mad at me again." She moves to nibble her lip, but I shake my head at her, stepping closer, closing the space. "Creature of habit?"

"Well, you are."

I kick open her legs and then drop to the floor in front of her. "Does this feel like a creature of habit?"

My tongue juts out and swipes at her skin.

"Yes."

I flatten my tongue and lick her faster. "How about now?" I mumble against her flesh.

"Yep." I thrust a finger inside her, then two. I pull away, looking up at her as I fuck her with my hand.

"Still boring?"

"Yes."

"That's it, you asked for it." I stand, pulling her with me, and then I move her until she's in front of my sink and thrust her to lean against the counter.

"Place your hands down," I order as I place my hand on her back, pushing her down for a better angle. Her body now bends slightly at the waist, and I bracket my hands around her waist to brace her.

I remove my right hand and thrust it between her thighs.

"Do you want me to fuck you against this sink?" I then dip my finger inside her. Her inner walls clench around me.

"Mmm, is that what you want, wife?" I continue to work my finger in and out, curling them up to hit the sweet spot inside. She starts to quake, and that's when I finally pull my hand away.

Not wasting another minute, I place myself at her entrance, then start to tease her by dipping just the tip inside. She moans in protest, so I answer her by slamming inside, seating myself deep in her core. Her walls contract instantly. She's already close to coming. Slowly, very slowly, I pull back out . . . then slam back in.

I can feel her, and the feeling is exquisite. The way her body tightens around me has me rushing to release too.

Once she does, she goes limp against my chest. After I come inside her, I kiss her neck, coming down from my own arousal, and then finally pull out from the warmth of her body.

"Am I still a creature of habit?"

"Debatable."

"For that, I'll punish you later."

"Promises, promises."

I fix myself and then zip up my pants.

"I'll be downstairs," I say, as I walk out the door and down the hallway.

When I'm in the foyer, I see Roberto walking my way.

"Everything scheduled."

"Yes. We are good to go."

"They will be there for the delivery tonight as planned."

"Good. When are you going?"

"Any minute." I hear the sound of her shoes. "Speak of the devil."

"I'm ready," Viviana says.

"I see you look gorgeous as always."

"Front or back?" Roberto's words pull me back from gawking at my wife openly.

"Either is fine," I tell him. "The route is secure. We're going to a restaurant. They already dropped off, right?"

Roberto's eyes go wide, but then he nods.

I haven't told him I told Viviana, but now I guess he knows. I walk the few steps to the stairs and take Viviana's hand in mine, and then I lift it to my mouth, touching my lips to her soft skin.

"Let's go."

Roberto opens the front door and leads us to the car we often travel in. Then, with my wife tucked in next to me, we head out for dinner.

As we drive, I stare at my wife, wondering how we got here. How in such a short time, I have grown to care for her.

I pepper kisses on her forehead and whisper all the dirty things I plan to do the moment we are back home. She giggles and smiles, making me wish we didn't have to go anywhere at all tonight, but we do, and when we go home, we're supposed to talk. My plans of seducing my wife again might have to wait.

Dinner, as always, is pleasant. We laugh and tell stories of funny things that have happened to us in the past. I notice that most of her stories are from when she's a girl. When I ask her about her teenage years, Viviana's mood changes, and she grows more somber. I change the topic back to small talk until it's time to head home.

On the way home, I notice the closer we get, the worse her mood is.

I know it's because she has to tell me all about her past. Tonight, she will unravel the mystery I have been trying to pull apart from the first time I saw her.

A well-guarded secret I'm still shocked I haven't figured out.

We pull up to the drive. After the car is thrown in park, I step out, and as usual, I open the door wider and take her hand to help her out. She's nibbling her lip.

I'm about to speak when the door flies open, and a frantic Lorenzo storms out. As soon as I see him, my hand drops from hers.

Roberto moves into position too.

"We were hit. Marco's was hit."

The words slash through the air, my brain spinning, as the only conclusion falls over me. It hits Roberto at the same time because he's pulling out the gun and aiming it at my wife's head. I move around, facing her.

She betrayed me.

"It was all a ruse," I spit. "The whole sob story a big fucking ruse." I pounce, pushing her up against the car. Locking her in with a gun to her head. . .

"I-I didn't do it."

"Like fuck you didn't. You're the only one who knew. No one else knows. I fucking *trusted* you."

"Matteo! Please. I wouldn't. I didn't. I love you!"

I laugh in her face. "Love. You love me?"

With love like that, who needs enemies?

Tears rush out of her eyes. I'll hand it to her. She's a great actress. She acts almost as good as she fucks.

"I didn't do this."

"You want me to believe that on the same day I tell you what we're holding, you didn't tip off your dad?"

"I-I didn't. Please. Please, you have to believe me."

I spin the barrel. A little Russian roulette.

"Matteo—" Luka cuts in.

"Shut the fuck up!" I roar. "Now back to you, *Princess*. A bullet to your brain here, or do I drop you on your father's step like the trash that you are?"

I spin the cylinder

Pressing the barrel to her skull.

"Anything to say, wife?"

"You have to believe me. We went out the front. They could have followed us . . ."

"If that was the case, they would have tried to kill me. But isn't it convenient they only did it once you were safe?" I watch as the tears fall from her eyes. I feel nothing toward her. Only betrayal. "Nothing more to say? Very well." She sobs uncomfortably. Her eye makeup is streaking down her face in dark rivulets.

The same kind of tears that in the past would hurt me to see, but the small part of me that was starting to feel has turned to stone.

The betrayal too much.

I pull the trigger.

# CHAPTER THIRTY-THREE

Viviana

TIME STANDS STILL AS I HEAR THE BARREL SPIN, THEN THE trigger is pulled.

Nothing.

Just a click.

I'm alive.

Even if only barely. My sobs come faster now. Tears streaming down my face.

What happens now? Will he pull the trigger again? Isn't that the game?

My body trembles.

When he pulled the trigger, I was sure I would die. Instead, my body fell to the ground because my legs are no longer able to hold me up.

"Please—"

"Stop speaking," he hisses through clenched teeth. He steps to the side, leaving me lying on the gravel.

"Get her in the car," he orders his men.

"No. You have to believe me."

He steps closer. The tip of his shiny black shoe is dangerously close to my face. "Do you have a death wish?" he spits out. Then he's stepping back. I have never seen hate before like the way he hates me.

"Please," I whisper through sobs, but it's too late. He's no longer looking at me. He's stalking back to the house. Rough hands grab my arms, and before I can object, I'm being lifted.

Then the doors open, and I'm thrown into the back seat of the car. I move to get out, but I'm stopped.

"Be happy you're not in the trunk. Actually, be happy you're not dead." I don't speak, but I nod. I should be dead. By all intents and purposes, that's what Matteo said he would do to me.

He thinks I'm a traitor. I'm not. We were foolish not to take precautions. It's obvious they followed us.

"We should just kill her," one of his men says to Roberto.

"Boss said to take her back." Take her back? Back to where? It feels like a red-hot poker is being thrust into my chest where my heart should be. However, my heart was already broken before I heard I was being dropped off at my father's. So instead, the stabbing sensation intensifies the closer we get.

The trip feels like it takes an eternity. With every turn, with every mile, I beg for them to listen to me. I cry for them to stop if they hear me, which I know they do, but they make no gestures to show me. Instead, the car eats up the distance the way a beast feasts off a decaying body.

When the car pulls to a stop in front of my father's house, the door is thrown open, and I'm thrust out and onto the driveway.

I hit the ground with a thud. A lone tear drifts down my cheek, like the first raindrop to fall before an impending storm.

There is no question the sky will open. It's just a matter of when.

I try to hold them back. With my head held high, I walk toward the house.

I would go anywhere else if I could, but this is the only place for me now. If I want to keep my loved ones safe, I have no other choice but to stay here and play by my father's rules again. I will have to endure living here again.

That's why Matteo picked this as my punishment.

Matteo knows this is the most painful place for me.

My own personal hell.

He wants me dead.

This is the equivalent.

My father won't rest until I suffer for my insolence.

Well played, husband.

I rub the wet skin and will no more to fall. It's bad enough I'm here. I won't let these people see me fall.

Below my pants, I'm sure my legs are cut from falling to the ground.

With each step I take, my legs scream, but I plaster on a large, fake smile.

*Do not show them pain.*

My smile is sharp enough to cut glass.

The car skids off, kicking up gravel. The air thick with the smell of burning rubber.

I stand tall and proud. With my shoulders pulled back, I walk with purpose to the giant,

mahogany door.

The door swings open, and my father is standing at the threshold. He looks pleased with himself.

"That didn't take long. I see he grew bored of you already." I refuse to let him see me suffer, so I plaster on a fake smile.

"We had a fight, and since I gave up my apartment, I decided to come here instead. There's nothing to gloat about. I'm sure everything will be back to normal by tomorrow,"

I lie. There is no way I'll fall apart in front of him.

"I doubt that. But believe what you want. I would have preferred you keep him on the hook a little longer, but I'm sure we can find another, more useful, way to use you. Maybe Salvatore will take his cousin's sloppy seconds."

"Why do you hate me so?"

He looks me dead in the eyes. "I don't hate you. You just hold no purpose, and without a purpose, you might as well be dead."

"I'm your daughter."

"Which is why I need you alive, but I'll be dammed if your little rebellious act has me losing my chances of something bigger. You will be useful to me." His words leave me feeling cold and empty. I walk past him into the foyer.

I'm not sure where my mother is, but I have to assume she's somewhere with a martini glass in hand. I head up the stairs and into the old room where I used to live before moving to the city for college.

Once I'm in the safety of my room, I fall apart. My soul is bleeding out of my body in warm streams of tears. This is a pain I have never felt before. What I said to Matteo is true. I did fall in love with him.

Somewhere along the way, I fell in love with the villain. And like all evil things, he took me apart piece by piece and then crushed what was left.

He ruined me.

I will never be the same.

# CHAPTER THIRTY-FOUR

## Matteo

"YOU LET HER LIVE," LORENZO BLURTS, AS SHOCKED AS I AM, stepping into my office.

"I didn't let her do anything. A game of Russian roulette allowed her to breathe air for another day."

"And who really knows for how long? I'm sure her father is still furious with her for going against his original plan. I'm sure by the end of the week, she will be sold off to Salvatore. Maybe even put on his chopping block."

Despite my anger at her betrayal, his words cause my fist to clench. I hadn't thought of that. I might want to kill my wife, but that life, a life of slavery, is not what I want for her.

We are both quiet for a minute, and then Lorenzo takes a seat across from me.

"Why did you let her go?" His voice dips. He's asking me a question I don't want to answer.

He's asking me if I fell for my wife.

Instead of answering, I reach my hand across my desk and grab the glass decanter sitting there. Beside it are empty tumblers.

"Care to drink with me?" When he nods his head, I pour us both a drink. I slide his to him, and I lift mine and take a swig.

"I am not in love with Viviana," I answer, but I can't deny there is a weird feeling inside me. It feels as though I am empty.

It's a feeling I've never felt before, not even when my parents died. But I don't say that to him. Instead, I drink another sip. This time when I place it on the table, the liquid sloshes against the glass.

"Killing her would've been too easy, and it wouldn't have helped our cause," I finally say.

"So, then you do have a reason for keeping her alive?" he asks.

"Her phone is still tapped. Her purse still bugged."

"You plan to use her."

"It only seems fair."

"And then if she's not helpful. What if her father doesn't fall into the trap?"

"Well then, maybe we get lucky, and she will end up in Salvatore's hands after all."

"And you will be okay knowing what he will most likely do to her?"

"Yes," I say, but the word feels bitter on my tongue. Chalky. Like dust is settling on it, and I want to cough it up.

"Boss, you've never lied to me before. You don't have to now."

I'm at a loss of what to say. Is that what she did to me? Do I feel something for her? Did I care? Is that why my words are hollow? Is that why the idea of my cousin having her feels like I'm chewing shards of glass?

"I don't love her," I say again, but this time, it sounds like a lie even to me. He nods and lifts his own drink, sitting then in silence. When both our glasses are finished, I set mine on the table and push away to stand.

"Make sure a man is listening to everything going on in that house. I don't want anything to go over without me knowing. Do you understand?"

"I do."

I move across the room, exiting and leaving Lorenzo alone. I make my way up the stairs, down the hall, and when I swing the door open, I'm hit with the knowledge that she really is gone. I know she betrayed me. I was prepared for this, but how wrong I was. I wasn't prepared. I am not prepared. Not for the way the room feels empty.

Or how quiet it is. Not for the lingering smell of her perfume in the air. Or the way her clothes still hang in my closet. It doesn't matter because I'm going to have to be okay with it. Just like I'm going to have to be okay with however the future plays out. There's a good chance she'll end up dead, or worse, but she betrayed me. Only in the quiet of my own room can I admit that yes, my wife had gotten under my skin. It doesn't matter, though. Her fate is sealed.

The next day, I find myself in my surveillance room, curious to see what the night had in store for my dear wife.

"Any phone calls? Anything of importance?"

"No. Nothing."

"And the bug in the bag, what was the audio?" My men look at me but don't speak.

"Tell me."

"She was crying. She held her own as her father chastised her, but then when the room went silent, she cried. Probably after he left her alone."

Hearing she cried should make me feel better, but it doesn't.

We don't know why she cried. Maybe because her father once again has her under his thumb, which is the truth. We always knew he did. We just didn't know the interesting thing she was going to tell me the night she decided to betray me. I turn back to Lorenzo.

"You need to find out now what her secret is."

"Don't you think our resources are better served by finding your cousin?"

He's right, it is, but I need to know anyway. A small part of me thinks that's the reason she ultimately decided to betray me. Whatever her father is holding over her is the key.

"Do both," I say, and then turn and storm out of the room.

Leaving my men frantically working in my wake.

# CHAPTER THIRTY-FIVE

## Viviana

MY EYES ARE SWOLLEN WHEN I WAKE UP. RED AND blotchy, the obvious signs of a night spent crying myself to sleep. It didn't come for a long time. Not until approximately four in the morning, and when I did finally fall into a slumber, it was restless.

Nightmares plagued me.

Over and over again, I saw Matteo standing above me.

Over and over again, he pulled the trigger.

Each time I woke up, I jolted out of bed with tears pouring down my face. I need to talk to him. I need to tell him I didn't betray him.

But the chances of that ever happening are few and far between. One thing I know is, Matteo doesn't forgive.

He won't hear what I have to say, and knowing my father, by the time Matteo has calmed down enough to speak to me, I'll be long gone.

I'm sure he's planning my annulment right now. I'm sure his lawyers are already here drawing up the papers. I'm sure Salvatore is waiting for me.

Salvatore, a man even Matteo says I should fear.

How can my father sell himself to this man? I stand from my bed and make my way over to the dresser, where I threw my bag, grab my phone, then I start searching to see if I have any missed phone calls.

Not that I would think Matteo would call me, but still I check, I hope, I dream, and then like expected, I'm disappointed. No, that's not a strong enough word.

I'm crushed.

A shaky, audible sigh escapes my mouth as I make my way into the bathroom that's attached to my room.

What's staring back at me is frightening.

My dark hair, normally straight, is wavy from the wetness of my tears. My eyes, as I suspected, are bloodshot and puffy. My nose looks swollen, and I know my lip has dried, caked-on blood from where I bit myself.

I turn around and turn the shower water on, then when steam billows around me, I strip off my clothes. I'm still in the same clothes I wore yesterday. Once naked, I step under the scalding water. My skin burns, but I welcome the pain. Everything hurts my skin, but it serves me right.

I never should've fallen in love with him. I never should've trusted him with my heart because now, he's crushed it. Part of me wants to figure it out, figure out a plan, but another part, a much larger part, wants to hide in my bed for the next three weeks.

It takes me a few more minutes to wash out the soap in my hair, and then I throw a towel around myself, get back into bed, and go to sleep.

---

Days pass.

I spend them doing exactly the same thing every day—I sleep, I wake, I eat, and occasionally, I shower. I haven't heard from Matteo.

I don't have the strength to speak to Julia. I don't want her to say I told you so.

I don't want her to say anything. I avoid my mother. I avoid my father. I walk around the house like a zombie, but I don't speak to anyone.

I see Julia's brother staring at me.

He gives me a nasty look. One that says he's happy I'm down on my luck.

There was a time long ago when we were friends, but ever since he started to work for my father, it's like he hates me.

Maybe he never liked me.

I guess that's what happens when you live in the basement of a house. You resent the woman who lives on top. Regardless of the things I've done to help provide for him, he still hates me. I always thought because of my friendship with Julia, he wouldn't, but he resents me even more for that.

Sometimes, I wonder if he knows the truth about that night, and maybe that's why, but then I remember the only people who know the truth are my father and myself.

Today, I venture downstairs. I can hear my father's voice bellowing through the air, screaming at God knows who. I keep walking, and this time Julia's brother, Jonathan, doesn't even pretend to ignore me.

"You look like shit," he says, and I think he expects me to say something, to argue, to do anything, but I don't. I'm too tired to do that, so I walk past him into the kitchen.

I haven't eaten anything today. My stomach growls at the lack of food I've consumed. It's been so long, I'm sure it has shrunk, so a banana is all I need.

When I take it and walk out of the room, I bump into my father. "You're out of bed."

"I am."

"Good, it's about time."

"Time for what?"

"Time for you to meet Salvatore."

"Why would I do that?" I'm confused.

"Because the plan will go on as previously planned. I will secure the support of Salvatore. You will play the part you were always meant to play." I wasn't wrong. I just thought I had more time. But I guess I was wrong.

My shoulders flop forward.

"Get changed and be presentable. He will be here shortly." I think that this could have been my chance. I could have told Matteo about this. I rush to my room and call him. He sends me to voicemail.

**Me: Please answer me. He's coming here.**

**Matteo: As if I would ever fall for your trap again. Be happy I didn't put a bullet in your head.**

I try to call him again, but this time my call doesn't go through. I'm truly alone. With no help coming from Matteo, I have no choice. I have to brave this by myself.

I fix my hair and pull out an old outfit from the closet, then I grab my purse. Who knows if we are going somewhere. Maybe I'll get the opportunity to kill him myself, but I highly doubt it.

I walk down the stairs and find my father in his office. In the corner of the room is Salvatore Amante. His eyes are trained on me, focused intensely. He crosses the distance. Eating up the space, like a hungry carnivore in a prairie of sheep.

"Leave us," he says to my father, and I'm instantly scared. I take a step back. My back hits the now closed door. He steps closer. His large body is looming over me. I look around the room, looking for a way to escape. I could use the door behind me. But the way his arms block me in, I'm not sure if I'd be able to.

"I see why my cousin stole you from me."

He leans down, his face too close to mine. I can feel his breath against my cheek. I move to turn, but his hand lifts and grips my jaw.

"Let me go," I say.

"No. I don't think I will." His sardonic smile makes a chill run down my spine. He looks scary, and for the first time, I'm genuinely afraid.

I was never this scared of Matteo.

His grip on my jaw is tight, but it loosens as it slides down my neck.

"From what I hear, my cousin was quite fond of you. I can see the appeal," he says as he continues to trail his touch down the column of my neck.

"Please don't touch me."

He licks his lips, and the fear inside me multiplies. Will my father really let him do this to me? Will he let him hurt me?

As if reading my mind, he smirks but lets go.

"Pity. I promised your father I wouldn't touch you, not until I kill my cousin and marry you. Apparently, he doesn't take me at my word that I will help him."

"Would you?"

He smiles again, the words he doesn't say as clear as day . . . no.

"Why me? Why am I important to this deal?"

"Other than the obvious, the deal with your father for full control of every port in New York and New Jersey?"

"Yes."

"Because Matteo took you, because he fell for you, and because of that"—his hand touches me again—"I will enjoy myself immensely."

"He left me. He doesn't care for me."

"That's where you're wrong. If he didn't, you'd already be dead."

His words spark the little bit of strength I have, and I push him off me.

"I said, don't touch me."

He laughs then, a sadistic laugh, his eyes glinting with the depth of evil I have never seen before.

"I will enjoy breaking you. And once I do that, I'll give you to my men."

"My father—"

"You will still be alive. You'll still be the woman on my arm. I'll make sure all your bruises can't be seen." I smack him against his face, and he just laughs. "Run away, little girl. I enjoy the chase."

And that is exactly what I do.

I run.

# CHAPTER THIRTY-SIX

Matteo

WAR IS IN THE AIR.

All my men and I are staying in the city compound. It makes more sense. Salvatore doesn't know of its existence. It however hasn't been as easy to make pick-ups.

Which isn't good for business.

They have blown up all the old warehouses I have kept. The original ones that date back to my father's time. Thankfully, they haven't found the one we currently use.

But we still need to make drops.

My men are anxious. Fuck, at this point, so am I.

There has been no word from any of the bugs on Viviana. It's like she's a ghost.

She doesn't try to call me again. Not that her call will come through if she tried, but still. She doesn't even try to call her friend. As for the bug on her bag, she hasn't gone anywhere at all. Even the GPS tracker shows she hasn't left the mansion in all the time she has been there.

The phone rings in the surveillance room. Roberto takes the call. I hear him speaking, but I don't make out very much. Then he hangs up.

"We were right."

"About?"

"Marino is going after his original plan," he clarifies.

I arch my brow.

"Salvatore was at the house a few days ago."

My fist hits the table. "Why am I only finding out about this now?"

*But you did know. She told you. She warned you he would be there.*

"Eddie couldn't get the word out to us."

"And Viviana?" My mouth dries as I say her name. "Is she—" I stop myself. What do I want to say: okay, hurt, dead? Fuck. I don't even know how I feel about all the options.

"Eddie says Salvatore was alone with her." My fist clenches. "But it wasn't for long, and he didn't hear anything."

It doesn't make me feel good, regardless. Who knows what happened behind a closed door?

"Was she carrying her bag?" I ask, and Tony turns to me.

"He didn't say, but I can check the bug."

The room around us goes quiet as everyone waits.

Then her voice pierces through the air. Her scared voice.

It feels like I'm being stabbed. The men around me are tense. Luka's jaw locked. Hearing her makes me remember, and I don't want to remember.

The more she talks, the harder it gets to listen, but it's my cousin's words that have my fist clenching, and my stomach feels like there are boulders inside me.

"Turn it off."

*I can't hear any more.*

Why do you fucking care? She's a traitor. Regardless of what I want to feel, the sound of her voice, the way she begged, pleaded, cried . . . I shake my head to myself. No.

She's the one who ratted me out. This was all a ploy. But she tried to tell you that Salvatore would be there. You could've been set up. It most probably was a setup. But wouldn't Eddie have known if it was and told us about it? Especially now, after the fact, that we didn't fall for it.

A sinking feeling barrels its way inside me. Maybe I didn't look at this right.

No.

I refuse to believe that. The timing was too perfect.

"What do you want to do?" Lorenzo asks.

He wants to know if I want to take back my wife.

"What do you think?" I ask. His eyes go wide. It's not often I ask an opinion from anyone, especially on something like this.

"We can grab her. Or we can leave her. She betrayed you. Who knows what else she will say? She can tell them about this place . . ."

I never even thought about that. Shit, are my men safe? Maybe she doesn't remember.

"I think we need to figure out a way to get her back. It's the only way to ensure this place stays safe. Once we get her back, you have to kill her." I nod my head. He's not wrong. She's a liability. She knows all the locations. She's been there, so she'll be able to tell them. I'm not sure why she hasn't yet, but I still don't trust her.

"How do we get her out?"

"We use Eddie. It's the only way."

"Call him up and arrange it. Have him bring her to a point near the estate."

Eddie doesn't know about this location yet.

It's not something I can put in writing, so the estate seems like a better idea.

"Okay. On it." Most of my men leave the room, but Lorenzo stays.

"What's up? You have something you want to say?" I level him with my stare.

"When the time comes, Boss, I can do it." Now I look at him

like I have no idea what he's saying. "I can kill Viviana for you, Matteo." His voice lowers as he clarifies what he means.

He thinks I fell for her. He's not wrong, but what he is wrong about is he thinks I'm too weak to kill the woman I love.

Yes. I love her. I figured that out after I pulled the trigger that night and didn't kill her.

When the barrel clicked, the feeling was not disappointment. No, instead, it was a feeling of relief. That's when I knew.

The fact still remains, she went against the family. Love or not, I'll pull the trigger this time.

I am not weak.

# CHAPTER THIRTY-SEVEN

Viviana

L UCKILY, I HAVE HAD NO RECENT RUN-INS WITH SALVATORE.
He hasn't been here. His presence, just a memory now,
like a mirage that fades away and you wish you never saw. It reminds you of how close you came to escaping a fate worse than
death, but as soon as you were saved, none of it was real.

I was close to tasting freedom.

If I had only done something about it sooner. Confided in
Matteo sooner. But unfortunately, I didn't, and now I'm stuck
here, biding my time.

The door to my bedroom opens, and I jump back, expecting
to see Salvatore. It's not him, and I'm surprised to see this man
standing in my room. He's never been anywhere near me. He's
never spoken to me.

"What do you want?" I hiss.

"I'm taking you out of here." He narrows his eyes.

"I don't understand."

His eyes are dark and unreadable. Why is he helping me?

"I spoke to Matteo. He wants me to get you out of here." My
heart starts to flip-flop around in my chest. He finally believes
me.

"Okay."

"Do you need anything?" he asks.

I look around the room, searching for anything I would want to grab. I take my purse and throw my phone in it.

"Anything else?"

"No." I shake my head.

"Okay, let's go. We have to go out the back, so no one sees us."

"Why are you helping me?" I ask again, not understanding.

"I'm working for Matteo," he clarifies. I squint my eyes but having a spy inside the house is something Matteo would do. Together, we take the back staircase and go down a long, narrow hall.

Eventually, it leads to the kitchen. It's completely empty, and I wonder if it's planned or just a stroke of luck. He swings open the back door and parked right past it is a black SUV.

"You'll need to duck down while we pass security."

I nod my head, getting into the back, and crawling on the floor until I'm almost tucked as close as I can under the seat in front.

Good thing I'm short, or this plan would never have worked. I can hear him speaking on the phone, but with my ears pressed against the carpet, I'm not sure who it is.

The car swerves and makes a quick right, and I'm pretty sure he's getting directions from Matteo and trying to confirm no one is following us at the same time.

We drive in silence, other than the occasional phone call he gets. He never speaks to me. He never says anything. My mind is going a mile a minute, wondering what will happen once I'm with Matteo again. Does this mean he believes me? Does this mean he forgives me, or does this mean something else completely? Either way, I'm happy that he got me out because I was pretty sure my father was going to try to use me as bait, eventually.

I think he hoped, at least.

That's what Salvatore implied, anyway. Maybe this way we can come up with a plan together. All cards on the table. It's time there are no secrets, which means I'll need to tell Matteo everything. I'll have to tell Julia and Jonathan too. But first, we need to get to Matteo, then I can worry about the rest.

The car starts to slow down, and I'm impatient to get up from where I'm crouched.

Surely, no one is following us now.

Not after the way we were driving. I move to my knees, and then I lift until I'm on the back bench of the car. I don't see anything. It's empty.

It's like it's an abandoned parking lot.

Is someone coming?

Is it Matteo?

Then I see the car pull up, as our car slows almost to a stop.

*It's him.*

As soon as it stops moving. I throw open the car door before he even hits the brakes. When I'm outside, standing directly in front of the hood of the other car, I hear two doors open.

One comes from behind me. From my car, the other in front.

Matteo steps out. He's standing close but not close enough. His eyes meet mine, but I feel as though I've been sucker punched. The look he gives me is the same look from the last time I saw him.

Still hatred.

Still pain.

Still his desire to see me dead.

And then I know the truth.

He is not here to save me. He's here to kill me.

I turn around swiftly, looking toward dark eyes that are narrowed. Pleading for him to save me. To take me back.

"Thank you, Eddie, for helping me get her back." Matteo laughs from behind me.

Dark and menacing. I should be scared. I should turn around and plead for my life, but I can't. Then something else hits me, and I'm frozen in place at the name he said.

Eddie . . .

I look at the dark eyes, dark like before, still menacing. For the first time, the eyes smile at me.

Fear, an unnatural fear, pours through my blood. My stomach feels as though it's being dropped to the floor. Now I know what this is. This isn't my trap.

It's Matteo's.

This man is not named Eddie . . .

This man is Jonathan.

My father's inside man.

Julia's brother . . .

And he's the traitor.

"No!" I scream, springing into action, turning to face Matteo. "It's a trap!" Everything happens so fast, and before I can stop myself or think better of it, I'm running, more like jumping, in front of Matteo.

That's when the world stops, and like a movie where the director switches to slow motion, everything halts . . .

Everything moves slowly.

Jonathan reaches behind him.

My heart beats in my chest as he pulls out his gun.

*Thump.*

He points.

*Thump.*

His finger pulls back.

That's when time catches up.

There's a click.

A shot rings through the air. A sharp bite of pain. And then . . .

*Silence.*

# CHAPTER THIRTY-EIGHT

## Matteo

Everything happens fast. First, I see my wife running toward me.

Something changes in her. The change was striking.

A look of understanding dropped over her features, and then she was diving in front of me.

The sound of the trigger, of a gun firing and a bullet traveling through the air echoes in my ears.

I brace for the impact.

But it never comes.

That's when I feel her. I can do nothing but watch. She's standing there, directly in front of me, and then she's not.

In the distance, I can see my men running toward Eddie. His gun is still in his hand, trained on me.

Lorenzo fires a shot, and he goes down.

I'm not sure if he is alive. I can't be bothered with any of it when I see Viviana fall to the ground.

Dropping to my knees, I move beside her. Turning her carefully onto her back.

My world stops when I see her usually blushed skin, now pale, pasty, and lacking life.

Her eyes are closed. I search her body, and that's when I see it. The red spreading across her stomach.

It soaks through her shirt, pooling on the white material. Her blood coats my hands as I try to stop the flow. It pours through my fingers. I press down, but no matter how hard I do, the current refuses to stop.

Her eyes refuse to open.

The puddle beneath her continues to spread. My heart pounds as I watch the scarlet pool that forms beneath her.

She isn't moving.

Why isn't she fucking moving, goddammit?

In the background, I hear shouts, fists connecting to flesh, but I can't see that now.

Not when she jumped in front of a bullet.

She saved me.

The sound of footsteps can be heard, and then Lorenzo is beside me.

"Is she dead?" he asks.

"I-I don't know," I answer, my voice low, my tone cracked.

Everything inside me cracks as I see the woman I love on the ground.

Lorenzo moves over her, leaning in.

I can't find the strength to check.

Normally strong, she has robbed me of my strength.

When she moved in front of me, everything changed.

"She's alive."

Like a button pressed on my heart, his words kick me back to life.

"We need to get out of here. We need to get her help."

"I'll call the doctor."

He doesn't need to clarify. We have a state-of-the-art facility in the compound. She'll be safer and more comfortable in the hospital I have. My doctor and the team he will bring with him will make sure she's okay.

"We need to move her," he says. "Carefully." Together, Lorenzo and I take Viviana and place her inside the back of the SUV. I get in with her, holding her head. She's unconscious. I press my finger to her neck, making sure she's alive.

For now, she is. But with each second that passes, her heartbeat's softer and softer. The good thing is, the compound is less than a mile away. It's one of the reasons we chose this location. It feels as though an eternity passes as we drive the distance.

Each second hammers on longer and longer.

I can't stop seeing her jumping. I can't stop hearing her scream. This whole time, I thought it was her, when, in truth, it was me. My man was the traitor. The trust I put in my man is the reason Viviana is lying in my arms bleeding out.

It should be me.

I should be the one shot.

I will never forgive myself if she dies. I know that with every ounce of my life.

And after this is done, I will burn everything down to the ground to stop my cousin, to stop Marino.

To seek vengeance.

Not just for what they have done to me, but because of this.

I should have trusted her, but I didn't.

I will spend the rest of my life trying to prove to her that I love her. Trying to be a better man for her.

I place a kiss on her lips.

Her head is resting on my lap. She doesn't move, but for now, she's still alive.

My finger still feeling the pulse that keeps her breathing. Even if it's slight, it's there.

Soon we are pulling into the gates, and then we are on the driveway.

My doctor is already there.

There's a gurney ready to whisk her away.

"Throw in an IV," he shouts. "Move! Move! Move!"

Everything happens so fast from that moment on. One minute she's lying in my arms with her head on my lap, and the next, she's in the house, and I am standing there on the circular driveway wondering how the fuck this happened. Lorenzo walks up to me.

"She's going to be okay, Boss."

"She better be, or there will be hell to pay. How did this happen? How didn't we know . . . and how did she?"

There are huge gaps in the story here. Ones I need to find out. "Where is he?"

When we left the field, we left all the other men behind with the traitor.

"On their way. Should be a few minutes behind us."

There was no time to wait before.

"I want him in the basement."

"In a cell? Or in the room . . ."

He doesn't clarify which room, but we both know which room, the torture room.

Yes, I kept my uncle's room in the basement intact.

As did my father.

But only for the guilty.

And Eddie . . .

Is that . . .?

The car pulls up then, kicking gravel up.

The piece of shit is lugged out of the car once it pulls to a stop. His face bleeding, his shoulder bleeding from what I can only presume is a gunshot wound from when he tried, unsuccessfully, to fire another shot to kill me.

Lorenzo signals my men to take him to the basement. "Tie him up."

That's all he says. They know the orders now. I start toward the house, walking in the door, and heading to the opposite end of the building.

I don't need to tell anyone where I'm going. It's written all over my face.

When I throw open the doors, I see the glass that protects the room.

I can see the doctor already pulling away her clothes and starting to work on her.

There are chairs in the room, but I can't sit.

How can I? There is too much energy coursing through me.

I pace back and forth.

I want to punch someone. I want to punch the shit out of the fuck in my basement, but I need to make sure my wife is going to be okay first.

"Any news, Boss? What's going on?" Lorenzo walks up behind me.

"The doc hasn't come out yet or updated me, but it looks like she's in surgery."

I start to pace. There is too much nervous energy inside me to stand still.

"Matteo, you can talk to me," Lorenzo says, and I turn to look at him.

Like me, Viviana's blood is all over his clothes. I shake my head. I can't talk. I can't find words. My throat feels like it is closing up, like it is filled with cement, and no matter how hard I try, I can't break free.

"I know you're my boss—" he starts to say, his eyes heavy and thick with pain. He's afraid too. He cares for her too. "But you're my friend first."

My chest expands as I take a deep breath, forcing the words out of my dry lips. "I can't lose her."

"You won't."

"How do you know that?" I fire back, not angry with him, but angry with myself. I could lose her, and it's all my fault. "I don't deserve her," I mutter.

"Who says who deserves who?"

"I'm the devil. The tyrant. I'm what her nightmares are made of. She would be better off if I took the bullet and was out of her life."

Lorenzo steps up to me, his hand reaching out and touching my shoulder. It's a strange move between boss and employee, but as my friend, as my family, I welcome the comfort right now.

"Who told you that?" he asks. "Not her. She loves you, man. She stepped in front of a bullet for you." He breathes in deeply. "We were all wrong."

"Most of all, me."

"It wasn't just you. It was me, Roberto, and it was Luka too. We all felt betrayed. We all thought—"

"It doesn't matter, she trusted me, and I let her down," I cut in, not willing to hear anything but voice my own pain, my own guilt.

"Well then, you spend the rest of your life making it up to her."

"I will."

"She'll be okay."

"I hope so."

*Because I don't want to live in a world where she doesn't.*

---

We spend the next few hours in the same state. Dried blood on our clothes, pacing the room. Then the door swings open, and my doctor walks toward me.

"She's out of surgery. Thankfully, there were no complications. We got the bullet out, and we stopped the bleeding. We were able to get her all stitched up and close the wound, but she needs to rest."

"She'll be okay?"

He nods. "She'll be okay."

I continue to pace back and forth. I'm not sure how long I pace, but eventually, the door opens, and one of the nurses pops her head out this time.

"You can come in and sit with her now, Mr. Amante."

Making my way into the room, I take the seat beside her bed.

"Viviana."

*Beep.*

"Please wake up."

*Beep.*

"I'm sorry."

*Beep.*

"Please open your eyes."

*Beep.*

"I don't know how to do this."

*Beep.*

"I don't know how to live without you."

*Beep.*

"I'm so sorry," I choke out. "I should have listened to you. I should have let you explain. This is all my fault. It should have been me. I should be dead. . . You saved me."

# CHAPTER THIRTY-NINE

## Viviana

B EEP.
    *Beep.*

*Beep.*

*The sound of a machine plays through my dream, beckoning me to wake up.*

I try to open my eyes. I try to push through the pain, but my lids are too heavy.

*Beep.*

*Beep.*

*Beep.*

Mustering all the energy in my body, I try again. This time my eyelids flutter open.

"Matteo . . ." They flutter open, and Matteo comes into focus.

I have never seen him look like this. He looks devastated and completely distraught. "I . . ." The words I want to say won't leave my mouth. Instead, my voice cracks, my throat burning in pain.

"Shh. You don't have to speak. Rest. You need to rest."

I blink my eyes at him. What happened? One minute, I could see my fate, he wanted me dead and the next . . . Jonathan.

"A-a-re you h-hurt?"

Matteo leans forward and places a kiss on my lips. "No, baby, I'm not hurt. You saved me."

Everything comes rushing back.

Panic starts to engulf me.

Is he here?

Did he die?

I can't breathe. It feels like someone is stomping on my chest.

"You need to calm down. Breathe, Viviana."

His hand touches my cheek, and I try to move away.

Matteo wanted to kill me. He was taking me back to kill me.

"What's wrong?"

My head shakes back and forth. My heart pounds in my chest, causing the sound of the machine to go crazy.

"Please calm down. This isn't good for you. No one will hurt you again."

"You hurt me," I whisper. "You were going to kill me." Tears pour down my face. "Why am I here?"

He reaches out and takes my hand in his. "You're here because you saved me. You're here because you were right. You're here because I love you." I must look stunned because he lifts my hand to his mouth. "I do. I love you. It took me a long time to realize, but you are everything to me, Viviana."

"But you wanted to kill me."

"I didn't truly. I thought I could. But when I pulled the trigger, I realized I loved you. I was too scared to admit the feelings I had. Too scared to allow myself this, but when I saw you lying on the ground, I realized I would do anything to protect you."

The room goes silent. His confession heavy in the air. My own declaration weighs heavily on my tongue, but I'm not sure if I can tell him. If I can trust him with my heart again.

"You don't have to say it again. I heard you. I was an asshole, but that doesn't mean I didn't. It doesn't mean that your words are not forever engraved on my heart." Sometimes I forget that Matteo can see through me. He sees everything. The only time he was blind, it was because he thought I betrayed him.

Can I forgive him?

Can I give us another chance?

After what he did to me and put me through. Can I move past that?

*Should* I move past that?

I stare up into his green eyes. Eyes I have allowed myself to get lost in time and time again.

All I see looking back at me is truth.

His truth.

He loves me.

"I love you," I whisper.

"I love you too. Can you forgive me?"

I let my lips tip up into a smile. "It will cost you."

His own mouth parts in a smirk. "I'll be happy to pay the price. Whatever price you deem fit."

"Groveling . . ."

Our mouths connect, and he kisses me as if I'm his oxygen.

We stay entwined for a few more moments, but eventually, Matteo pulls back and looks down at me.

"How did you know?"

"About what?"

"That it was a trap."

What does he mean . . . didn't he already know this? I furrow my brow. "You don't know?"

"My men are still interrogating Eddie. Did you hear something when he was working in your father's house?"

"Who do you think *Eddie* is?"

"What do you mean? He worked for me. He was my inside guy."

My eyes widen, and I grab his hand. "Matteo. That's not who he is. He was never your guy. He's my father's."

"What?"

"His name isn't even Eddie. The man who brought me to you, his name . . . it's Jonathan. He's Julia's brother."

"This whole time—fuck." His hand lifts and pulls at the roots of his hair. "How didn't I see it? I even looked into Ana's family, but no—I never recognized him. He got through my security checks."

"When he first started working for my father, his appearance changed drastically. I thought it was because of the new job, but now I see it was to change his appearance to deceive you. My father really did think of everything. But what I don't understand is why try to kill you? Why would he do anything for my father like that? Unless my father told him the truth. Unless he's blackmailing him too."

"Blackmail? Truth? What aren't you telling me?"

I have put this off long enough. It's time I told him everything.

"When I was a child, I had a nanny. She started to work for my parents when I was a little girl. She lived in our house. Back then we lived on a large estate, similar to this. It belonged to my mother's family. My mother had the money. I grew up with Jonathan and Julia. They were the closest thing I had to siblings. When I was ten years old, I had a crazy idea. I wanted to bring Ana a cake for her birthday. I didn't have a cake, so I took one of my cupcakes and put a candle on it. Ana wasn't in her room when I went. I looked for her, and that's when I saw the light in the playroom on. I heard her voice because she was talking to someone. I left the cupcake there on a table next to the playroom. It was an accident. There were papers on the table, the whole thing went up in flames. I don't know how but Ana was stuck in the room, the door was blocked. I don't remember anything. I don't remember how any of it happened."

My tears come out faster now. My words a hiccup. "All I know is once she was gone, my father told me I had killed Ana. I didn't understand then. My father told me I would be sent to jail. That worse than that, her family would have nothing. At ten, I didn't realize it, but I made a deal with the devil. He agreed to always take care of her family, pay the bills, and all I had to do was keep my mouth shut about my part. I didn't know then that the plan was to hold it over my head. Forever. And I didn't know the worst part . . ." I sob harder.

"What he's holding over your head?"

"First, the secret. He told me I would go to jail. I would be taken away from my home. When I got older, I realized he lied, that they couldn't take me away for that. . . That's when he threatened to stop paying for Julia and Jonathan. See, I knew they were poor. My father had a private detective take pictures of them. They were only kept together because of the money my father gave their new guardians. He was able to hang this over me. Showing me images, making me bend to his will. When they finally graduated from high school, I thought I could get out, but I was wrong again. They couldn't afford college, and so I did what he asked, always, and the worst part was what I found out . . ."

With my head down, I whisper the rest of my secret. All of it. Every detail I know. When I finally stop crying, I sit quietly for a minute, wondering if he will say anything, but he doesn't.

"Do you think Jonathan knows the truth? Do you think that's why he did this? Because of his mother."

"I don't know, but when you're up for it, why don't you come downstairs and find out yourself."

# CHAPTER FORTY

Matteo

As soon as Viviana falls asleep, I feather a kiss on her cheek, and then I tell the nurse I'll be back.

I don't like leaving her here by herself, but I know she'll be okay.

When I'm downstairs, I let myself into the room where we are holding the bastard I now know as Jonathan.

Flinging the door open, I step inside.

He's been tied to the chair since he arrived.

He's fully dressed still, but blood soaks the shirt.

I'm sure my men already patched his gunshot wound, but the wound could still be fun to play with if he doesn't answer my questions.

"Jonathan."

"Guess she's not dead," he chides.

I have to hold back from taking out his tongue. Unfortunately, he can't talk without it. Instead, I'll have to come up with some other means of torture.

I settle on a punch across his face.

Hard enough that he spits out blood, now there is more on his shirt.

He's a fucking mess.

"Were you working for him the whole time?" He looks up at

me, blood pouring from his mouth now. "I take it the answer is yes, seeing as who you are." Jonathan's eyes go wide. "Yes, she told me everything about you. And yes, to answer the question you haven't asked, she's fine. Perfectly fine. You're a lousy shot."

"I wasn't aiming for you."

"Why?"

"Why not?" He shrugs. He's not going to talk, at least not yet. He needs more time to stew.

"I'll be back."

That was a waste of time.

I head back up the stairs and into my makeshift hospital.

Viviana is still attached to all the machines and resting. Her eyes flutter open when she hears me come in.

"Everything good?" Her voice is drained of all energy. Raspy like she needs water.

I move to the side of the room and do just that, filling a cup and bringing it to her.

"Here. Drink this."

I place a straw in the cup and tilt it so she can take a sip. When she's done, I place it back down and then move to sit next to her in the chair.

"Can you sit with me?"

"I already was planning to stay here with you all night."

"Can you sit here, I mean." She pats the bed beside her.

"I don't think that's a good idea."

"Please."

I can't say no to this woman. Not now. Not ever.

I give her a small incline of my head and then get into the bed beside her.

"You're lucky this isn't a real hospital."

"We'd never fit in those beds."

She's right. This bed is a full size, which although a tight squeeze it's at least doable.

"Sleep." I place a kiss on her temple.

"What happened to Jonathan?"

"Don't worry about him, right now. You need your rest."

When her breath grows shallow, and she finally falls asleep, I allow myself to finally breathe.

I don't think any more about Jonathan, Marino, or Salvatore.

I'm just happy to have her in my arms again.

The next morning comes before I know it.

When I open my eyes, I see that hers are still closed. She looks peaceful while she rests. I don't want to wake her. She needs to gather her strength. We don't have the luxury of not retaliating soon. This means the next few days are key to taking down my opponents. If she's up for it, she's going to need to come with me to talk to Jonathan. It's all tied together. Her father, my cousin, and this would-be killer I have locked in a cage in my basement.

"Morning," she says.

"Morning." I gently pull her closer to me, careful not to hurt her.

"How are you feeling? Are you in pain?"

"No. I'm okay." She sighs into my chest, and I know, for now, she is.

Regardless of that, I also know now more than ever, I need to take care of the threat once and for all.

Viviana will never be safe in a world where her father walks free, nor in a world where my cousin breathes.

I need to kill them.

# CHAPTER FORTY-ONE

## Viviana

TIME MOVES RATHER SLOWLY WHEN YOU ARE CONFINED TO A hospital bed and can't get up. But as the days pass, Matteo never leaves my side.

He reads to me, too.

Beside my bed is a stack of the classics.

All the books I grew up reading.

If there wasn't a hole in my stomach from where a bullet was ripped out, I would say the time we've spent together in this room have been perfect.

There is one thing, though, and in the back of my mind, even as Matteo cares for me, there is also the issue of Jonathan.

He's somewhere in this house.

Locked up.

For all I know, he's being tortured.

The thing is, I should hate him. He shot me, but something tells me there is more to this story.

Lots more.

Beside me, Matteo stirs, and then he is moving his body until he hovers over mine. He is careful not to rest his weight on me, although for a little pain, it would be worth it. I've been home for days, and other than a small peck on the lips, he hasn't touched me.

"Don't even think about it," he says, his early morning voice rough and husky.

"Think about what?" Mine is coy.

"You know what. You're still healing." He scolds me as though I have just been summoned to the principal's office.

"Fine, but you're no fun." I pout, and he shuts me up with another damn kiss.

He laughs against my lips, and the sound is heavenly. It also reminds me that we can't live in this bubble for long.

We do have to deal with the mess in the basement first.

"I'm ready," I blurt out, and the confused look in his eyes is cute.

It's funny how much he's changed over the course of this week. I saw glimpses of this man before, sweet and caring, but now that he's admitted he loves me, it's so much more.

"Ready for . . ." he trails off. "Sex? I thought I just said no."

I playfully swing at him. "Not sex, perv. I'm ready to go down to the basement and talk to Jonathan."

His mischievous stare from only a second ago is now long gone. It's replaced by narrow eyes and a line between his brow.

A deep scowl across his face.

"Are you sure?" Even his voice has changed. There is no lightness at all. This is all mob boss. The playful and dutiful husband replaced by a killer.

"Yes. Help me up."

He stands from the bed and pulls me up to be beside him.

Although the doctors have had me walk each day, it still feels weird to be on my legs. Like a fawn learning their first steps, I'm wobbly and unsteady.

Matteo helps me into the bathroom, and as I get ready to go downstairs, so does he.

It takes me a good hour to get myself pulled together. I might have miscalculated the extent of my injuries.

"You sure you want to do this?"

"Yes. I need too. I need to know what he knows."

The truth is, that's the scary part. I'm not sure if my father told him anything, and I'm not sure how he will react if he doesn't know the truth.

My stomach churns with nerves.

"You okay?"

I nod my head, but Matteo places his finger on my lip, the lip I'm currently biting, my tell.

"Talk to me."

"What if he doesn't know the truth? What if my father finds out I told?"

"Do not worry about your father," he scolds. "I'll handle him, and I will take care of everything. You will never have to worry about being under your father's thumb again. Do you understand me?"

"Yes."

"Good. Now, let's go."

Each step we take seems harder than the last. Heading toward the basement feels like I'm a prisoner walking to death row. I'm scared, but I keep my head held high.

After we walk down the stairs and turn the corner, I see him.

He's in a cell.

Tied up.

He's dressed, his clothes ripped and shredded.

His hair is dirty, filled with grease from the days he's been kept here.

There is a stink in the air.

In the corner of his cell is a toilet, a bucket of water, and an old tray of food.

At least they are feeding him.

"Look what the cat dragged in," he chides from behind bars.

"Jonathan," I say, stepping closer. "Why?"

"As if you really have to ask," he fires back.

"I think we need to talk."

"The time to talk was twelve years ago, don't you think?" he bites out.

If I ever wondered why he had such animosity toward me, now I know.

"Are you ready to talk?" Matteo asks, throwing the gate open. At first, I'm afraid he will spring out and attack us, but that's when I see that in the corner of the cell a metal chain is attached to his foot.

Bile collects in my stomach as I remember the story Matteo told me.

Seeing this place, I realize how important it is that we don't let Salvatore succeed.

Not being able to look at his smug face, I step up to Jonathan and slap him across the face.

"How could you work with him?" I hiss. "Look around you . . . do you have any idea what he wants to do? My father is willing to turn a blind eye to Salvatore's desires . . . but you. How would you feel if Julia was traded like sheep? Locked in here like an animal."

"And it's okay, what your precious husband is doing? I'm trapped here like a 'sheep.'"

It hurts when I cross my arms at my chest, but the move makes me feel safer, tougher as I fire back at him.

"You are an animal who tried to kill him. You deserve everything coming to you. But the innocent women you wish to hurt . . ." I take a deep breath in, trying to calm the emotions inside me. "They don't deserve that. Are you really willing to give them that fate?"

"Like you care about the innocent."

"Whatever my father told you . . ." My eyes fill with unshed tears at the memory, at all the lies I have told. "There is more to it. Let me explain."

"I don't want to hear anything from you."

"Then you will hear from me." Matteo steps up, and something is gleaming in his hand. A knife. Not just any knife at that, this one looks like a kitchen cleaver.

I'm about to say something to him, object to this form of torture. No matter what Jonathan did to me, he's still my best friend's brother. But Matteo shakes his head at me, knowing full well what I was about to do.

"Were you always working for my cousin?" Matteo asks.

Jonathan refuses to answer.

"Fine. You want to play it that way, that's cool, but I'll get you to talk . . . eventually. Tell me this, before the fun starts. What was the plan? Or did you even have a plan? Was it just to kill me?"

"I was going to kill both of you, actually."

"Jonathan—" I start, but then I don't know what to say. He just admitted to wanting to kill me. How do I even explain everything I have ever done was to protect him and his sister? I step closer to him, ready to say more. To tell him everything I'm sure my father didn't when I hear a scuffle and footsteps.

Jonathan's eyes go wide, looking over my shoulder to where the sound is coming from.

There, walking with tape over her mouth, is Julia. I bolt out of the cell and toward my friend. My hands lift as I push Roberto off her. The moment I make the movement, I realize my mistake, and pain radiates through me from the gunshot wound.

"What the hell are you doing, Roberto?" I turn to face Matteo. "Why is she here?" I scream at my husband. There better be a good reason, or he will be my soon-to-be ex-husband.

"What the fuck are you doing with her?" I say again, and this time, Matteo approaches me, hands raised, like he's an animal trainer trying to wrangle in a wild beast.

"You thought she was innocent?" Matteo asks, clearly perplexed by me, and when he realizes I did, his eyes soften in sympathy. I really have no one but him who cares about me. He reaches his hand out and takes mine in his, then he squeezes it gently. "She's been working with her brother the whole time." His voice is lower than normal, treating me like a wounded bird that might fly away.

"Is that true?" I ask my friend, a woman who has basically been my sister.

Roberto rips the tape off. "It's true." Julia smirks. The betrayal stabbing me in the heart.

"But—" A lone tear betrays me by falling down my cheek. "Why are you doing this?"

"You took my life. You took my mom. You killed her. You are the reason she is dead. Your father told us everything. Every day for twelve years, you betrayed me. You looked in my eyes and betrayed me. You are despicable, and I only wish I knew sooner. Because then I would never have allowed myself to love you."

Every emotion I thought I would feel at this revelation is completely wrong. The pain I feel of hurting her morphed by the anger and hatred I feel toward my father right now.

In the end, he used them.

He used my friend in a convoluted plot to kill my husband and get back at me for going against him.

"He lied to you."

"Cut the shit, Viviana. Why else would you be at his beck and call? It's because you killed my mother, and he was covering up your secret."

"Because your mom isn't dead."

# CHAPTER FORTY-TWO

## Viviana

"W-WHAT DO YOU MEAN?" JULIA STUTTERS, HER VOICE weak, and her lips pale, teeth rattling.

"She is alive. He's been lying for years."

"But then, how do you know?" Jonathan spits out from behind me, and I turn to face him.

"My father told me. He threatened me and showed me the papers to prove it."

"How long? How long did you know my mother was alive and not told me?"

"Not long. I found out by chance. I don't think he planned to tell me. But when I told him I wouldn't marry Salvatore, he did. That's when things got bad. Really bad. My father—I had no choice but to agree to his terms. If I helped him in his plot, he wouldn't hurt her. He has been blackmailing me for years. For different things. But this was the worst. He threatened to stop her treatment. Threatened to put her out of her misery. Threatened to stop supporting you. I didn't know what to do. I had no one."

"You had me."

"But don't you see? That's the catch-22. If I told you, he would have killed her."

I take a step closer to Matteo. To my husband, who has promised to help. "When Matteo came to me, I thought this could be it. He would have the power to stop this. It took me a long time to trust him, but when I was finally ready to ask him for help, Marco's place was raided. Was that you?" I ask Julia.

For the first time since she has been brought down here, she looks down at the floor. She is finally starting to understand what her actions cost her.

I understand what mine have cost. I will always feel the pain in my heart.

"Why?" the soft voice sounds foreign coming from Jonathan. It reminds me of the little boy I once knew. The one who used to play with me and Julia, my once friend. "Why would he lie? Why would he keep her there? It doesn't make sense." He starts to ramble to himself. I can't make out most of it, but one thing is clear. I have always wondered the same question.

I turn to Jonathan. "This has plagued me for months. This same question. When I found out he lied to me and that she wasn't dead, I asked myself why. What good was it to spin this web of lies? What did he have to gain?"

"What did you find out?" Julia asks.

Even though it hurts, I start to pace.

"Nothing. I couldn't find out anything. I wasn't sure if what I had read was true. The moment I saw the intake papers he had, I should have come to you guys, but by that time—"

"He was blackmailing you?" she asks.

"I wish you would have told me," Matteo says.

I nod. "I'm sorry I didn't trust you. I just—" Matteo steps up to me, tilts my head up, and places a kiss on my lips.

"I didn't deserve your trust. I would have used her against you too."

I shake my head. "You wouldn't have."

His brow arches, and I know he doesn't see the man I do. The man I love.

"I'm sorry," Julia says from behind me, and I move to face her.

"I-I." Her eyes are focused at my stomach, and where the bulky bandage is clearly visible through my shirt. "You could have died. Jonathan and I—"

I lift my hand to silence her. "This isn't your fault. It's mine."

"Like fuck it isn't," Matteo interjects. His voice rough with anger. "They tried to kill you."

"I do believe we were actually trying to kill him."

"Speak for yourself. I was trying to kill both of them." We all turn around to face Jonathan. He shrugs from his cell. "No reason to lie. I was. Now that I know the truth, I obviously feel like shit, but it's the truth nonetheless."

Everything feels so confusing, my legs start to sway under me.

Matteo catches me in his arms, and before I know it, Roberto is pulling a chair under me to sit in.

"Are you okay?" Matteo is now eye level with me. Staring at me like he's afraid I'm going to die.

"I'm fine." I reach my hand out and touch his jaw. "Let Jonathan go." My words shock even me, but in truth, now that the truth is out there, I'm not afraid of him. If anyone should be afraid, it's my father.

"Are you insane?" I level my eyes on him. "Viviana, I can't let him go."

I look over Matteo's shoulder, staring directly at Jonathan now. "Can he let you go? Are you going to kill us?"

Jonathan looks tired—not just physically but also mentally.

"I'm not going to hurt either of you."

"No." Matteo's voice is louder than I expect. "He hurt you."

"Look at it from his side. He thought I killed his mother. What would you do if you had a chance to kill the person who killed yours?"

Matteo's hand wraps around my arm and pulls me out, away from everyone.

"It doesn't stop me from wanting to kill him for hurting you."

"I know."

"No, you don't know!" His anger no longer sizzles on the surface. Now, it's a raging inferno, one I'm not sure how to douse. "I thought I lost you. I thought you died. You are everything to me. You are my life. Do you hear me? You are my life."

I lift my hand up and touch his jaw. His rigid jaw that I think will snap in half. "It's okay. I'm okay."

His head hangs down. "You could have died, and it was because of me. I didn't protect you."

"I forgive you, Matteo. Now it's time you forgive yourself. I love you. You can't hold this inside you." Taking his hand, I walk us back to stand in front of the cage.

"I can't let him go. I can't get over that he tried to take you from me."

"But I can. I forgive him. Do this for me. Trust me. Please . . ."

Matteo lets out a long-drawn-out sigh and then nods his head to Roberto. He clearly looks as shocked as Matteo that I would even ask this of them.

"If you so much as look at my wife, or even me for that matter, I don't care what she says, you are dead."

"It was never against you," Jonathan says.

"It sure felt that way when you had a gun pointed at my head."

"Marino said he had more information about my mother. He promised if I took care of the problem, he would tell me."

An audible gasp escapes my mouth. "He was blackmailing you too. Do you think he was going to tell you she was alive?"

"At this point, no. I think he was using Julia and me to do his dirty work. Once Matteo was out of the picture, I have no doubt that he wouldn't have."

"I don't know," I mumble under my breath.

"What don't you know?" Matteo asks me.

I stand from the chair and walk to Jonathan's cell. His chains drop to the floor, the clanking sound of the metal echoing off the concrete.

"Why go through all this trouble to tell you anything?" I ask Jonathan. "When did he tell you about your mother?"

"After you married Matteo."

"And before that, why were you working for him?"

"He approached me about the job. I was going to move away, and he told me to stay. At first, I did odds and ends. Then he approached me to work undercover with Matteo, to sell myself as someone he could trust. He did tell me a lot, but seeing as he had always supported me, I thought I owed it to him." His fists clench at his side.

"So many things don't add up."

"No, they don't."

"I think there is only one solution," Julia says from beside me. "You need to take us to our mother."

"She's at a hospital that my father runs. Can you get us in?" I ask my husband. If anyone has the connections, it's him.

"I can."

"Good, then let's go."

"There's only one thing," I say. "Where does Salvatore tie into this? None of that makes sense."

"It could be as simple as money. The port access is a billion-dollar profit as is. Add in the women he plans to bring in. Triple it."

"This is all about money for him?"

"And to get back at me. I think Marino and Salvatore also are doing this as an opportunity to combine forces, so that they can kill two birds at the same time. Help each other out in a mutually beneficial way."

"There is something I have to tell you," Julia whispers.

"At this point, just spit it out," Jonathan says to his sister. "She will find out, eventually. Obviously, everything is a big giant ploy, and we were the fucking pawns." The anger and venom are not lost on any of us.

"The man I was dating . . ."

I vaguely remember her telling me she met a man at a club.

Oh my God.

"No."

She nods her head.

"It was Salvatore."

# CHAPTER FORTY-THREE

## Matteo

E ACH PIECE OF THE PUZZLE STARTS TO FALL INTO PLACE. So many variables we were all blind to.

Now that I know the part my cousin had in this whole mess, I'm not surprised. He used false information Marino gave the twins and then sweetened the deal to get them to play right into his hands.

It almost worked too.

If Viviana hadn't stepped in front of a bullet for me, we would all be dead. Then to think of the countless women who would have been hurt.

I pull my wife toward me and hug her. Puzzled by my move, she looks at me. "What was that for?"

"For saving me."

I'm not just talking about the bullet this time.

"Always."

After I place a kiss on her mouth, I pull back.

"Let's go." I turn to Lorenzo. "Have Price hack into the facility. I want no eyes on us."

"Got it, Boss."

From there, everything moves rather fast.

We make it from the compound to our destination in less than an hour.

Instructed by Jaxson Price through an earpiece, we are able to avoid security using a back door and a security code he hacked.

I'm going to need to give this boy a raise, that or convince him to work only with me.

Once inside, we are led through the hallways. We walk as though we belong, even though we don't.

No one stops us.

A part of me wonders if this is too easy or a trap, but then it dawns on me. Marino probably thinks his daughter is dead. He probably thinks I'm dead.

Or he thinks Jonathan is, and seeing as I'm quick-tempered, we were never able to get to the bottom of this.

When we open the door to the room, Julia falls to the floor. There, in the corner, is a woman who looks like her. Except instead of blond hair, it's gray and oily. Her eyes are dull and lifeless.

There is a large burn mark across her face, leaving her disfigured.

I look further and see that her arms are badly burned as well. The fire was real.

Now everything that happened after that is still a mystery.

"Mom." Julia runs to her. Beside me, Viviana is quietly sobbing. I brace my arms around her, letting her cry into my chest.

"She's alive. I know he told me . . . but he wouldn't let me see her."

Ana, the twin's mom, looks heavily sedated.

She doesn't look at her children, but she does start to speak.

Her words make no sense.

Just repeats them over and over again.

I'm not sure if it's from her medication or if it's from the accident that happened so long ago, but it's obvious that the woman they know and love is long since gone. If she will ever return is the question.

"What are you doing here?" the nurse barks at us, but then

when she sees Julia on the floor beside her mother crying, she understands.

"She's my mother," Jonathan says, stepping up from behind to walk up to his sister. He places his hand on her.

"She can't have visitors."

"Please, she's my mother." Julia weeps. "Don't make me go."

"He won't let her have visitors. You can't be here. If he finds out . . ." Her face is pale, and she doesn't need to tell us who she is talking about.

Marino.

"He won't know we are here. Please tell us anything you can about her case."

As if on cue, Ana starts to babble again.

"Does she speak?"

"I don't really know. I'm new here, but for as long as I've been here . . . no."

"Is it from the fire?" Viviana asks, clearly devastated by what her actions might have caused.

"I don't know," the nurse admits.

"So, it could be from the drugs?"

"Maybe. I'm new, I don't want to get into trouble. I only hand out the medicine the doctor provides."

I nod my head, knowing she is scared. "We are going to fix this," I tell everyone in the room, and I mean it. No matter what happens, I will make sure Ana is no longer in this hellhole. "Is there anything more you can tell us? Anything that could help?" She shakes her head. Ana starts babbling again. "What is she saying?"

"Doll."

"I'm not entirely sure, but I think doll."

"You have to go. They are starting rounds again. I only came in because I heard you. If I can hear you . . ."

I turn back to Julia, who is now holding her mother's hand.

"Julia, I promise I will do everything in my power to get her out, but first, we have to get out of here."

"Okay," she whispers before leaning in and kissing her mother. Jonathan is next, followed by Viviana, who tells her she's sorry.

---

Hours later, we are all back at the compound.

It's funny how only earlier today, I was sure I would be killing both of them, and now, as I sit in my chair, scotch in hand, I watch them all cry together over what we just found.

But the question still stands, why did Marino have her?

"What was to gain from keeping her?"

"That's my question too. Why would he go through all this trouble to keep her hidden?"

We all go silent as the question lingers in the air.

Why?

"An insurance policy. She knows something, and by keeping her in the state she is in, she can't talk."

A myriad of emotions play over everyone's faces.

Anger. Sadness, and then relief.

Because if this is the case, then maybe Ana will come back to us.

"You think she is in there, still?"

"There is no way to know," I tell the group. "Years of medication . . . but maybe. She did speak, so maybe."

"What was she saying?" Julia asks.

"The nurse said she always babble the same thing . . . doll. Maybe dollhouse."

"Oh, my God."

"What?" everyone asks Viviana at the same time.

"That's from when I was a child."

"What do you think it means? Do you think that was her way of telling us she knew we were there?"

Viviana shakes her head. "No. The nurse said the staff was trying to figure out what it meant for years. That it's the only thing she says."

"We need to find it. Maybe it means something."

"Where is it Viviana?"

"With my stuff."

"And where would that be?"

"In the governor's mansion."

# CHAPTER FORTY-FOUR

## Viviana

STEP ONE, TAKE DOWN MY FATHER. STEP TWO, DEAL WITH Salvatore. In that order.

I'm not sure how we are going to find the dollhouse, but we have to try. Even if it means dying.

I turn to Jonathan.

"You have to take me back."

He inclines his head and gives me a look like he thinks I'm batshit crazy.

"And how exactly do you suppose I do that?"

"Tell my father I escaped. Say I got shot. Say anything, but sell it. I need in that house."

"Do you honestly think your mother still has it?"

"You don't understand. Of course, she does. This dollhouse isn't any dollhouse. It's passed down from generation to generation. I guarantee she does. It's symbolic of her family."

"And where would she keep it?"

"If it was me, it would be in the basement or the attic."

"Hope it's not either. Those places are creepy," Julia interjects.

We're still in the car. This time instead of going home, we are headed to the governor's mansion.

"Maybe we should just break in? It would be easier."

"Better idea," Matteo announces to the car. "We are walking

in the front door. I will tell him you tried to run away. Jonathan went after you, and I decided I didn't want you. I shot you . . . and now 'cause I don't want your death on my doorstep, I'm dropping you off."

"There is no way he will believe that."

"Well, I guess you better sell it then, baby."

I look between Jonathan, who is all bruised, and my bandaged lump in my shirt, and nod, and then I rip off the bandage.

"What the fuck are you doing?" Matteo hisses.

"Selling it." I wink. "Someone give me a knife."

"Fuck no."

"I need blood on my shirt for him to believe it."

Matteo growls, but he reaches into his pocket, pulls out a knife, and slices his own arm. My eyes bug out of my head, but before I can object, he's rubbing the blood all over me.

"I guess that works too." I roll my eyes.

Twenty more minutes pass before we are at the house, then Matteo whispers an, "I'm sorry," before he's forcefully pulling me out of the car. Lorenzo has the whole gang in tow.

Security must have tipped off my father because when we make it to the front door, it flies open, and he's there. My mother gasps and tells us to come in.

She's hemming over the blood not to get on anything.

I hate her. She has condoned his behavior, and maybe she wasn't directly involved, but she condoned it. She is just as culpable.

"I need to speak to you now, Marino."

My father looks back and forth and then follows Lorenzo, Roberto, and Matteo out.

"Mom. Where is the dollhouse?"

"What?" she asks, her voice giving way to confusion.

"The dollhouse, Mom. The one Ana and I played with. Tell me where it is!" I whisper-shout.

"Basement. Storage room."

"Let's go," I tell Jonathan and Julia, and then we are taking off in that direction. The stairs that lead down are pitch-black. We look for the lights, but when we can't find them, Jonathan uses his phone flashlight.

We take the stairs faster than I should in my condition, and then we are basically running to the storage room.

There it is.

In the corner. Exactly how I remember it.

"Quickly, is there anything there?"

The dollhouse is old, probably in my family since the 1920s at least. We search each room with a flashlight. Then we start to turn over the furniture. The kitchen, the bathroom . . . when we get to the bedroom, I pull out the bed and flip it over.

My breath leaves my body in a gasp.

Taped to the bottom of the bed is a USB drive.

"Holy crap. I found it. Quick, let's go."

This time as I run, I can feel the immense pain in every step I take, but I power on. Needing to get out of here and find out what's on the USB.

Sending a call to Matteo, I tell him we have to leave now.

I'm not sure how we are going to pull this off, but for some reason, I think I'm stuck here.

The sound of my father's footsteps is all I can hear now. There is no way for us to leave this house unscathed. Not without him knowing we are up to something.

Matteo is walking with his men beside him.

"I didn't kill her out of courtesy," Matteo says. "I didn't kill your little errand boy either. I expect you to consider this a peace offering. Consider my deal. Let me know your answer."

Matteo's done speaking. He walks up beside me, caging me in against the wall.

"Your father has convinced me to grant you an annulment

and not kill you. Do not attempt to come back to me. I don't want you." His tone is wicked, but I know what this is. I know Matteo better than anyone.

"No." I play along, throwing my arms around him. "Please." I place the USB in his hand.

"You were such a disappointment," he spits, and then like the evil mob boss he is, he walks away from me . . .

USB in hand.

# CHAPTER FORTY-FIVE

## Matteo

"YOU THINK HE BOUGHT IT?" ROBERTO ASKS WHEN WE GET into the car.

"Let's hope so. I left my fucking wife in that house," I grit out, not happy about it at all.

"She'll be okay."

"She better be because if I lose her . . ."

"You won't."

This plan isn't ideal. I have the USB, and Jonathan and Julia both want to know what's on it.

They'll have to wait, though. Marino would have known if I took them with us. And seeing as Viviana is hurt, I need her to have Julia with her.

As soon as we make it back to the compound, we head into the surveillance room and fire up the monitors.

Document after document is pulled up.

My eyes go wide.

Holy fucking shit.

Marino will no longer be a problem.

Thanks to Ana, I now have the governor by his balls.

Now, how to handle it is another question.

The first thing I have to do is tell Julia and Jonathan what I found. But there is no easy way to do that.

Not without hurting them. Not without hurting Viviana.

I have made this trip more than I should. But after today, I'll never have to do this again.

They announce my presence. Then I'm waiting in the foyer.

The need to see her is all-consuming, and when she does take the stairs down, I know I'll want to cross over to her and take her in my arms.

I don't have the time for that.

The cops will be here soon. The evidence scheduled to hit the detective on my payroll's inbox any minute.

We will be long gone before I allow myself to be tied to this mess. This needs to be done in private, but time is not on our side. We no longer have the luxury of waiting, so even though it's not ideal, I will do this now. Because with each moment that passes, there is a bigger chance Marino will do something drastic, and I can't risk leaving Viviana here any longer.

The first person I see is Jonathan. His sister is on his heels behind him.

"What was on the USB drive?"

I take a deep breath and hand him the printout copies. He starts to rummage through them. I can see the way his pupils widen as he reads through the words. The way his fist clenches every now and then.

I see when he comes across it.

When the vein in his forehead looks like it's going to explode.

The moment he realizes who he really is. How his presence really hits into everything. Julia is next to look at the reason her mother is locked in the purgatory of her mind.

The sobs can't be mistaken.

The way she falls to the floor . . .

It's not every day you find out a truth like this.

It's not every day you find out you are the illegitimate daughter of a monster.

It took me a while to comprehend what Ana had saved. From the evidence gathered, Marino and Ana had an affair. She was his mistress when she became pregnant, and it was decided she couldn't tell.

Political dreams and all. I'm not sure if he threatened her, or if she stayed out of love . . .

Only Ana can tell that story, but what I do know is somewhere along the line, she found out a secret about her lover, about the father of her children.

The secret so big, I'm not sure if Viviana ever had anything to do with the fire.

In the documents is all the proof we will ever need to keep Marino behind bars for life, and if my cousin ever found out, Marino would be dead.

There, documented, were all the crimes.

All the women.

Somehow, Marino had gotten his hands on incriminating evidence about Salvatore's father's human trafficking operation. There were pictures of both the girls taken and the men who purchased them. All the records of years of abuse were saved.

He wanted to keep the mob boss in his pocket. But with the files he received, he forgot to remove the ones on himself. The ones that proved his knowledge and his own participation in the operation. *He was apparently a very loyal client.*

"Holy crap," Jules says, as she finally pulls herself together.

"Fuck." Jonathan's voice cuts in next. "He's our father," he whispers. "Our fucking father."

"We need to tell Viviana first. Where is she?" I ask.

"I'll go get her." Julia walks off, heading up the stairs.

"What are you doing here, Amante? I thought I made my position perfectly clear. When I didn't answer, I didn't want your deal."

"Deal's off the table, anyway. The only deal you should be considering right now is with the DA."

"What the fuck are you going on about? I own this state. No one is coming for me."

"Are you sure about that?" I collect the papers and toss the file at him nonchalantly.

His nostrils flare, his eyes going wide with anger.

"Where the fuck did you get this?"

"Wouldn't you like to know."

"I should have killed the bitch when I had a chance."

And then the other shoe finally drops. A gasp reverberates through the space as understanding hits Jonathan.

"You . . . You did this to her?" There is no need to clarify. "You put her in that place, and you let us all believe that—holy fuck. You let us believe our sister did it. You were going to have us hurt our sister. Fuck. I almost killed her." Jonathan now falls to the floor, devastated by everything that transpired.

From behind me, I hear footsteps. I turn to see Viviana, but it's only Julia.

"Where is she?" I ask her.

"She wasn't there."

I turn to Marino. "Where the fuck is my wife?"

"You're too late."

I step forward, my hands circling his throat. "Speak."

"Salvatore has her, and knowing him . . ."

# CHAPTER FORTY-SIX

## Viviana

H IS EYES ARE VOID OF EMOTION. DARK AND SINISTER.
He had come to my father's house and took me. My father offered me up to him like a prize pig ready for the slaughter.

Now I'm in what seems to be an abandoned warehouse.

Alone, waiting for him to tell me what he wants from me.

The shackle around my ankle makes chills run up the back of my neck. But it's the bed in the corner that truly terrifies me. I would rather die than be this monster's plaything.

Kill me.

But not before he hurts me, not before he makes me pay for defying him.

I knew when this plan was set in motion that this could happen. I had hoped we would be able to pull it off.

But now, in the darkness of this dank space, I know I was just fooling myself. This was always the outcome.

Regardless if I had never married Matteo, this was my fate.

I don't regret a minute.

Not one if it brought me to Matteo.

The sound of heavy footsteps has me scooting back and trying to hide. But there is nowhere to go.

His sinister laughter echoes through the air, and my gaze flies toward him. He's stalking toward me, large and menacing.

"What are you going to do to me?"

"If you're worried I'm going to rape you, don't. You're more trouble than you're worth."

"Then why am I here?"

"Come on, Viviana, you're smarter than that."

"Bait."

"Ding. Ding. One point for the mafia queen."

"He won't come for me. He doesn't care."

He laughs again. "You better hope he does. If not, I'll have to send you to him piece by piece until he has no choice but to pick up your scraps."

"You assume too much," I choke out, even though I know I'm lying. I just hope he doesn't come. I would gladly die to protect him.

"My cousin loves you. And he will come for you. When he does, I'll be here to kill him. And after, if you give me trouble . . ." He lets the threat hang in the air. "I'm going to call him soon. Is there anything you want me to tell him for you?" His lips tip up into a smirk.

"Go fuck yourself."

His smile broadens, and he looks downright sinister in this light.

"With a mouth like that, I hope Matteo doesn't come. I'll make a shitload of money on you. Ironic with who your father is."

My confusion must play across my face. "Oh, you don't know? Didn't you ever wonder why I got into business with him? Why I knew he wouldn't be against my ideas for expansion?"

It hits me in the gut, and the wind is knocked out of my lungs at his declaration.

I always knew my father was evil, but this . . .

Tears fill my eyes, but I refuse to let them fall.

I can't show him my sadness or my fear. He will consume it like a succubus prays on the weak.

"How sweet, you didn't know."

I'm frozen in place at his words as my mind spins frantically.

Strange pieces I didn't know of a puzzle falling into place.

My body is twisted around, no longer able to look at him.

I can't.

He's the harbinger of death.

It's only a matter of time.

# CHAPTER FORTY-SEVEN

## Matteo

S HIT IS TENSE IN THE CAR ON THE WAY BACK TO THE COMPOUND. We have no idea when he grabbed her or where he took her. When we get back, we stand in the foyer with no direction on how to proceed. The only option now is to call my cousin. I know this. My men know this.

We have to sacrifice the king to save the queen.

Lorenzo finally breaks the silence, saying, "What do we do?"

"We have to figure out where she is, and then we have to go in and get her."

"It's not that simple." Lorenzo starts to pace back and forth. "You can't surrender. That's what he wants."

"If that's the way I save her, that's exactly what needs to be done."

"I know where she is." We all turn to where Julia is standing. No one speaks, just stares at her. "I know." This time her voice is stronger and full of conviction. "Let me help."

"This smells like a trap."

"It's not. She is my best friend. She-she's my sister. I would never do anything to hurt her."

Lorenzo steps forward, essentially caging her in. He looks like a beast next to her. "You already did," he sneers.

"And I apologized. I feel awful. It's my fault she was hurt, but I'll never make that mistake again. You have to believe me."

"I don't think it's a good idea," Lorenzo mutters. Clearly, he does not trust Julia at all. I don't trust her, either. But it's beside the point.

"I think it's the only one we have," Jonathan says. "And trust me, I don't say that lightly. There's a good chance Salvatore will call you. When he does, you're walking into a trap. The only thing we have going for us is the element of surprise." Jonathan points at his sister. "She brings that element."

"No." I shake my head. "There are too many unknown variables. Just tell us where she is, and we will take him out."

Jonathan interjects. "And risk her getting hurt?"

I'm about to say more when Julia walks over to me and places her hand on my arm.

"I'm going. You have no other choice. Please . . . trust me." It's true, we don't. "Use me as bait. Then kill Salvatore once and for all."

"Matteo, can I speak to you . . . alone?" Lorenzo says to me, and I nod my head and then turn to Roberto. "Stay with them."

Once we are alone, he crosses his arms at his chest. "You're going to work with them?" I nod. "It will make you look weak."

"It's not weak to admit you need help. They are our in. Our only in, and before you argue about the past, I get it. I don't blame them. I would have done the same thing to find out about my parents."

———•———

If we are going to let her go in, we will make sure it's not a trap.

"Get Jaxson Price on the phone."

The phone rings through the car speakers.

"Matteo. I'm starting to think I should up my prices. What can I do for you now?"

"Salvatore has my wife."

There is a pregnant pause at my words, followed by a cough. "Fuck, man. I'm sorry. What do you need?"

"We have a location, but I need to know if it's legit," I tell him.

"You want me to check if there are people?"

"I want you to tell me exactly where they are, so I'm not blindsided."

"No problem."

I feed him the location, and in the background, I can hear him typing furiously on the phone.

"Okay, I hacked into a satellite. There are two men outside in the front and two in the back. Once you get inside, there are only two more."

"You sure about this?"

"One hundred percent. Unless your cousin is wearing an ice suit, the heat index won't lie."

"You sure you don't want to come work for me directly, Price?"

"I'm not for sale."

"Everyone has a price."

"You couldn't afford me."

"Debatable, but right now I have to get my girl, so let's table the discussion." I turn to my men. "You guys ready?" I ask.

"What's the plan?" Lorenzo asks.

"If Julia isn't lying, and she's been here before, his men should know her," Roberto says, obviously still not trusting her.

"I'm not lying. I understand why you don't believe me, but I'm not."

"As Roberto was saying, we send in Julia . . . when she is distracting Salvatore, we take out the men on the outside. But we have to do it quietly. Let's put on an earpiece. That way, she can hear us, and we can hear her. Once we signal that everyone is dead, we come in guns blazing." I turn to Julia. "Can you handle this?"

"Yes."

"Okay, let's go. Pull the car over a block outside the factory. We go on foot.

"Roger that."

Roberto pulls to the side of the abandoned road before the turn that will lead to where Viviana is.

When we are all out of the car, Julia gets in the driver's seat.

"Can you hear me?" she whispers.

"Loud and clear."

"Okay, I'm pulling up."

The line goes silent, the only sound coming from her rapid breathing.

"Calm down, Julia," her brother says through the earpieces we are all wearing.

"Sorry," she mumbles so low we can almost not hear it.

The sound of the car door opening is the only indication of what is happening.

"What are you doing here?"

"Here to check in with Salvatore." It's obvious she was deeply ingrained in this plot as there is no objection. Instead, we hear the sound of the heavy, metal door opening.

Then the sound of her footsteps on the concrete.

"The bitch is still alive."

"Julia?" Viviana says, her voice clearly shocked. I wonder if she knows this is all a part of the plan, or if somewhere inside her, she fears her friend has gone against her one more time. She doesn't know yet about what we found on the USB drive.

"Yep, it's me. Although I have to say I'm rather disappointed that you're here, and to be honest, you don't even look hurt," she snarls, but now we know Viviana isn't hurt.

"What are you doing here?" Salvatore's voice booms through the earpiece.

The sound of footsteps echo again. "I missed you."

When we hear the sound of Julia kissing Salvatore, I lift my hand, signaling my men.

"Let's go."

At the same time, with silencers on our guns, we launch a synchronized attack.

Guns lift.

"On three."

"One. Two. Three."

*Pop. Pop. Pop.*

The men drop like dominos falling.

"We're coming in," I announce into the mic, letting Julia know to take cover.

At that, we bust open the door, guns raised. But as soon as we do, Salvatore moves too fast. His gun is now aimed at Julia's head.

"Let go of the girl," I hiss.

"And lose my own bargaining tool?"

"She's not some tool, you shit," Jonathan steps up, gun raised.

Salvatore looks at all of us. There are more of us than him, so there is no way he can get out of this alive. However, he doesn't seem upset at all.

It's almost like he knows something we don't. Then I hear it, and I know it's because he does.

Cars screeching to a halt, doors slamming, heavy boots moving our way. It's a fucking ambush.

His lip tips up, and then he laughs. "The moment you hit Marino's, I knew you were coming. Julia showing up alone was the icing on the cake."

"You let us kill your men outside?"

"Casualties of war."

The crazy motherfucker allowed his men to be bait so we would come in here, essentially trapping us.

"Spread out. Protect the girls!" I scream, but with Salvatore holding Julia hostage, that will be harder.

It takes a moment to realize what's happening, but then like a flash of lightning, Julia thrusts her head back, and at the same time, Jonathan charges.

All hell breaks loose.

It's complete pandemonium.

Salvatore lifts his gun and fires. Jonathan flops to the floor. He didn't even make it two steps before he was hit.

However, it was enough time for his sister to escape and run for Viviana and enough time for me to lose focus and almost get knocked out by my cousin. Luckily, I right myself as he comes barreling into me, and only my gun drops to the floor.

All around me, a war is waging. Guns fire.

My men are taking cover and firing back.

From the corner of my eye as I stand, I can see Julia flipping the bed over to give her and a chained-up Viviana protection from the gunfire.

"I should have killed you too." He throws the first punch. I block and jab back.

"Too?"

An evil smirk and dark eyes tell me all the answers I need to know. He chuckles to himself, clearly amused. "Seriously, you really don't know?"

"You killed my parents."

"Of course, I did. Your father killed my father. He took away my legacy. He stole my throne, and you put yourself on it. You never belonged there. It was always mine. I let you warm it for a few years, but I'm taking it back."

"Like fuck you are."

Even without my gun, I'm going to kill him.

I charge him again. This time, I allow the full weight of my body to collide with his.

We struggle on the floor.

Blood splays between us. He grabs my head, attempting to bash it into the concrete, I brace for impact, but as he moves, I headbutt him, busting his nose and flipping us over. Now straddling him, my hands wrap around his neck.

I hold tighter and tighter.

His life slipping through my fingers.

It's almost over.

From the corner of my eye, I can see his gaze change, his arm reaching out. I follow his line of sight. His fingers are now dangerously close to the discarded gun.

If he gets it, I'm dead.

If that happens, my wife will meet a fate worse than me. I know it. She knows it. Salvatore knows it. No matter what happens, I can't let that happen, even if I have to die to protect her. Letting him go is a calculated move as my hands slip from his neck. Oxygen rushes into him, and it's enough to give me the leverage I need. I jump.

He's quick to follow.

My fingers feel the metal.

My hand wrapping around it.

I grab the gun, and then I aim.

*Bang.*

The sound rings through the air.

Thunderous.

Right in the head.

I've killed my cousin.

I've avenged my parents.

Most of all, I've saved the love of my life.

With his body now on the floor, lying in a pool of his blood, I move to stand so that I can make my way over to Viviana.

His men are all subdued, some dead. Julia is grasping keys from one of the bodies and is working on freeing my wife.

I'm tired, so very fucking tired, but then I see her running, and despite her healing injuries, she's barreling toward me. Throwing her arms around my neck and kissing me as if she was sure I had died.

It was close.

But in the end, we prevailed.

"I love you. Don't ever do that again."

"I can't say never."

And that's the honest truth. I can't. Not in my line of work.

Can I give it up?

Could I walk away?

She looks at me like I'm her salvation, not her damnation, and I know right then and there I can.

For this woman, I can give it all up.

Maybe not today.

Or tomorrow.

But soon.

# EPILOGUE

## Viviana

It's only been three months since everything went down. Things were crazy at first. They arrested my father. It was an open and shut case. The proof Ana had collected of his involvement with Matteo's uncle's human trafficking ring was substantial. He won't be getting out of jail soon. I haven't spoken to my mother since Salvatore took me, and I don't plan to. Last I heard, she left the country, and is living with some family we have in Sicily, far away from any scandal regarding my father.

Matteo and I have settled into a comfortable routine, whatever comfortable can be when you're married to the mob.

We spent the first few weeks making sure we got Ana the best care available. Now that she's in a good place, a safe place, I have been brainstorming what I want to do with the rest of my life.

As much as I love lazy days with my husband, I need to work.

Julia often brainstorms with me, and we come up with some great ideas, but nothing concrete yet.

I hear the footsteps before I see him.

Turning over my shoulder, I smile up at him as he walks into the room.

"Is he potty trained yet?" he asks, looking down into my lap. Snuggling against me is the rescue puppy we adopted last month. We aren't exactly sure what breed he is, but if I had to harbor a guess, I would say he's a mix of a cavalier and a poodle. Matteo claims we needed a big scary dog, but when I saw Bruce, I knew he was for me.

According to the shelter, someone left Bruce on the side of the road.

The moment I heard the story, I felt an instant connection. Not that I was left on the side of the road, but I knew what it was like not to be wanted by your family.

Since then, I have spent almost every waking hour with the tiny bundle of fur. Matteo, however, has been slower to warm up, not appreciating the fact that Bruce doesn't like to pee outside. Instead, he prefers to pee on furniture and carpet . . . and well anywhere that drives my husband crazy.

"He's getting better," I offer as my answer.

"So, he's still shitting everywhere?"

"He's not shitting everywhere," I mumble under my breath.

His right eyebrow lifts, challenging me.

"Fine. He had an accident . . . or three today." Matteo's eyes go wide at my words. "But he's totally trying."

"Whatever you say." Matteo walks farther into the room before stopping closer to me. My jaw chooses that moment to rattle from the chilly air. "Are you cold?"

The blanket wrapped around me and the puppy sitting on my lap do little to warm me.

"A bit."

"Let me start a fire."

"That's okay . . ." I trail off, looking down at the floor. His hand touches my jaw and lifts it, so I'm once again looking into his eyes.

"Viviana." His voice is powerful yet comforting as he says my name.

"Yes," I whisper.

"Do you think I would ever hurt you?"

My head shakes back and forth. "Of course not."

"Do you think I would let anything hurt you . . ." He leads, and I know exactly what he's implying. My irrational fear of fire.

"Well, no. But—"

"No buts. I won't. So right now. Right here. In our house, I'm going to teach you how to light a fire. I'm going to show you how to keep it controlled."

He reaches his hand out to me to take and I stare at him blankly. I know my fear is stupid. I haven't even allowed myself to light a candle, or fire since. Even when we lost power so many months ago and Matteo lit them, I couldn't control how my heart raced.

"It's stupid. I don't know why I can't."

He grasps me and pulls me up, Bruce stepping off me and curling into a ball, watching us from where he now rests as Matteo pulls me toward the fireplace. Beside it are logs.

"We are going to start by placing two pieces of wood on the grate." He moves to grab it, doing the work for me. I'm relieved by it, but something tells me he's going to make me light it. Once he sets the logs down, he grabs a few pieces of newspaper that he has resting on the table, ready for this exact moment. He crumples it up. Once it's ready, he turns to me. "Are you ready to light the kindling?"

"No."

"You can do this. You went up against my cousin, you took a bullet for me, you can light it." His voice leaves no room for objection.

I look down at the match, and the paper now stuffed between wood.

Taking the match in my hand, I stare at it. How can something so little be so scary?

That's when I realize to think how, sometimes, Ana would say different quotes to me.

What had she said about fear?

A quote from Aristotle . . . *"He who overcomes his fear will truly be free."* That was it.

Right now, I realize the truth to those words. No matter how far I have come, how amazing my life now is, I'll never be able to move forward until I conquer my fear.

Without a second thought, I strike the match and place it in the fireplace.

It comes alive.

Breathing life into flames.

I watch as it dances before me, Matteo's hand takes mine, and together, we feel the warmth.

The heat that no longer burns.

---

## Matteo

*Nine months later . . .*

Things have calmed down since the crazy night in which I got my wife back.

Since then, I have been a tyrant. *The* tyrant.

I never let her out of my sight. Every now and then, she complains, but I know she secretly loves it.

She loves it when I'm a possessive ass.

The only time she's alone is when I go to work, but soon that will change too.

Viviana spends those times with her sister. That came as a shock, but now that time has passed, it's the most natural thing in the world for her.

Today, when I arrive home, I find her in the library. Viviana is pulling books to donate to the free library she and Julia have started.

It started off as a little project, but now, by the looks of what's going on in the room, it's going to take up her time.

"Hi." She smiles up at me from the floor.

"Looks like you have your hands full."

She laughs. It's a beautiful laugh, one that I can, and will, spend the rest of my life listening to.

Placing the books down, she stands up and places a kiss on my lips.

"How was your day, dear?" she jokes. It's her new favorite way to greet me, as if we were just a normal couple, and I didn't run the mafia.

I pull her closer, deepening the kiss, and she giggles against my lips. "That good."

"I have something to talk to you about," I say as I pull away.

"That sounds serious." I walk over to the couch, and she follows suit.

"It's done."

"What's done?"

"I stepped down. Lorenzo is taking over for me."

Her mouth hangs open. "What . . . are you sure you're okay with this?"

"I am. I'm not going to stop working. I'll run the legitimate parts of the business. This is what my father always wanted too. He just never had the opportunity because of his brother. But now that Salvatore is dead, I can live his dream."

Viviana jumps from where she is sitting into my lap.

"I'm so happy for you." She lets out a sigh of relief, and now I'm sure I made the right decision.

Every day that I left her these past few months, I could see the fear in her eyes. Now it's gone.

"I have one more surprise."

"Another? Eeep," she squeals. "I love surprises!"

I stand from the couch and hold out my hand for her to take.

Now, together, we walk out of the library. I lead her to the foyer.

That's where Julia and Jonathan are waiting with the surprise.

When she turns the corner, a gasp leaves her mouth.

It was a long road, a long year, but all the hard work was worth it.

"Ana . . ." A sob breaks through her lips, and tears flow down her cheeks.

The woman who raised my wife stands in the doorway.

She's still frail, and sometimes her mind gets jumbled from the years of medication, but every day, she gets a little better with the help of the best doctors in the world. A part of her once lost is restored.

"My girl, my Vivi." The term of endearment makes my wife cry harder.

Slowly, she walks up to her, and they embrace.

They hug for a minute before we escort Viviana and the family into the den. Tonight, a dinner will be prepared to celebrate family.

Lorenzo will be joining us too, as well as Roberto. My family.

Life has changed for me over the past year, but I realize now, power is not important. Neither is money and fame.

All that matters is this . . .

Having people to cherish, people to love.

That's when you are finally complete.

The End

# ACKNOWLEDGMENTS

I want to thank my entire family. I love you all so much.

Thank you to my husband and my kids for always loving me. You guys are my heart!

Thank you to my Mom, Dad, Liz and Ralph for always believing in me, encouraging me and loving me!

Thank you to my in-laws for everything they do for me!

Thank you to all of my brothers and sisters!

Thank you to everyone that helped with Ruthless Monarch.

Jenny Sims

Marla Esposito

Karen Hrdlicka

Champagne Formats

Hang Le

Jill Glass

Jaime Ryter

Sarah Sentz

Viviana Izzo

Grey's Promotions

Thank you to The Cover Lab for such a great image.

Thank you to Sebastian York, Vanessa Edwin, Kim Gilmour and Lyric for bringing Ruthless Monarch to life on audio.

Thank you to Sebastian's Addict for your support.

Thank you to my AMAZING ARC TEAM! You guys rock!

Thank you to my beta/test team.

Parker: You rock even if you send weird gifts . . .jk I adore you.

Leigh: Thank you for always being there for me. I love you!

Kelly: Thank you for all your input and proofing my audio.

Lulu: Thank You!

Suzi: Thank you so much!

Jill: Thank you for all your help.

Melissa: Thanks for everything.

Harloe: Thanks for always being there.

Mia: Thanks for always talking shop ie plots and helping me write my blurbs.

Mary: Thank you for reading an early copy and helping come up with ideas.

I want to thank ALL my friends for putting up with me while I wrote this book. Thank you!

To all of my author friends who listen to me complain and let me ask for advice, thank you!

To the ladies in the Ava Harrison Support Group, I couldn't have done this without your support!

Please consider joining my Facebook reader group Ava Harrison Support Group

Thanks to all the bloggers! Thanks for your excitement and love of books!

Last but certainly not least...

Thank you to the readers!

Thank you so much for taking this journey with me.